The Walls of Jericho

The Walls of Jericho

Rudolph Fisher

MINT EDITIONS

The Walls of Jericho was first published in 1928.

This edition published by Mint Editions 2024.

ISBN 9798888970713 | E-ISBN 9798888970768

Published by Mint Editions®

 MINT EDITIONS

minteditionbooks.com

Publishing Director: Katie Connolly
Design: Ponderosa Pine Design
Production and Project Management: Micaela Clark
Typesetting: Westchester Publishing Services

For Glendora—
May her laugh be silver,
like her hair

JERICHO

Despite the objections of the Dickties, who prefer to ignore the existence of so-called rats, it is of interest to consider Henry Patmore's Pool Parlor on Fifth Avenue in New York.

The truth about Fifth Avenue has only half been told, that it harbors an aristocracy of residence already yielding to an aristocracy of commerce. Has any New Yorker confessed to the rest—that when aristocratic Fifth Avenue crosses One Hundred Tenth Street, leaving Central Park behind, it leaves its aristocracy behind as well? Here are bargain-stores, babble, and kids, dinginess, odors, thick speech. Fallen from splendor and doubtless ashamed, the Avenue burrows into the ground— plunges beneath a park which hides it from One Hundred Sixteenth to One Hundred Twenty-Fifth Street. Here it emerges moving uncertainly northward a few more blocks; and now— irony of ironies—finds itself in Negro Harlem.

You can see the Avenue change expression—blankness, horror, conviction. You can almost see it wag its head in self-commiseration. Not just because this is Harlem—there are proud streets in Harlem: Seventh Avenue of a Sunday afternoon, Strivers' Row, and The Hill. Fifth Avenue's shame lies in having missed these so-called dickty sections, in having poked its head out into the dark kingdom's backwoods. A city jungle this, if ever there was one, peopled largely by untamed creatures that live and die for the moment only. Accordingly, here strides melodrama, naked and unashamed.

Patmore's Pool Parlor occupied the remodeled ground floor of a once elegant apartment-house: two long low adjacent rooms, with smaller one in the rear. You could enter either of the larger two from the street, and a doorway joined them within. There were no pretenses about these two rooms: one was a pool room, its stolid, green-covered tables extending from front to back in a long squat row; the other was a saloon, with a mahogany bar counter, a great wall mirror, a shining foot rail and brass spittoons. In the saloon you could get any drink you had courage and cash and use any language you had the ingenuity to devise. The third room was off the pool room and behind the saloon; this gave itself over to that triad of swift exchange, poker, black-jack, and dice.

Such was Pat's standing in the community that you might at anytime find in this little rear room a policeman sitting in a card game, his coat on the back of his chair, his cap on the back of his head. For men, Pat's was supremely the neighborhood's social center, where met real regular guys and you rubbed elbows with authority. Henry Patmore was no piker, no sir, not by a damn sight.

In Patmore's the discussion concerned a possible riot in Harlem, a popular topic among these men who loved battle.

Jinx Jenkins and Bubber Brown led the argument on opposite sides, reinforced by continuous expressions of vague but hearty agreement from their partisans: "Tell 'im 'bout it!"

"That's the time, papa!"

"There now—shake that one off yo' butt!"

Jinx and Bubber worked at the same job everyday, moving furniture. At this they got along tolerably, but after hours they were chronic enemies and were absolutely unable to agree upon anything.

Jinx was thin and elongated, habitually stooped in bearing, lean and sinewy, with freckled skin of a slick deep yellow and a chronically querulous voice.

"Fays got better sense," said he. "Never will be no riot no mo' 'round hyeh."

Bubber was as different from Jinx as any man could be, short, round and bulging, with a complexion bordering on the invisible.

"'Tain't due to be 'round hyeh," he corrected. "It's way over Court Avenue way. Darkey's gonna move in there to-morrer and fays jes' ain't gon' stand fo' it." Bubber spoke with a loose-lipped lisp, perfected by the absence of upper incisors.

"Who he?" Jinx inquired.

"Some lawyer 'n other name' Merrit."

"The one got Pat in that mess with d' gover'ment?"

"Well ef he's a lawyer he sho' mus' know what he's doin'."

"Don' matter what he is," argued Bubber. "Ef he move in that neighborhood, fays'll start sump'm sho—and sho' as they start it, d' boogies'll finish it. Won't make no difference 'bout this Merrit man—he'll jes' be d' excuse—man, you know that. Every sence d' war, d' boogies is had guns and ammunition they stole from d' army, and they jes dyin' fo' a chance to try 'em out. I know where they's two machine guns myself, and they mus be a hund'ed mo' in Harlem."

"Yea," said Jinx. "Heard 'bout that, too. But I don't think no shine's got no business bustin' into no fay neighborhood."

"He got business bustin' in any place he want to go. Only way for him to git any where is to bust in—ain' nobody gon' invite him in."

"Aw, man, whut you talkin' 'bout? Hyeh's a dickty tryin' his damnedest to be fay—like all d' other dickties. When they git in hot water they all come cryin' to you and me fo' help."

"And they git help, what I mean. Anytime dickties start fightin', d' rest of us start fightin' too. Got to. Dickties can't fight."

"Jes' 'cause they can't fight ain' no reason how come we got to fight fo' em."

"'Tain' nothin' else. Fays don' see no difference tween dickty shines and any other kind o' shines, One jig in danger is ev'y jig in danger. They'd lick *them* and come on down on us. Then we'd have to fight anyhow. What's use o' waitin'?"

"Damn' if you'd ever go out o' yo' way to fight f' no dickties," Jinx taunted.

"Don' know—I might," Bubber said.

"Huh!" discredited Jinx. "You wouldn' go out o' yo' way to fight f' y' own damn self—and you far from a dickty."

"Right," cheerfully agreed Bubber. "I'm far from a dickty, no lie. But I ain' so far from a rat." Jinx missed the meaning of this, so Bubber sidled up close to him and drove it home. "Fact I'm right next to one."

Encircling grins improved Jinx's understanding. "Next to nuthin'!" exploded he, giving the other a rough push.

"You know what you is lots better'n I do." Whereupon he did a triumphant little buck and wing step, which ended in a single loud, dustraising stamp. Dry dust and drier laughter floated irritatingly into Jinx's face. Jinx was long and limber but his restraint was short and brittle. Derision snapped it in two.

"So's yo' whole damn family nuthin'!" he glowered, heedless of the disproportion between the trivial provocation and so violent a reaction. For it is the gravest of insults, this so-called "slipping in the dozens." To disparage a man himself is one thing; to disparage his family is another. "Slipping" is a challenge holding all the potentialities of battle. The present example of it brought Bubber attention from their gin.

The bystanders began "agitatin'"—uttering comments deliberately intended to urge the two into action. The agitators concealed their grins far up their sleeves, presenting countenances grave with apprehension and speaking in tones resigned to the inevitability of battle.

"Uh-uh! Sho' mus' know each other well!"

"Wha' I come fum, dey fights fo' less 'n dat."

"Ef y' can't stand kiddin', don' kid, I say."

"I don' b'lieve he's gon' hit 'im, though."

"I know what I'd do 'f anybody said that 'bout my family."

As a matter of fact, the habitual dissension between these two was the symptom of a deep affection which neither, on question, would have admitted. Neither Jinx and Bubber nor any of their associates had ever heard of Damon and Pythias, and frank regard between two men would have been considered questionable to say the least. Their fellows would neither have understood nor tolerated it; would have killed it by derisions, conjectures, suggestions, comments banishing the association to some realm beyond normal manhood. Accordingly their own expression of this affection had to take an ironic turn. They themselves must deride it first, must hide their mutual inclination in a garment of constant ridicule and contention, the irritation of which rose into their consciousness as hostility. Words and gestures which in a different order of life would have required no suppression became

RUDOLPH FISHER

precisely opposite aspect, concealed a profound attachment by exposing an extravagant enmity. And this was a distortion of behavior so completely imposed upon them by their traditions and society that even they themselves did not know they were masquerading.

Bubber, his round face gone ominously blank, drew slowly closer to Jinx, who, face thrust forward a little and scowling, stood with his back to the bar counter, on which both elbows rested.

"Mean—*my* family?" inquired Bubber.

Jinx dared not recant. "All the way back to the apes," he assured him "—and that ain't so awful far back."

"The apes in yo' family is still livin'," said Bubber, "but they's go'n' be one daid in a minute."

"Stay where you at, you little black balloon, or I'll stick a pin in you, you hear?"

By this time Bubber was almost within range and an initial blow was imminent. Absorbed in the impending clash, no one had noticed the arrival of a newcomer. But now this newcomer spoke and his words, soft and low though they were, commanded immediate attention.

"Winner belongs to me."

Everybody looked—spectators holding their drinks, Bubber with his blank black face, Jinx with his murderous scowl. They saw a man at one end of the bar counter, one foot raised upon the brass rail, one elbow resting on the mahogany ledge; a young man so tall that, though he bent forward from the hips in a posture of easy nonchalance, he could still see over every intervening head between himself and the two opponents, and yet so broad that his height was not of itself noticeable; a supremely tranquil young Titan, with a face of bronze, hard, metallic, lustrous, profoundly serene. He repeated his remark in paraphrase:

"I am askin' fo' the winner. I am very humbly requestin' a share in his hind-parts."

It was apparent that the bristling antagonists bristled no longer, had limply lost interest in their quarrel.

"You know what I'm talkin' 'bout you freckle-face giraffe, and so does 'at baby hippopotamus in front of you. We got that Court Avenue job in the mornin', and if I got to break in one rooky on it, I might as well break in two." The voice, too, was like bronze, heavy, rich in tone, uncompromisingly solid, with a surface shadowy and smooth as velvet save for an occasional ironic glint.

"This boogy," explained Bubber, "thinks he's bad. Come slippin' me 'bout my family. He knows I don't play nuthin' like that."

"Need'n git uppity 'bout it," mumbled Jinx sullenly.

"Ain' gittin' uppity. Jes' natchly don' like it, thass all. Keep yo' thick lips off my family ef y' know what's good fo' y'."

He who had interrupted queried blandly, "Ain't there gonna be no fight?"

Jinx said to Bubber—"Aw go 'haid, drabble tail. Ain' nobody studyin' yo' family."

And this questionable apology Bubber chose to accept. "Oh," said he. "Oh—aw right, then. Thass different."

The atmosphere cleared, attention returned to gin and jest, and Bubber approached the giant, who now was grinning.

"Certainly am sorry th' ain' go'n' be no hostilities," sighed the latter. "Been wantin' to spank yo' little black bottom ev'y sence you broke that rope this mornin'."

"Aw go 'haid, Shine. That boogy's shoutin' 'cause you was hyeh to protect 'im. I'm go'n' ketch 'im one these days when you ain' 'round, and I'm go'n' turn 'im ev'y way but loose."

"Don't let 'im surprise y'. He kin wrastle the hell out of a piano."

"Piano don't fight back."

"Don't it? Well—neither will you if he get the same hold on y'."

"Humph. Who the hell's scared o' that—freckle-face giraffe?"

Patmore, the proprietor, appeared, a large, powerful man with a broad, hard face, a bright display of gold teeth, and the complexion of a guinea hen's egg. He wore brown suit, of which the coat was large and boxy and the ample trousers sharply creased but so long that they broke about his ankles in cubistic planes and angles. Smoke and the caustic vapors of rum had rendered his voice rough and husky, and when he spoke you had an irresistible impulse to clear your throat.

Pat addressed Bubber. "You and Long-Boy still at it, huh?"

"Aw—at string-bean's crazy. I'm gon' snap' im in two and string 'im one these times."

"Know what I'm go'n' do with you two?"

"Whut?"

"See that door over there?"

"Yea."

"That's the cellar door, see? Next time y'all start anything in hyeh, I'm go'n' send the two of you down there and let you settle it once and for all. Best man come out—other one drug out. See?"

"Any rats down there?"

"Yea—and y'all 'll make two more."

"Well," grinned Bubber, "when I walk out, them rats'll have some bones to gnaw on anyhow," and he moved off toward the pool room.

Ignoring Pat's attempt to play the genial host. Shine had already returned to his drink with an indifference hardly short of insult. He now replenished his glass from a pint bottle in his hand, and slipped the bottle into his own hip pocket.

Pat's green eyes narrowed. "That'll be only three bucks to you, Shine."

Shine looked up. "What?"

"Anybody else—four."

"This," said Shine, "is *good* licker."

"'Course 'tis. All my licker is good."

"This ain' never been yourn—'scription licker."

unconcern, the one unmistakably for his drink, other for his company.

Pat feigned incredulity. "Mean that's *your* licker?"

"'Tain' my brother's."

"Mean—" Pat's unbelief mounted "—mean—you buy licker somewhere else and bring it in my place to drink?"

Shine tossed off the rest of the glass, set it down on the bar counter, and looked upon Pat, who was almost as tall as himself, with a wearily tolerant smile.

"Sho' takes you a long time to see a thing," he remarked. "You hear me say it's 'scription. You ain' runnin' no drugstore, are y'? You see me drink it. You ain't blind, are y'? Yea, I bought it. Yea, I brought it here. Yea, I'm drinkin' it. Now what the hell 'bout it?"

A smaller man equally "bad," equally convinced of the necessity of being hard, but aware of physical odds against him, would have said this with sneers and sarcasm, thus bolstering his courage against his handicap. Shine however had never found it necessary to be nasty as well as bad. He had spoken with an air of amusement, and there was but a touch of challenge in his terminal remark.

Pat stood silent a moment. Eventually he said, "Nothin' 'bout it, big boy. Nothin'. Jes' askin' f' information, that's all." And rather too abruptly he walked away.

Shine stared long into his third glass of 'scription liquor before he lifted it to his lips. Good whiskey is not like gin. Gin makes you forget, good whiskey makes you remember. Perhaps it was at the memories in this, his third glass of good whiskey, that Shine now stared.

A boy, overgrown, bigger by far than his fellow orphan asylumites, so much bigger that they never challenged him to do battle as they frequently challenged the others. As big, almost, as the superintendent, about whom the smallest thing was his pebble of a heart. They were all at work in the truck garden, overgrown one whose name was then Joshua Jones. They were picking tomatoes, mostly green ones, to be taken to the kitchen and made into "pickalilly." They were seeing who could pick most in the hour allotted to them for the work.

And Shrimpie, unaware that they were being watched from the window of the nearest cottage, suddenly stopped, staring in surprise and delight at a big, red, prematurely ripe tomato his hand.

"Y'all kin work fast as you please," Shrimpie declared. "I'm gon' stop and eat this hyeh one."

Three bites out of the luscious thing—and the superintendent's hand was on Shrimpie's shoulder. Three cruelly vehement shakes of Shrimpie's little body—and a hard green tomato sped through space and broke on the super's cheek.

The red face became redder, the super dropped Shrimpie and turned toward the big boy, enraged. Made for him—dodged another tomato—came on. Grappled, scuffled, slipped, fell, and found the boy astride him. Pounding on his head—pounding—gone quite crazy, pounding. The super was stunned less by the pounding than by the fact that the boy kept doing it. Even after he was shaken off, the boy kept fighting aggressively. Without a rod it wasn't so easy to tame as overgrown sixteen-yearold devil. When they both let up, it was at least spiritually Joshua Jones's round.

A BIGGER BOY NOW, ALMOST a man; well over six feet tall, but still ribby and hungry-looking. Eighteen now. Shining shoes in front of a Lenox Avenue barber-shop. Making nine, ten, sometimes twelve dollars a week.

The head barber liked to stand in the doorway and kid the boy about being so big.

"Great big husky—" he would draw out the "great" till it was as long as Joshua himself—"great big husky like you—it's a shame. You oughter be movin' pianos 'stead o' whippin' shoe-leather. Benny, come 'ch. Look at dis boy. When he stoop over his heels is higher 'n his head."

little. "Shine?" was the most he ever uttered, and from this the men dubbed him Shine.

Nobody called him Shine, however, but Negroes. A fay patron, with no other intent than to be genial, once repeated the name Shine after hearing the head barber use it. "How do you get to the subway from here, Shine, my boy?" he asked, paying his bill.

Shine looked him up and down, and after a moment inquired, "How'd you know my name was Shine?"

"Guessed it," smiled the patron.

"Guess how to get to the subway, then."

The patron stared, gaped and departed mystified at so sudden hostility.

But the head barber, looking on, grinned and approved. "Tight kid," he commented. "What I mean, *tight*."

A TIGHT KID MAKES A hard man—two hundred and twenty pounds of hardness in this case, wrestling daily with pianos; pianos equally hard and four times as heavy; two hundred and twenty pounds of strength; not the mere strength of stevedores hooking cotton bales on a wharf; you can't hurt a bale of cotton—it can't hurt you; tumble it, hook it, kick it what the hell? But pianos—even swaddled in quilting—pianos must be handled like glass. Not mere strength do they require, but delicacy and strength; not muscles driving out or yanking in with abandoned force, but muscles held taut, precisely controlled under however great tension, released or restrained at will. You are protecting not only the instrument but yourself and your partner at the other end. The soft edge of a cotton-bale won't hurt a fellow's foot—the hard one of a piano will break it.

A piano is a malicious thing; it loves to slip out of your grip and snap at your toes, with an evil chuckle inside. Push up its lip and see it sneer; touch it and hear it rumble or whine. Ponderous, spiteful, treacherous live thing—a single spirit in a thousand bodies, one of which will crush you soon or late.

A malicious thing. Only today they were putting a piano into a third-story window of a house on a busy street. They had used

Cornices aren't supposed to bear weight—an inferior mixture will do. One hook came Shine was reaching out of the window to catch hold of the suspended instrument and guide it through the frame. He heard the crackle of broken cement above, saw the instrument sag a little while over it showered crumbs of broken cornice. With the hand already extended he grabbed the nearest leg of the upright and pulled it part way through the window just before the other lost its hold above. The greater part of the piano however was still unsupported outside the window—the longer arm of a lever that all but broke even Shine's tremendous strength. Straining back with all the power of his back and arms, his knees braced against the lower edge of the window-frame, he held the instrument there slipping on the sill till Jinx and Bubber reached him. Someone must have been hurt in the crash that would surely have come otherwise.

"Thing nearly pulled me out the winder," he remarked when the piano was again under control. "Why the hell didn' y' let it go, then?"

Shine looked rather blank. "Damn' 'f I thought of it," he said and grinned at his own stupidity.

Joshua Jones, whom his fellows called Shine, came out of his reverie, to observe the return of Jinx and Bubber, arm in arm and quite happily drunk.

"This yeh freckle-face giraffe, he's a good boogy," Bubber declared. "Good boogy—yassah. He's my boy. Ain't you my boy, biggy?"

"No lie," Jinx agreed. "Tell 'im 'bout that licker we ruint."

"Try some good licker," Shine invited, turning the rest of his pint over to them. "Go 'head—I got enough."

"Jes' had some good licker, I tell y'-Pat saw us go—"

"Y'all drink," Shine ordered, "and let me do the talkin'."

"Talk, then—talk. Don' nobody have to listen jes' 'cause you talk. Talk."

"I told y'all 'bout that Court Avenue job in the mornin'."

"What d' hell you so worried 'bout that job for?"

"Might have to get me some extra hands. Boss told me find somebody."

There was quick and sober resentment on the part of Jinx and Bubber. "Extra hands—fo' whut? Ain' no job too big fo' us three."

"Trouble, maybe," Shine explained. "You know what's happened already. Guy tried to move in on One Hundred Forty-ninth Street, this winter and they dared 'em to take the stuff out of the van. Jes' las' month, four blocks from where we go tomorrow, somebody put dynamite under a shine that moved in on his hardness. Well, boss is making this dickty pay for risk this time, and we get a bonus, see? But we got to get the stuff in safe, else—no bonus. And we got to keep our eyes open, or we may leave some of our hips right up there on that Court Avenue asphalt."

"Won't leave none o' Jinx's," Bubber prophesied.

"How come?" challenged Jinx.

"'Cause you ain' got none to leave, you doggone eel."

"So be ready for anything," Shine said. "Five bucks extra apiece if the junk gets in o.k."

"Well—" Bubber was uncertain, "—five bucks is five bucks, but they's a lot mo' five buckses loose in the world 'n they is hips.

tight around the waist. "See them? It's took me twentyfive years git them. And you talkin' 'bout let tin' somebody throw dynamite at 'em fo' five bucks. Huh. Man down at Coney Island once offered me *ten* bucks a day jes' to let 'em throw baseballs at my haid-and baseballs don't explode."

"Furthermo'," Jinx added, "you could spare that haid. 'Twouldn' be no loss whatsoever."

"Point is," said Shine, "five bucks or nothin', I'm jes' tellin' y' to be ready, see? If anybody bother us jes' up and knock hell out 'n 'em, that's all."

"You a pretty hard boogy, Mr. Shine," Bubber observed, "but I ain' never see you knock the hell out 'n no dynamite."

"Far as I'm concerned," contributed Jinx, "I'm ready now— to run. I been haulin' furniture, and I been haulin' pianos; but when they starts plantin' dynamite, this baby's gonna start haulin' hindparts!"

"Be the first honest haulin' you ever done, too," commented Bubber.

To Shine this banter was merely pledge of allegiance in case of crisis, assurance that the hiring of extra hands would in no event be necessary. Beneath the jests, the avowed fear, the merriment, was a characteristic irony, a typical disavowal of fact and repudiation of reality, a markedly racial tendency to make light of what actually was grave—a tendency stressed in Jinx and Bubber by the us habitual perversion of their own conduct toward each other. Members of another race might have jest said simply:

"What the hell do you think we are—quitters?"

So between them they killed the rest of the pint and mourned its death with laughter.

PATMORE RETURNED, GRINNING.

"You two," he directed Bubber and Jinx, "catch air. I got a bug to put in the big boy's ear." And when they had eventually obeyed, he went on to Shine: "Jes' to show y' they's no hard feelin's, I got a scheme that means bucks, and if you got two good eyes, you kin see how to make some of 'em."

"Listen. You don't specially like no dickties, do y'?"

"I ain' none too fond o' rats."

"But dickties give you a very special pain, don't they?"

"Lot's o' places. No lie."

"Me too. Now that's where you and I are alike, see?"

Shine's silence admitted nothing; but Pat went on:

"Heard you say sumpin' 'bout movin' this dickty Merrit."

"Did?"

"Yea. Now there's a guy I can't see with field glasses."

"No?"

"No.—Tell sumpm'." Pat looked about to be sure of privacy, leaned closer to the bar counter. "If Merrit died tomorrer—I wouldn' send 'im no flowers."

"What you got 'gainst 'im?"

"Plenty." There came a characteristic confidential twist to one side of Pat's mouth. "He put me in sometime back, see? Damage suit—ten thousand berries. Hit a guy crossin' the speedway—knocked him f' a gool, the dumbbell. Well—it was pay off or see jail, and naturally I wasn' go'n' see jail. Coulda' got out cheaper may be, on'y this bird Merrit wouldn' listen to reason. Claim' he was go'n' bring in my occupation and lots o' other stuff if I didn' come clean—forcin' my hand, see? Knew I had cash and knew he could make me pay off by threatenin' to squeal. I ought 'a' crowned him then, but he was too wise—knew where to meet me and when. So all I could do was pay off. Ten thousand bucks to stay out o' jail"

"Ten thousand bucks wasted," Shine said.

Pat misunderstood. "Yea," he agreed. "Nothin' to show for it. Know what I could 'a' done with that much at that time?"

"What?"

"I could 'a' bought in a fay neighborhood and held on for a price. I could a' made fifteen thousand that ten. Same as he's doin' now."

"So now you figger on a comeback?"

Pat was almost reproachful. "'Course not—that ain't the kind o' bird I am. Hell, I ain't evil, Shine. Anyway th' ain' nothin' I kin do 'bout it now anyhow, is they?"

"All I want is his trade, man. Bygones kin be bygones, far as I give a damn. Gittin' even is woman's stuff—man don' hold no grudges. But if I kin sell him and his friends licker regular, it'll mean a lot to me, see?"

"Unscheme yo' scheme, boogy."

"Listen. I'm handlin' a Canadian Club that'll sell itself, no stuff. If I kin git him to sample it, he'll take it—order it for himself and recommend it to his friends. It's bound to go big, see? But hych's the thing: if he knows I sent it he'll figure I'm tryin' to poison him and be scared to touch it, see? Now I got half a case on hand he kin have and I got ten bucks you kin have if you deliver it along with his things in the mornin'."

Shine's brows lifted. "Yea?"

"Yea. You're my agent, see? Only don't tell him—let him think you're handlin' it y'self. They'll be more later not only to him but his friends, and you kin collect ev'y time. How 'bout it?"

Shine's answer did not come promptly.

"Fact," Pat pursued, "with yo' job, you could work up a wonderful delivery service for me—no suspicion attached to it, see? Hyeh's yo' chance, man—start out as my agent.'

"Agent yo' hiney," said Shine. "Listen. Ain't you heard 'bout me?"

"'Bout you?"

"Sho', man. I done started already."

"Bootleggin'?"

"No lie. I got a regular business. Ain' but two people in it, though, the bootlegger and the customer. I'm both of 'em."

Once again Pat eyed Shine in silent frustration and, after an angry moment, turned away wordless.

Watching him go, Shine grinned, then frowned and muttered to himself:

"Wise guy. Aimin' to choke Merrit and throw the blame on me. Jes' 'cause I bring my own licker in and pass up his kerosene. Can y' beat it? Wonder how many kinds of a jackass that bozo thinks I am?"

By way of contrast, it is of further interbest est to drop in on a little group of dickties, superiorly self-named the Litter Rats, who were assembled informally this evening in the dwelling of one J. Pennington Potter, their current president.

This particular meeting of the Litter Rats' Club had been set apart for the discussion of The Negro's Contribution to Art and The Lost Sciences of Ethiopia. But when Fred Merrit announced that he had bought a house on Court Avenue, most exclusive of the residential streets adjacent to Negro Harlem, scheduled discussions were for the moment forgotten; and when he added that he intended to live in the house, and to do so whether a riot resulted or not, the dozen men about the room came promptly to the edges of their chairs.

"Preposterous!" said J. Pennington Potter, a plump little sausage of a man, whose skin seemed stuffed to the limit with the importance of what contained.

"Why so?" inquired Merrit.

"This colony," Potter pronounced, "should extend itself naturally and gradually—not by violence and bloodshed."

"The extension of territory by violence and bloodshed strikes me as natural enough," Merrit grinned. "I haven't much of a memory, but I seem to recall one or two instances—"

"Progress is by evolution, not revolution," expostulated J. Pennington Potter. "And you may be sure that race progress is no exception."

"Who the deuce said anything about race progress or about extending the colony?" asked Tod Bruce, the young and far from fundamentalist rector of St. Augustine's. "Why is it that a shine can never do anything except as a shine?"

"Well," commented Langdon, an innocent looking youngster who was at heart a prime rascal and who compensated by writing poetry, "if Fred will just keep his hat on, none of his neighbors will know he's a shine."

"Or he could try Stay-Straight for those kinks—" someone suggested.

primarily with the racial aspect of the thing—"

"He ought to be!" exploded Potter.

"I am," said Merrit coolly. "All of you know where I stand on things racial—I'm downright rabid. And even though, as Tod suggests, I'd enjoy this house, if they let me alone, purely as an individual, just the same I'm entering it as a Negro. I hate fays. Always have. Always will. Chief joy in life is making them uncomfortable. And if this doesn't do it—I'll quit the bar."

"Well, Fred," said Langdon, "don't forget the revenue. They'll pay you double the value of the place just to get you out, you know."

"I had that in mind, but hell—what's money? They won't pay me what I'll ask anyhow, and I won't sell for less."

There was a certain grimness about Merrit, for all his rosy cheeks and cherubic grin. He was anomalous in certain important particulars. Fair as the northernmost Nordic, his sandy hair was yet as kinky as that of any pure blooded African; and not the blackest of Negroes could have hated the dominant race more thoroughly.

"You know," he said, "I especially wanted my mother to live there. How she would have queened it—it would have been part compensation—"

It was another of Merrit's anomalies that, though he hated his lineage in general, he had been especially devoted to his mother. She had always seemed to him a symbol of sexual martyrdom, a bearer of the cross, as he put it, which fair manhood universally placed on dark womanhood's shoulders. Of all those whom he blamed and cursed for his own mongrel heritage, she was the one exception; for her, the only one he had actually known, he had only racial pity and filial devotion. She had recently died, late enough in her own life, but too early in his, to enjoy the luxuries he had just become able to give her. And so in addition to what she already represented, she had now become a symbol of motherhood unrewarded, idealized in memory far beyond what had been true in life.

"I think," he added, "my housekeeper'll give the neighbors enough of a shock, though. She's as colored as they come."

"Good!" grinned the cherubic Fred.

"They'll set fire to the—place they'll blow it up—the way they did Morris and Peters."

"Insurance is a marvelous invention, isn't it?"

"Uncalled for distress. I thoroughly disapprove of deliberate, intentional havoc. It's just what we're trying to prevent." This was to be expected of the extremely proper J. Pennington Potter, a "social worker" with a windy, pompous voice and a deep devotion to convention.

"Well," moderated Bruce, "Harlem began its growth by riots. I remember when I was a youngster, I used to be scared to stay out after dark. It was pretty bad then—either a crowd of fay boys would catch a jig and beat him up or else a crowd of jigs would get a fay boy and teach him the fear of the Lord. In either case the thing would be the first skirmish of a pitched battle somewhere on the frontier. The shines tricked a half dozen Irish lads into One Hundred Thirty-fourth Street one night, I remember, and two of them never came out. Cops—there weren't any black cops then—always went in threes at least. And I recall one day when twelve mounted policemen came galloping up One Hundred Thirty-Fourth Street after one little West Indian ice-man—and galloped back without him. It was really comical."

The others gave Bruce attention, watching him as he spoke. He too was fair, but less so than Merrit, and his skin was uniformly pallid. His face was lean, his features prominent and severe to the point of austerity, the nose large and narrow, the chin advancing, the mouth wide, straight, and thin-lipped. As if to offset the ascetic in this countenance, his eyes were deep-set and black, and in them some curious passion gleamed constantly like a flame. As he spoke these eyes engaged everything that might hold a drop of interest, comprehended it, drained it, left it; swiftly flashed from this to that, paused, penetrated, abandoned; sought further, halted, penetrated again, departed—a pair of black wasps.

"Those were the happy days," he went on. "People kept kettles of hot lye on the stoves and carried them to their doors whenever the bell rang. And you could go upon the roof of your knocked down and the bricks stacked at front room windows for ammunition. And say—one night a bunch of bad jigs—like those over on Fifth Avenue now—mistook me for a fay, and I had a Merritt is devil of a time proving I was a Negro, too!"

"I had the same experience," said Merrit. "You should've seen me exhibiting my kinky head."

"It was probably straight for a while," grinned Langdon.

"It's the old, old story," said Bruce. "War—conquest of territory. But our side of the thing isn't all there is to it. The fays have a side too, you know."

"I know," Merrit protested, like the lawyer he was, "but we aren't supposed to see that."

"Well, I don't know. It's easy to laugh now. But the fact is, it was tragedy. Black triumph is always white tragedy. We won—we won territory. All the fays had to get out, make way, make room for us. What did they do? Resist, of course—why the devil shouldn't they? Clung to their district, tried to recover. And we broke their heads with chimney bricks and bathed their bodies in hot lye. How do you suppose they felt about it?"

"Best thing that ever happened to 'em," grinned Fred.

"But tough on *them*, you'll admit."

"What of it?"

"Only this—that when you move up there on Court Avenue, you're opening up all those old scars. Just as Pott says, they'll resist. They'll warn you with threatening notes. They'll try to buy you out. If these don't work, they will probably dynamite you."

"I've received one warning already."

"You have?"

"You heard about Gamby, last month," said someone. "They had a gang of toughs on hand and they wouldn't even let the movers land his stuff on the sidewalk. Had to get the police."

"Glad you mentioned that," said Merrit. "I'll my worst stuff first, and I'll get the toughest furniture—movers in Harlem."

"Nowadays," Bruce observed, "we grow by—well—a sort of passive conquest. The fays move out, and the jigs are so close no more fays will move in. So the landlord has to rent to jigs and older method, I don't think it will do any great harm to the rest of us. He's taking all the risk. And even though he claims a racial interest, he has admitted that the chief motive is personal after all. It's his business."

"There is absolutely no excuse for it," was J. Pennington Potter's final dictum.

"Who the hell asked for an excuse, Pott?" was all that Merrit answered.

C ourt Avenue is a straight, thin spinster of a street which even in July is cold. There is about it an air of arched eyebrows, of skirts drawn aside and comments made with a sniff. It is adorned in sparse, lean, scrawny maples, all suffering from malnutrition, and these tend to stress rather than relieve the hardness of dry, level pavements.

The dwellings are all the same pale gray and are all essentially alike, four stories tall, thin to gauntness, droop-eyed with drawn shapes, standing shoulder to shoulder in long, inhospitable rows. Stone stoops, well withdrawn from the sidewalk, lend an air of inaccessibility, and the tiny front yards that might dispel this illusion by only a bit of grass or a flower are instead uniformly laid away beneath slabs of expressionless concrete.

Twice a day, when sunlight touches the windows of this side in the morning and again of that side at night, Court Avenue smiles a chilly, crystalline smile. It is the sort of smile that goes with the words, "My dear! Can you imagine such a thing!" and you might suppose that the street was returning even the sun's genial greeting and warm farewell with a disapproving sneer.

In short, Court Avenue is a snob of a street. Yet it is somewhat to be pitied in its pretense at ignoring the punishment that is at hand: the terribly sure approach of the swiftly spreading Negro colony.

ISAACS' TRANSPORTATION COMPANY, WHICH IS to say old man Isaacs, would have trusted Joshua Jones with any moving job whatever. It was work that Shine loved because of the challenge it presented to his personal strength and skill. He took charge, accepted responsibility, helped execute the orders he gave. Whenever a staircase or hallway presented a difficult turn or an insufficient dimension, he was at hand to decide just how the problem should be solved. Whenever a valuable piece of ungainly size had to be dismembered, and afterwards reconstructed, his knowledge of the mysterious anatomy of furniture was wholly important item: himself selected and anchored the tackle and guided the instrument through the window that was chosen to admit it.

Pianos indeed, were his particular prey, his almost living archenemies. He personified them, and out of controlling them, handling them, directing them helpless through midair, he derived a satisfaction comparable to that of a tamer of beasts. There was a superstition that a piano would "get" a man one time or another. Jinx and Bubber had both suffered injuries from instruments that slipped from their grips. But Shine laughed at this superstition, not because it was a superstition, but because he knew that he simply couldn't be "had."

Even the four-ton van was to Shine a beloved companion. He called her Bess, and Bess was the only thing on earth that he coveted. She was padded within and especially designed for the moving of things fine and fragile; her engine was responsive and smooth, her treads pneumatic, single in front, double in the rear. She rode like a private ambulance and she could make forty on a level. It was Shine's ambition one day to win her away from old man Isaacs.

The crew was usually made up only of Shine, Jinx, and Bubber, and these three in two years of cooperation had come to work together in a fashion beyond fault-finding, carefully, quickly, punctually, untrailed by patrons' complaints.

This early summer morning Shine swung Bess, loaded with Merrit's possessions, into the chilly Court Avenue atmosphere, and, with deliberate malice, sped up to a roar, then coasted, shifting his spark to make the motor spit.

"That'll wake up somebody," he grinned as Bess bang-banged like an automatic. "Come on you bomb-throwers—do your stuff—let's go!"

"Boy, lemme out this cab," said Bubber. "This darkey done gone crazy."

"Shuh!" complained Jinx. "Ain't go'n' be no rough stuff in this neighborhood. Deader'n Strivers' Row."

three-thirteen. The door opened and Merrit himself came out to meet them. He wore his usual air of nonchalance and his usual cherubic grin.

"Hello, fellows," he greeted. "Get it all on one load? That's clever."

All three stared. Such cordiality in a dickty was nothing short of astonishing, and it put the suspicious workers immediately on guard.

While Jinx and Bubber unfastened van-doors, Merrit went up to Shine and leaned carelessly against a tree. "What do you think of this?" he said, producing a letter.

Shine accepted the proffered note without enthusiasm. It was without heading or salutation, typewritten, and lacking a signature:

> You are not wanted in this neighborhood.
> If you move in, we'll move you out.

"Where'd you get it?" Shine asked Merrit.

"Found it in the vestibule when I came up to look around yesterday."

"Humph," said Shine. "Jes' let 'em start sump'm while we're here, that's all." And because he disliked dickties and wanted no talk with anyone of them, he changed the subject rudely. "Where you want us to put this stuff?"

"Anywhere. Spread it all over the first floor. My housekeeper'll come in from the country-place and have it arranged later."

"Hear that?" Jinx said to Bubber, out of sight at the rear of the van. "Thass what I say 'bout a spade. Spade can't git a little sump'n without stretchin' it. His housekeeper. His country-place. Humph—what's a use lyin' like that—?"

"He ain' lyin', fool. That jasper's got mo' bucks 'n you got freckles. Got a swell place on the upstate Pike, not far out o' town. Throws big parties and raises hell jes' like d' fays. Folks up there didn' know he was a jig till he had a party—and they offered him a million dollars fo' the place jes' to git him out. He wouldn' leave, though."

"Uh-huh."

"And he wouldn' leave?"

"Uh-huh."

"Huh! You lie wuss'n he do." Merrit's words came to them repeating, "Mrs. Fuller will take care of everything later."

"Thare now," commented Jinx, "y'see?"

"See what?"

"Soon as a old crow gits up in d' world, he got to grab hisse'f someother guy's wife."

Bubber regarded him with pity. "How you figger dat out?"

"*His* name ain't Fuller, is it?"

"No. And yo' name ain' Sherlock. Don't you know what a housekeper is? And ain't you never heard of sech a thing as a widow?"

"Aw man, whatyou talkin' 'bout?"

"You ought to be a policeman, brother."

"How come?"

"'Cause you very suspicious and very, very dumb."

These two had been unwrapping carefully covered hindmost pieces of furniture. Shine came around to lend a hand, and Merrit moved along the curb to a position such that he could observe them.

Now he indulged in another astonishing speech.

"Don't be too damn careful about these things. Flat didn't have anything but junk in it, anyway. Good stuff's in the country—won't move it in till fall. Just chuck this stuff in and let it lay."

What manner of dickty was this? He greeted you like an equal, casually shared his troubles with you, and did not seem to care in the least what the devil you I did with his furniture.

Jinx said sullenly to Bubber. "All he wants is for us to scratch up sump'm, so he kin call the five bucks off."

Bubber said to Jinx, "That ain't it. He's jes' makin' sure o' friends in case d' fays start sump'm." Shine said to himself, "If this bird wasn't a dickty he'd be okay. But they never was a dickty worth a damn."

into the emptied van—burlap and canvas wrappers, quilting, hemp rope, leather straps.

Merrit had just turned the key in his door and was facing about for departure, while Shine was on the point of climbing into the cab. At this juncture, simultaneously, everybody made an observation. It was the only observation that they all would have been likely to make at one time, and it held Merrit at attention on the stoop, rendered Shine motionless with one foot upon the step of his cab, and halted Bubber in the act of throwing a gunnysack over Jinx's head. Along the hitherto empty street a girl was briskly approaching.

You could see that she knew they were staring, so completely did she ignore them, and the ease with which she did so, the queenly unconcern with which she passed, indicated that she was accustomed to being stared at and did not mind it at all.

There was quite obviously no reason why she should have minded it. Certainly her attire invited no criticism—a brief frock of cool black satin, sheer gun-metal hose, and trim patent-leather pumps. Nor did she herself. She was tall and her face was pretty, and her body slenderly invited, though her legs perversely eluded, the persistent caress of the sedulous soft black satin.

Even if this had been all—a pretty girl on that gaunt empty street at this solitary hour, the staring would have been pardonable. But there was in addition an especially extenuating circumstance: the girl was not white.

Before she quite passed beyond earshot Jinx and Bubber were indulging in low enthusiasms:

"Boy, do you see what I see?"

"Law-aw-aw-dy!"

"Mus' be havin' a recess in heaven!"

"No lie. Umh-umh-umh—" Grunts to signify admiration far beyond words.

"Lady, you kin have all my week's pay—ev'y bit of it." Bubber dived elaborately into his empty pockets, while Jinx vowed:

"I'm gon' get religion and die so I kin go to heaven and meet that angel—yassuh!"

house the girl turned in, traversed the short cement walk, mounted the stoop, unlocked and entered the front door. Merrit raised his brows in a characteristic expression of surprise. Shine saw him do so and had a swift interpretation for that expression:

"Figgerin' on a jive already the doggone dicky hound. Why the hell dickties can't stick to their own women 'thout messin' around honest workin' girls"

Bubber was rapturizing without restraint, "Man—oh—man! A honey with high yaller laigs! And did you see that walk? That gal walks on ball-bearin's, she do—ev'ything moves at once." He illustrated his idea with head-wobblings, shoulder-rollings, and loose backward protrusions and retractions of buttocks. "See what I mean? Tail-conscious, man, tail-conscious—"

"You jes' a damn liar," came unexpectedly from Shine. "She walks like what she is, a lady—and you talk like what you is, a rat. Come on, it's gettin' late—let's go from here." Whereupon Jinx looked at Bubber and Bubber Jooked at Jinx. Here was indeed something new, Shine championing a woman.

"Well, kiss my assorted peanuts!" exclaimed Bubber.

"Guess that's the dynamite," was Jinx's dyspeptic surmise.

UPLIFT

M iss Agatha Cramp had, among other mthings things, a sufficiently large store of wealth and a sufficiently small store of imagination to want to devote her entire life to Service; in fact, to Social Service on a large scale. And because Miss Cramp took very personal interest in her successive servants, it came about that this Social Service was directed towards definite racial groups. When her maid had been French, Miss Cramp had organized a club to assist rebuilding demolished French villages; when her maid had been Polish, she had taken up with a Society for the Aid of Starving Poland; and shortly after hiring a Russian girl, she became a member of the Russian Relief Committee.

Thus Miss Cramp had devoted the more recent years of her life to Service, and now, with a colored maid on hand, she had no outlet for her urge.

For two weeks she had been idle, and idleness drove her to distraction. She felt worse and worse day by day, until at last her doctor said what she paid him to say: that she was on the verge of a nervous breakdown and would simply have to go to bed and rest.

She rested three days; whereupon an ironic Court Avenue sun revealed to her something of which she had hitherto been unaware: her colored maid, bringing in her breakfast, looked somehow amazingly pretty. And although Miss Cramp had no very generous eye for beauty, she was so struck by the discovery of what hitherto had mysteriously escaped her that she was moved to exclaim:

"Why, Linda, what've you done to yourself? You look so nice this morning."

Linda stood stiff in astonishment, eventually managing what might have been construed as a reply:

"You—feeling better, Miss Cramp?" The twinkle in the maid's eye escaped her mistress.

"I believe I am, Linda. I really believe I am."

attention to the tray just placed on her lap; inspected it, looked through it absently.

"Something else, Miss Cramp?" asked Linda.

"No. This is very nice, Linda. Very nice. But don't go. I want to talk to you. Something has just occurred to me."

It had indeed. For fifteen years Miss Cramp had been devoting her life to the service of mankind. Not until now had the startling possibility occurred to her that Negroes might be mankind, too.

The bare statement is extravagant; the fact is not. The only Negroes Miss Cramp had ever spoken to were porters, waiters, and house-servants of acquaintances. These were the only ones of whose existence she had been even remotely aware. Negroes to her had been rather ugly but serviceable fixtures, devices that happened to be alive, dull instruments of drudgery, so observed, so accepted, so used, and so forgotten. Had all the dark-skinned folk in the country been blotted out by some specific selective destruction, Miss Cramp would not have missed them in the least, would not have been glad nor sorry, would have gone serenely on unaware, tehk-tchk-ing perhaps over the newspaper account, but remaining wholly untouched in her sympathies.

Not so with remoter disasters: Over the slaughter of Armenians by Turks she had once sobbed bitterly and even over the devastation of the Japanese by earthquake she had mourned a little; because, though she had never known Armenian or Japanese, she had thought somewhat about them; though they had never approached her person, they had penetrated her intellect a little. But Negroes she had always accepted with horses, mules, and motors, and though they had brushed her shoulder, they had never actually entered her head.

But now something had occurred to her.

"Linda you're quite different from most—er—colored people, aren't you?"

To Linda, who had no idea what "most colored people" might mean, this was a baffling question. "I don't know, Miss Cramp," she said.

really quite pretty." She was experiencing the difficulties familiar to all who itch with curiosity but prefer not to be seen scratching.

"You're so light, you know."

Linda's lips twitched. "Why I'm not so awfully light, Miss Cramp. And plenty folks lighter than I am are far from being pretty."

"Yes—of course," Miss Cramp considered. "Even white people. To be sure. But of course you meant—er—colored. But your hair now—it isn't kinky." At once an assertion and a question.

The only answer was, "No, Miss Cramp."

"And how can you afford to wear such nice looking things on eighteen dollars a week?"

"Well," Linda said, "'course I could do better on twenty."

Miss Cramp did not hear this, but observed, "Patent-leather pumps and a black satin dress—"

"They're cheap shoes," Linda explained. "Just look nice 'cause they're new. The dress I got down on Eighth Avenue for seven dollars."

"But your skin, my dear. You might pass for a Sicilian or an Armenian."

Linda was not sure about these. "I was a gypsy once in a concert," she admitted.

"A concert?"

"At church."

"You go to church?"

"I like to go very much."

"Now that's just what I wanted to ask you about. Your people are very religious creatures aren't they?"

"Well, some are and some not."

"I thought—er—slavery, you know, would have made you very religious."

"Maybe it did," said Linda. "I wouldn't know 'bout that."

"But don't you have your own hymns? Spirituals, I believe they are called."

"Not in my church," Linda said.

"What church is that, Linda?"

"Episcopal!" incredulously. "Why *I'm* an Episcopalian." The tone indicated clearly that there must be some mistake.

A little devilishly, Linda smiled, but all she said was, "Is that so?"

"But you—" began Miss Cramp, then reconsidered. "But you must sing spirituals. All Negroes sing spirituals, don't they?"

Doubtfully Linda ruminated. "Wh—I remember some jubilee singers gave a concert of 'em once at the Parish. And I've been to Methodist revival meetings where they sang 'em just like jazz. We only went for fun, to see the folks get happy and shout. I've never heard them at my church in regular service, though."

"Well," said Miss Cramp. And again, "Well." Then, "What I was getting at was—do your churches make any effort to improve conditions, to render real service to your people?"

"Oh, yes. We have an employment agency. They sent me to the one that sent me to you."

"No, no, Linda." So stupid a reply restored Miss Cramp's self-assurance. "That is not what I mean, my dear. I mean the people that are mentally ill, the criminals, the dope-fiends, the fallen women. Do your churches try to help them?"

"I don't think so—not unless they're members."

"There must be some organization to do such work among your people," Miss Cramp insisted.

"Well," Linda suggested brightly, "maybe the same organization does it that does it among your people."

"Of course—of course. One would think so, wouldn't one? But I haven't come in contact with—of course, I haven't worked in colored communities—"

After a vacuous pause, Linda said, "Maybe you mean the G.I.A."

"G.I.A.? What's that?"

"General Improvement Association."

"What do they do?"

"Well, they collect a dollar a year from everybody that joins, and whenever there's a lynching down south they take the dollar and send somebody to go look at it."

RUDOLPH FISHER

"I don't know, Miss Cramp. Seems like they just want to make sure it really happened."

"Well. Then what do they do?"

"Well, by that time the year's up and it's time to collect another dollar. So they collect it."

"Why don't they turn their attentions to conditions here at home?" Miss Agatha wanted to know. "There must be much to be done here among you—an alien, primitive people in a great, strange metropolis. Why don't they do something here?"

"Well, nobody gets lynched here."

The simplicity of this response did not satisfy Miss Cramp, who could never have suspected that her colored maid would dare make game of her ignorance or play upon her credulity.

"Why I can't understand—I really can't. Here is a situation that surely needs attention, and the people do nothing—absolutely nothing about it. Lynchings—of all things! When right here in New York City there are How many of you are there here, Linda?"

"Two hundred thousand, according to Father Bruce."

"Oh, that's an exaggeration, of course. But even if there are as many as ten thousand, a great work could be done among them. This organization you mention—"

"The G.I.A."

"Yes—quite evidently someone needs to point the way. Their attention is entirely in the wrong quarter."

"Whyn't you help them out, Miss Cramp?"

"That's just what occurred to me Linda. Exactly what occurred to me. When I saw you this morning and noticed for the first time how different you were from most colored people, I said to myself, 'There now—why can't they all be like that?' And I said, 'Why they can be if they have the right sort of help. Some organization that could render real service, that's just what they need!' Then you mentioned this G.A.R.—"

"G.I.A."

"—and told me of the mistake they were making, and I said, 'There now, there is an instrument that can be turned to good use out. I really do think I will."

"They'll certainly appreciate it, Miss Cramp."

"Of course. . . well, that's all, Linda. Thank you very much. Linda, bring me the 'phone book when come back, won't you? I presume they have a telephone?"

"Who, Miss Cramp?"

"This G.I.R. Society."

"A telephone? I don't know, Miss Cramp." Linda was elaborately uncertain, eventually concluding, "They might have one. They might at that. I'll bring the book, Miss Cramp."

There is at least one occasion a year when Manhattan Casino requires no decorations, the occasion of the General Improvement Association's Annual Costume Ball. The guests themselves are all the decoration that is necessary.

This is not only because many guests attend in costume, but also because, of all the crowds which Manhattan Casino holds during the year, none presents a greater inherent variety: There is variety of personal station that extends from the rattiest rat to the dicktiest dicky, for this is not an exclusive, invitational "function" but a widely advertised public affair; and it is supported by everybody, because the proceeds are to be given over to Negro advancement. There is variety of personal appearance that ranges from the dingiest dinge to the most delicate pink; variety of age, from little brown gnomes of nine or ten to Cleopatras of sixty; variety, finally, of occupation, related of course to variety of social standing. At the So-and-So's Dance you would find chiefly doctors, lawyers, and undertakers; at the Speedway Club Dance, bootleggers, big-time gamblers, professional politicians; at the Barbers' Ball, tonsorial artists, chauffeurs, and head-waiters. Anybody may achieve admittance to anyone of these, but the crowd somehow remains in large measure distinct and characteristic. Not so with the G.I.A. Costume Ball. This is the one occasion in Harlem when everybody is present and nobody minds. The bootleggers raise no objection to their rivals, the doctors. The K.M.'s are seldom if ever seen to turn up their noses at the school teachers. Elevator boys and gamblers together discuss their ups and downs: and the richest real estate man in the colony greets his bootblack with a cordial smile. The bars are down. This is for the Race. One great common fellowship in one great common cause.

There was the great dance floor, large as a city block, with a fifteen-piece orchestra exhausting itself at the far end. On either side of this dance area, separated from it by railings and extending the length of the building between the dance floor and the lateral walls, a raised level or low terrace, occupied by a tangle midway by a wide staircase, that turned at right angles and led up alongside the wall to the upper level, the level of the tier of boxes that encircled the hall and roofed in the two lateral terraces below.

Those who between dances repaired only so far as the terraces and sat at the round-top tables and drank Whistle, perhaps tinctured with corn, were either just ordinary respectable people or rats. But those who mounted the stairs and crowded into or about the boxes, who kept waiters busy bringing ginger ale, which they flavored from silver hip flasks—those were dickties and fays.

Of the people downstairs, a few of the girls wore inexpensive costumes; others wore gaudy habiliments that were just as truly costumes but were probably not so intended. The men wore anything, from clothing so inconspicuous as to attract no attention to outfits positively stunning—light gray suits, cerise crêpe ties and bright yellow, broad-toed oxfords.

Of the dickties, the women were all extravagantly dressed. Whether they wore costume or evening frock, it quite obviously had to outglitter everyone's else. The men, however, uniformly clad in dinner-coats, performed well their sole esthetic function of background.

Of the usual sprinkling of fays, a few were the friends and guests of dickties; several were members of the Executive Board of the G.I.A., professional uplifters, determined to be broad-minded about this thing; and accompanying these two groups, a third consisting of newcomers to Harlem, all gasps, grunts, and ill-concealed squirms, or sighs and astonished smiles. The first group coming to enjoy not the Negroes but themselves, hence perfectly at ease; the second coming to raise up the darker brother, hence sweetly beaming and benevolent; the third coming to see the niggers, hence tortured with smothered comment and stifled expression. On the whole corresponding pretty well to their hosts, these visitors: usually dull and ordinary, occasionally bright and substantial, once in a blue moon brilliant or beautiful.

So swept the scene from black to white through all the shadows and shades. Ordinary Negroes and rats below, dickties the roof over the heads of the other. Somehow, undeniably, a predominance of darker skins below, and, just as undeniably, of fairer skins above. Between them, stairways to climb. One might have read in that distribution a complete philosophy of skin-color, and from it deduced the past, present, and future of this people. . . out on the dance floor, everyone, dickty and rat, rubbed joyous elbows, laughing, mingling, forgetting differences. But whenever the music stopped everyone immediately sought his own level. One great common fellowship in one great common cause.

D ownstairs at one point on the terrace were Jinx and Bubber, oblivious to everybody, arguing heatedly over the relative speed of corn and gin as intoxicants. Neither had either. At another point a group of girls dressed as gypsies sat laughing around a table. The prettiest of these was Linda, not the dry and quiet Linda that served Agatha Cramp her meals, but a vivacious lighthearted child, out on a lark, being herself. Not far away, leaning against one of the pillars that supported the tier of boxes, stood Henry Patmore, calculatingly watching Linda. Further back, unnoticed, like a great shadow against the wall, Shine stood with his hands in his pockets, motionless, watching Patmore.

He had not long to wait before what he anticipated began to happen.

Henry Patmore was acknowledged among his friends a perfect ladies' man. He had all the qualifications: money to burn, with a constant large supply of banknotes on his person, after the fashion of bootleggers; excellent taste in dress, as exemplified tonight by a sack suit of light greenish gray, a shirt of slate radium silk with collar to match, a bright green satin cravat caressing a diamond question mark, and a breast pocket polka dot handkerchief, whose crêpe border matched the tie. He was large and self-assured with an engaging manner and a flashing smile. Some people might not have cared for the fishy blankness of Patmore's gray eyes, nor for his tough-looking tan skin, thickly bespecked with small brown freckles, nor for his rather heavy jowls nor his rather thick neck with its two deep transverse creases behind. But so courteous was his manner with ladies, so deferential, so flatteringly humble his approach, that almost never did a girl deny his request for a dance, whether she knew him or not.

Further, there was about him the reassuring deliberateness of complete self-confidence. He was thirty-five years old, as free of the uncertainties of youth as of the infirmities of age; on the one hand debonair but not dashing, on the other, solid but not set. He had reached a point where his person might still inspire did Patmore's manner suggest his motive.

It follows that Patmore's conquests were many and his reputation enviable. Nor can it be denied that he made the most of this reputation among his fellow men, taking little pains to conceal either the nature of his activities or the identity of their object. He even allowed it to be suspected that there were dickty homes where he made it convenient to deliver liquor only during the hours when the head of the house was absent. Of this he did not openly boast, of course—not, at least, when he was sober. That would have been bad business indeed, just as it would be bad business tonight to mount the stairs and try to mingle with his many patrons in the boxes. Occasionally, however, his own liquor did make him excessively talkative. He would stride into his establishment proclaiming his own excellence in this or that particular, and not in frequently the particular was conquest of ordinarily inaccessible women. Accordingly his fellows declared him to be a "jiver from way back." And while, drunk or sober, he did not deny this, still he always insisted that he was business man first of all.

For today however his business was done. He had provided more of the life of this party than any other single person, and he now fell back with a clear conscience upon the pursuit of his avocation.

As a field for such an avocation, the uniqueness of Harlem is that there are always new realms to conquer. Incredible, bewildering variety. Consider the mere item of complexion, you whose choice may run only from cool white to warm rose-andolive. Harlem offers its cool white too, with blue eyes and flaxen hair, believe it or not; proceeds on through the conventional shades to the warmth of rose-and-olive; and here, where the rest of Manhattan ends, Harlem has just begun: on through the creams, the honeys and high-browns, the browns, the sealskins and chestnuts—a dozen gradations in every class, not one without its peculiar richness. And if white be cool and olive warm, must not chestnut be downright fever? Harlemites swear that the Queen that Cleopatra could have been but a honey at the fairest. And for evidence they will point out a dozen Shebas and any number of Cleopatras in the flesh.

Here is every variation of skin-color, every variety of feature-form, every possible combination of these variations and varieties. And of course every imaginable result, from the most outrageous ugliness to the most extraordinary beauty. Harlem is superlatively rich in diversity.

Accordingly Henry Patmore enjoyed almost boundless choice, and it was no mean tribute to Linda's beauty that tonight his wandering eye fell and lingered upon her. He saw that she was with other girls and therefore probably unattended—legitimate prey. And if he caught something vaguely different about her, it but served to heighten his interest.

Shine too had seen Linda and recognized her as the girl of the Court Avenue comments. It had given him strange and moving sensations, this recognition, had made him stare again just as foolishly as he had stared that morning a fortnight before. For him the rest of the picture thereupon faded into background, grew abruptly distant—people, laughter, shouting, music—while this darkeyed girl in her gypsy attire, scarlet, gold, and black, became and remained the center and reason of it all.

Joshua Jones, be it confessed, was himself no cipher among the ladies. There had been girls aplenty: Sarah Mosely, Babe Merrimac, Lottie Buttsby, Becky Katz, Maggie Mulligan, and others. An acknowledged master of men is usually attractive to women, and in his world of sinew and steel, Shine had the necessary reputation; there was no end of stories about what he could do with his hands.

But his general philosophy of conduct, of being impenetrably hard, of repudiating sentiment and relaxing toward no one and nothing, shielded his spirit if not his body from the women he so far had known; and while he might have claimed some excellence as a man of affairs if he had so chosen, it would not have been the same in degree or kind as that attributed to Patmore. Patmore's victories had been achieved, Shine's had been thrust upon intentionally eluded.

"Women," Shine had often said, "don't mean a man no good. Always want sump'm. Always got they hands out. Gimme. Any bird that really falls for a sheba is one half sap and th' other half sucker."

It did not matter that he had derived this conclusion from observation rather than experience. He believed it firmly. And so it was that triumph to Patmore would have been defeat to Shine, and the former's reputation was to the latter nothing at all to brag about. Indeed, this reputation of Pat's was one of the things about him that Shine most disliked. It summed Pat up as less of a man to be so much of a sap.

A NEW DANCE BEGAN, AND from the orchestra, keyed up now to its very low-downest, there issued a current of leisurely, compelling rhythm, a rising tide of rhythm which floated couple after couple off the bank into midstream. Presently Linda was left alone at her table.

Henry Patmore went forward. To request the dance, less accomplished beaus would have simply extended a hand toward the girl, an audacious gesture, bordering on the presumptuous. Not Patmore. In addition to the slightly extended hand, he bent forward in a most ingratiating bow, smiled the metallic smile which revealed so much of his wealth, and said earnestly:

"Would you do me the favor, miss?"

Linda, however, how dismiss strangers. She looked up, smiled very, very sweetly, and said with great finality, "No, thanks."

The average sheik would have passed on. Patmore was not the average sheik; and perhaps Linda had smiled a little too sweetly to convey sarcasm. Said he:

"The nex' one, maybe?"

"I'm leaving after this one," the girl lied easily.

"My, my. What a shame, both of us wastin' it."

He drew up a chair and sat down, his manner indicating clearly that though she might not dance with him, she could have no objection to his sharing her table. And he casually continued the conversation.

Linda silently annoyed, was on the point of rising to leave. His next remark detained her:

"I'm one o' the judges, y' know."

Her brows went up and he knew that now, at least, he had her interest. It quickened his own. A girl who was wise would have answered, "Yea—and I'm Norma Talmadge."

Linda, instead, exclaimed without irony, "Are they really going to give prizes?"

Patmore grinned within, congratulating himself on his own good fortune. "Ripe in the body and green in the head. What more could a man want?"

"No lie," he assured her. "And I'm gonna vote for you—unanimous."

Of course, if you happened to be wearing a costume and unexpectedly found a prize in sight, there was no sense in throwing a chance away. And if this courteous man was a judge, that meant he must be Somebody and not just an ordinary masher as she had supposed.

"I been noticin' you specially," he said.

She was decently silent.

"That's why I ast you to dance. Wanted to find out all about you." He took out his business address book, which contained the names and addresses of many prominent Harlemites, and wrote the words which he repeated after her aloud:

"'Miss Linda Young. Three hundred and nine Court Avenue, Washington Heights.' Fine. Fine. Miss Young, the first prize is twenty-five dollars, and it's as good as yours right now."

"Oh, no—"

"Deed so. Now listen, Miss Young. My name is Patmore—Henry Patmore—and we might jes' as well be friends. And if you'll finish this dance with me, I'll see that th' other judges gets a good look at you."

Shine, several yards away, could hear nothing that was said, but he saw the whole thing: first, the girl's obvious reaction to being approached by a stranger; despite this, the ease with which she had been engaged in conversation; then the promptness with

RUDOLPH FISHER

the new friend's notebook. Now he saw her smile and rise and let Patmore steer her to the dance floor. In a moment more the pair was engulfed in the stream.

The scene occasioned in Shine a curious reaction: not an intensification of his contempt for Patmore, as might have been expected, but an unaccountably violent revulsion of feeling toward the girl. His inordinate admiration turned to equally inordinate scorn.

"As easy as that!" he scowled. "Well, I be damned!

Course he now fell back on his own unfailing gospel.

"See?" said he to the cock-eyed world, "that jes' goes to show y', see? One mo' sheba, that's all. Mo' different they look, less different they are. Bet he offered her a stick o' candy or sump'm. . . and here I come near gettin' excited jes' lookin' at her. Can y' beat it?"

But though this might be only one more instance of a far-reaching general truth, somehow the cynic did not dismiss it with customary casualness. As the evening progressed, he admitted this to himself, indeed could not deny it. For even after he had danced through "Do it, Daddy," with Babe Merrimac, who vamped him desperately without avail, and through a slow and easy, somewhat disturbing "Shake That Thing" with the voluptuous Lottie Buttsby, the earlier incident still stuck fast in his mind. Babe and Lottie both complained of finding him even less enthusiastic than usual; he was, they avowed, downright leaden, and Lottie specified precisely where anyone interested could find the lead. But neither succeeded in bantering him into promising to see her safely home after the shout.

He caught sight of Linda occasionally, dancing with boys, nice, Sunday-Schoolish boys he did not know, and he blamed these occasional views of her for the persistence in his of what he had seen. He began to resent that persistence:

"What the hell I keep thinkin' 'bout *that* for?"

Then, by way of excuse, "Well she sho' is good to look at. Ain' no sense in a woman bein' that good-lookin'. Ain' no excuse for it. Dangerous, what I mean. Ought to be locked up somewheres where she couldn' do so much harm."

He encountered Jinx and Bubber and they did nothing to help him forget. "Boy!" exclaimed Bubber, "'member that sheba we seen that mornin' on Court Avenue?"

Shine grunted assent.

world. We jes' seen 'uh-right over yonder. Great Gordon Gin—talk about one red hot mamma! "Dressed like a fortuneteller—wish" she'd tell mine. Anything she say 'd be awright with me. Tell me I go'n' die tomorrer, I'd go right on and die happy."

"I *mean*," Jinx agreed. "And when I was dead and buried, all she'd have to do 'd be walk over my grave, see?—And damn if I wouldn' git up and follow 'uh. Boy, she's got what it takes, and papa don' mean maybe!"

"She's the owl's bow'ls," Bubber epitomized. Shine looked at them scornfully. "You guys," he observed, "mus' both have glass eyes."

When he had glumly departed, they looked at each other a long time solemnly; then they grinned and finally laughed aloud.

"What's a matter with my boy?" Jinx wanted to know.

"Nothin'. She jes' done put d' locks on 'im, thass all."

"Nothin' different. And then up and give him lots of air."

"Seems lak," Bubber grew serious, "our boy has been smote sho' 'nuff, though, don' it?"

"Smit," corrected Jinx.

"Smote."

"Smit."

"What you know 'bout language?"

"Mo' 'n you. Don' nobody talk language down yo' home in South Ca'lina."

"What they talk, then?"

"Don' talk 'tall. Jes' grunt."

"Yea—and so did that man grunt what run you out o' Virginia, too."

"Thass aw right 'bout that. Fact is, ev'y time you forgit you up nawth, you start gruntin' in yo' native language."

"Maybe. But what I mean, you don' never *forgit* you up nawth—and ain' nobody never heard you sing that song 'bout 'Carry Me Back to Old Virginny' neither."

"D' word is smit."

"Smote."

"Smit, I say."

somebody *write* y', it's *wrote*, ain't it?" "

"You listen, Oscar. When you git a hole in yo' hiney where some dog *bite* y', you *bit*, ain't y'?"

THE DEBATE BETWEEN THESE TWO was no more undecided than another, conducted within the mind of Joshua Jones. The question at issue was this: If Henry Patmore had so easily picked up the girl, why should not he pick her up also? Or—why should he?

On the one side were all the customary objections of his avowed attitude toward women. On the other were a number of obscure things, imponderable as vapor, but just as present and annoying: an impulse to win her favor just to have the pleasure of discarding it, compensating somewhat thus for his own recent disillusion; a plaguing curiosity to observe the girl at close satisfy the suspicion that she couldn't be all that range and she seemed to be at a distance; a thought of riling Patmore by outdoing him at his own game and robbing him of this, his latest triumph; these but the half-conscious excuses, really, for a far simpler, unadmitted urge: the unquestionably compelling attractiveness of the girl herself.

This debate terminated suddenly and decisively. Linda finished a dance with one of the "Sunday-School" boys, and now, completely bored, shooed him off into the crowd, insisting that otherwise the following dance would begin before he could find his next partner. She came now unaccompanied toward the low terrace, reaching it just as the orchestra struck up a new number. Here she and Shine met face to face and the argument was settled; she was alone, she was at hand, and a new dance was beginning.

Their eyes met and he grinned and said:

"Didn' you promise me this one?"

It was a good grin, wide, honest-looking, a trifle amused, a trifle audacious. His chin assumed more than its usual challenge, and the flash of his teeth set up twinkling echoes in his eyes. It was a perfectly spontaneous, disarming grin and it ought to have turned the trick. But it failed.

puzzled; then with a little smile of comprehension and disdain, brushed past him without a word.

The superiority of that smile was far and away more telling and convincing than any scornful toss of the head or sneer or gesture of anger could have been. It placed the notion of dancing with him beyond anger, resentment, or contempt. It stamped such a possibility as too absurd to be aught but a trifle amusing. And it raised Shine's temperature.

On the impulse of his anger he turned and followed her the short distance to her table, and when she sat down and looked up, there he was. She was mildly astonished.

"Wrong number," she said briefly and smiled that smile again.

He sat down and put his arms on the table and leaned forward as she drew back in surprise. He spoke very gravely, and his voice, though low, suffered no loss of clarity by reason of the bedlam 'round about; indeed the merry confusion seemed to lend them a certain seclusion.

"Listen, Long Distance—who you kiddin'?"

"Wrong number, I said," the girl repeated less generously and pushed back her chair to rise.

"One moment please, operator," returned Shine. "What number'd you think I was callin'?"

"The number on that policeman's badge," she said, although "that policeman" was nowhere sight.

"Where?" He looked about unconcernedly.

"Or—one of the officials."

"Officials?"

"Yes officials!"

"Oh. They all friends o' mine."

"Mr. Henry Patmore, I suppose?"

"Who?"

"Henry Patmore." She knew that would settle him.

"Pat? . . . Well I take it back. I know him well but he ain't no friend o' mine."

There was but one way to keep him from imperturbably trailing her the rest of the evening—she had recourse to insult:

That went wide. "What official is he—official bootlegger?"

"He's a judge—and a gentleman."

"Judge? Judge of what?"

"Of costumes—and of people that try to be sheiks."

He looked at her as she sat on the edge of the chair, a bird poised, postponing flight only for one last jab at the snake; and instead of laughing aloud at what she had said about Patmore, he scowled and muttered, "Judge. Humph. So that was his jive. Huh. Judge."

This piqued her curiosity and further delayed her departure. "Yes, judge."

"What else did he tell y'?"

"Nothing else about himself—but a whole lot about you."

"Me?"

"Yes you."

"Me? How he come to?"

"I saw you looking and asked him." She rose at last. "I promised him this dance, if"—no missing the sarcasm this time—"if you will excuse me."

"No—wait a minute—listen." He too was standing now, towering over her, leaning a trifle toward ber, and perhaps less composed than he'd ever been in his life in the company of a girl. If she had been interested enough to ask Pat about him, there was no sense in releasing her now so easily, just because she was playing tight. Or maybe she wasn't playing. Maybe she was scared. "Listen—I admit I got you all wrong. But it looked—listen. I'm standin' over there, see? And Pat comes up and puts on his jive—anybody can see you don' know 'im. But lap it up. You swallow it whole. I mean that's the way it looked. Naturally I figger I can get away too, see? Y' can't kill me f' that, can y'?"

From Shine this was abject apology. Babe would have taken it so, or Lottie, and been delighted and amazed. But Linda, to whom his implication was insult, stiffened as if something unclean had touched her, while her eyes dilated with anger and resentment. Then her body relaxed into an attitude of casual contempt and her look became tranquil scorn. She said quietly, as if verifying a memory:

merely stuck in his ears unrealized and meaningless, like the monotonous pulse of the orchestra's bass drum. Then suddenly, as if their beating had finally broken through a wall, they burst full into consciousness and throbbed in his head like pain.

He stood quite still, experiencing new and terrible feelings. Rat. Well enough from an equal—but from this girl—Rat. Dirty rat. Patmore *said* you were just a dirty rat.

Linda saw the change come over his face; saw the brows contract, the eyes gleam, the jaws tighten, the lips set; saw his body go taut like a rope under tension and the bronze skin lose its life and turn dirty copper. Linda had not the sophistication nor the cultivated self-protective cruelty of most beautiful women. She did not see that she had achieved her purpose, had effected a serious wound, and could now perhaps go on her way unafraid. She saw only that her thrust had gone too deep and said impulsively:

"Oh, I'm sorry—I didn't really mean that—"

Then in a flutter of contrition and fright she whirled about and fled.

For yet a while longer he did not move. Music, dancing, laughter—tumultuous silence, uproarious, crowded solitude. Presently he was aware of a voice periodically snarling "R-r-rat!" and after a while realized that the trap-drummer was executing a series of rolls each swelling to a terminal snap like the epithet. "R-r-rat!"

That woke him. The stupor had been the recession of a wave, withdrawing only to gather impetus. Now again it rushed over him, hot and impelling. He looked about a little madly and very grimly, and he said aloud:

"Judge. Hmph. Show me that judge. I'm go'n' give 'im sump'm to judge."

U pstairs in the box of J. Pennington Potter, who was one of the dozen vice-presidents of the General Improvement Association, an incredibly ill-chosen variety of personalities squirmed. It was J. Pennington Potter's conviction that only admixture produced harmony between races. He argued quite logically. Prejudice and misunderstanding were due to mutual ignorance and ignorance due to silence. This silence must be broken. How break it save by acquaintanceship—how acquaint save by admixture? Social admixture—there was the solution to all the problems of race.

And so he proceeded to admix. There was himself, proud, loud, and pompous, and his wife, round, brown, and expansile, who always seemed bursting with something to say, but had never been known to say it; a woman so inflated with her husband's bombast that one felt she'd collapse at a single thrust. There was the Hon. Buckram Byle, an ex-alderman from the twenty-ninth district, whose presence was intended to give the party some notion of the dignity of a Negro public servant. This he assuredly did, his habit being to stand apart, alone, with folded arms, motionless, silent, scowling, in the deeps of meditation. But few suspected the real basis of this air: that Mr. Byle was simply very angry at his young and pretty wife, Nora, who had managed to elude his jealously watchful eye all evening; and that the scowl, as usual, evidenced his resolution to take her straight home the moment she should reappear. There was Noel Dunn, the Nordic editor of an anti-Nordic journal, who missed no item of or conversation that he thought he could use for copy. Dunn's readers gobbled up pro-Negro pieces, not because they were pro-Negro so much as because they were anti-white, and he and Mrs. Dunn were frequent visitors to Harlem, finding the Pennington Potters convenient wedges in effecting several profitable entrances.

The Potters were very proud of this friendship, and J. Pennington never missed a chance to mention, parenthetically night before last The Dunns were known among their friends to mention these excursions also, but not at all parenthetically. The Dunns always explained elaborately about the "wealth of material" to be found in Negro Harlem, and they punctuated their apologies with different intonations of the word "marvelous." Everything in Harlem, to the Dunns, was simply "marvelous!"

A friend of the Dunns, one Tony Nayle, who was visiting Harlem for the first time, was absent from the box at the moment. He had found the music and Nora Byle an irresistible combination; and Nora admitted later that she had continued dancing with him not merely to aggravate her jealous spouse, but also to verify what at first she could hardly believe. Nora always insisted that fays danced with a rhythm all their own, if any. She found Tony Nayle to be the first fay partner she'd ever known, so she said, to dance as though he paying any attention to the music at all.

And finally, side by side in the front of the box, sat Fred Merrit and Miss Agatha Cramp.

It would have been enough to kill the spirit of any party just to have the inarticulate Mrs. Potter as its hostess; enough to distress any company just to inject into it a chronically jealous husband like Byle, let alone bringing his pretty wife, Nora, into contact with the attractive and willing-to-learn Tony; enough to insure discomfort in any group to include guests whose purposes were so different—amusement, profit, uplift; difficult enough to bring together unacquainted, dissimilar people without attempting to mix diverse motives as well. But to have put Fred Merrit and Miss Agatha Cramp side by side—this was the master touch; only a J. Pennington Potter could have done that.

ONE VIEW ONLY DID THEY all have in common, the scene on the floor below.

"Marvelous!" said Mr. Dunn.

"Marvelous!" echoed Mrs. Dunn.

"Wonderful!" said J. Pennington Potter with a certain air of discovery.

the next, that an observer from above might easily have lost the sense that these were actually people. They seemed rather some turbulent congress of bright colored, inanimate things, propelled by a force over which they had no control. The couples were like the leaves and petals of flowers strewn thick on a stream; describing little individual figures and turns, circling capriciously in groups here and there, but all borne steadily onward in one common undertrend. Each seemed to answer with a smile the whim of every breeze; all actually obeyed unaware the steadfast pull of the current.

"Marvelous!" duoed the Dunns. "Wonderful!" said J. Pennington Potter.

"M-m—" grunted the Hon. Buckram Byle.

"Don't you think, Penny," said Noel Dunn, "that your organization would be more specifically defined if it were named The General Negro Improvement Association?"

"Why, yes. Yes indeed. That is, perhaps. As a matter of fact we originally conceived the name as the General Negro Improvement Association. But it was I myself who contended, and without successful contradiction, that any improvement of the American Negro would inevitably improve all other Americans as well. There was therefore—ah—no point, you see, in including the word 'Negro,' and I succeeded in having it deleted."

Mr. Dunn smiled, noting that the trap-drummer was at the moment very amusing.

Meanwhile Miss Agatha Cramp sat quite overwhelmed at the strangeness of her situation. This was her introduction to the people she planned to uplift. True to her word she had personally investigated the G.I.A. and been welcomed with open arms. Certain members of the executive board knew her and her past works—one or two had been associated with her in other projects—and her experience, resources, and devotion to service were unanimously acclaimed assets. And nobody minded her excessively corrective attitude—all new board members started and that would be enough to upset anybody's ideas of revision.

Never had Miss Cramp seen so many Negroes in one place at one time. Moreover, never had she dreamed that so many of her own people would for any reason imaginable have descended to mingle with these Negroes. She had prided herself on her own liberality in joining this company tonight. And so it shocked and outraged her to see that most of these fair-skinned visitors were unmistakably enjoying themselves, instead of maintaining the aloof, kindly dignity proper to those who must sacrifice to serve. And of course little did she suspect how many of the fair-skinned ones were not visitors at all but natives.

When she met Nora Byle, for instance, she was first struck with the beauty of her "Latin type." To save her soul she could not help a momentary stiffening when Buckram Byle, who was a jaundice-brown, was presented as Nora's husband: Intermarriage! She recovered. No. The girl was one of those mulattoes, of course; a conclusion that brought but temporary relief, for the next moment the debonair Tony Nayle had gone off with the "mulatto," both of them flirting disgracefully.

It was all in all a situation which robbed Miss Cramp of words; but she smiled bravely through her distress and found no little relief in sitting beside Fred Merrit, whose perfect manner, cherubic smile and fair skin were highly comforting. She had not yet noticed the significant texture of his hair.

"Well, what do you think of it?" Merrit eventually asked.

"I don't know what to think, really. What do you think?"

"I? Why—it's all too familiar now for me to have thoughts about. I take it for granted."

"Oh—you have worked among Negroes a great deal, then?"

Merrit grinned. "All my life."

"How do you find them?"

That Merrit did not resist temptation and admit his complete identity at this point is easier to explain than to excuse. There was first his admitted joy in discomfiting members of the dominant race. Further, however, there was a special complex of reasons closer at hand.

Byle and Tony Nayle than had been even Miss Cramp herself, and with greater cause. His own race prejudice was a bitterer, more deep-seated emotion than was hers, and out of it came an attitude that caused him to look with great suspicion and distrust upon all visitors who came to Harlem "socially." He insisted that the least blameworthy motive that brought them was curiosity, and held that he, for one, was not on exhibition. As for the men who came oftener than once, he felt that they all had but one motive, the pursuit of Harlem women; that their cultivation of Harlem men was a blind and an instrument in achieving this end, and that the end itself was always illicit and therefore reprehensible.

It was with him a terribly serious matter, of which he could see but one side. When Langdon once hinted gently that maybe it was a two-way reaction, he snorted the suggestion away as nonsense.

That he should allow it to disturb him so profoundly meant that it went profoundly back into his own life, as it did into the lives of most people of heredity so diverse as his. The everyday difficulty of his own adjustment engendered in him an unforgiving hatred of those past generations responsible for it. Hence every suggestion that history might repeat itself in this particular occasioned revolt. If there could be no fair exchange, said he, let there be no exchange at all.

He knew that no two ardent individuals would ever be concerned with any such formulas, but the very ineffectuality of what seemed to him so just a principle rendered its violation the more irritating. And in the particular case of Tony and Nora— well, he rather liked Nora himself.

And so beneath his pleasant manner, there was a disordered spirit which at this moment almost gleefully accepted the chance to vent itself on Miss Agatha Cramp's ignorance. To admit his identity would have wholly lost him this chance. And as for the fact that she was a woman, that only made the compensation all the more complete, gave it a quality of actual retaliation, of parallel all the more satisfying.

RUDOLPH FISHER

better than white people."

"Oh Mr. Merrit! Really?"

"You see, they have so much more color."

"Yes. I can see that." She gazed upon the mob. "How primitive these people are," she murmured.

"So primeval. So unspoiled by civilization."

"Beautiful savages," suggested Merrit.

"Exactly. Just what I was thinking. What abandonment—what unrestrain—"

"Almost as bad as a Yale-Harvard football game, isn't it?" Merrit's eyes twinkled.

"Well," Miss Cramp demurred, "that's really quite a different thing, you know."

"Of course. This unrestraint is the kind that is hostile to society, hostile to civilization. This is the sort of thing that you and I associologists must contend with, must wipe out."

"Yes indeed. Quite so. This sort of thing is, as you say, quite unfortunate. We must educate these people out of it. There is so much to be done."

"Listen to that music. Savage too, don't you think?"

"Just what had occurred to me. That music is like the beating of—what do they call 'em?—Dum—dums, isn't it?"

"I was just trying to think what it recalled," mused Merrit with great seriousness. "Tom-toms! that's it of course. How stupid of me. Tom-toms. And the shuffle of feet—"

"Rain," breathed Miss Cramp, who, since her new interest, had deemed it her duty to read some of Langdon's poetry. "Rain falling in a jungle."

"Rain?"

"Rain falling on banana leaves," said the lady. And the gentleman assented, "I know how I once fell on a banana peel myself."

"So primitive." Miss Cramp turned to Mrs. Dunn, who sat behind and above her. "The throb of the jungle," she remarked.

"Marvelous!" exhaled Mrs. Dunn.

"These people—we can do so much for them we must educate them out of such unrestraint."

at the box entrance; and Tony, descendant of Cedrics and Cæsars, loudly declared: "I'm going to get that bump-the-bump dance if it takes me the whole darn night!"

"Bump the what?" Miss Agatha wondered.

"Come on, Gloria," Tony urged Mrs. Dunn.

"You ought to know it, long as you've been coming to Harlem. Mrs. Byle gives me up. You try." Mrs. Dunn smiled and quickly rose. "I'll say I will. Come along. It's perfectly marvelous."

"FURTHERMORE," EXPOUNDED J. PENNINGTON POTTER, "there is a tendency among Negro organizations to incorporate too many words in a single designation with the result that what is intended as mere appellation becomes a detailed description. Take for example the N. O. U. S. E. and the I. N. I. A. W. There can be no excuse for entitlements of such prolixity. They endeavor to encompass a society's past, present and future, embracing as well a description of motive and instrument. There is no call you will agree, no excuse, no justification for delineation, history and prophecy in a single title."

"Quite so, Penny," said Mr. Dunn. "Mrs. Byle, may I have this dance?"

"Certainly," said Nora, smiling a trifle too amusedly.

"We're going home after this one," growled her husband as she passed.

MISS CRAMP SAID IN A low voice to Merrit: "Isn't he a wonderful person?"

"Who?" wondered Merrit.

"Mr. Potter. He talks so beautifully and seems so intelligent."

"He is intelligent, isn't he?" said Merrit, as if the discovery surprised him.

"He must have an awfully good head."

"Unexcelled for certain purposes."

"I had no idea they were ever so cultured. How simple our task would be if they were all like that."

"Like Potter? Heaven forbid!"

Negroes deserve at least a few leaders like that."

"I don't know what they've ever done to deserve them," he said.

Unable to win him over to her broader viewpoint, she changed the subject.

"Mrs. Byle is very pretty, isn't she?"

"Yes."

"She is so light in complexion for a Negress."

"A what?"

"A Negress. She is a Negress, isn't she?"

"Well, I suppose you'd call her that."

"It *is* hard to appreciate, isn't it? It makes one wonder, really. Mrs. Byle is almost as fair as I am, while—well, look at that girl down there. Absolutely black. Yet both—"

"Are Negresses."

"Exactly what I was thinking. I was just thinking—now how long have there been Negroes in our country, Mr. Merrit?"

"Longer than most one hundred percent Americans, I believe."

"Really?"

"Since around 1500, I understand. And in numbers since 1619."

"How well informed you are, Mr. Merrit. Imagine knowing dates like that—why that's be tween three and four hundred years ago, isn't it? But of course four hundred years isn't such a long time if you believe in evolution. I consider evolution very important, don't you?"

"Profoundly so."

"But I was just thinking. These people have been out of their native element only three or four hundred years, and just see what it has done to their complexions! It's hard to believe that just three hundred years in our country has brought about such a great variety in the color of the black race."

"Environment is a powerful influence, Miss Cramp," murmured Merrit.

"Yes, of course. Chiefly the climate, I should judge. Don't you think?"

Merrit blinked, then nodded gravely, "Climate undoubtedly. Climate. Changed conditions of heat and moisture and so on."

The northern peoples are very fair—the Scandinavians, for example. The tropic peoples, on the other hand are very dark—often black like the Negroes in their own country. Isn't that true?"

"Undeniably."

"Now if these very same people here tonight had originally gone to Scandinavia—three or four hundred years ago, you understand—some of them would by now be as fair as the Scandinavians! Why they'd even have blue eyes and yellow hair!"

"No doubt about that," Merrit agreed meditatively. "Oh yes. They'd have them without question."

"Just imagine!" marveled Miss Cramp. "A Negro with skin as fair as your own!"

"M-m. Yes. Just imagine," said he without smiling.

The comments of the occupants of nearby boxes would have been illuminating to J. Pennington Potter's party, the box, for example, containing Cornelia Bond's guests. Among these were young Dr. and Mrs. Peter Long, Mrs. Hernie Boston, Conrad White, who was a writer of stories about Negroes, and Betty Brown, his fiancée. Miss Cramp would have found their comments vulgar, unforgivable of Con and Betty, who had a way of forgetting all about the fact that they were white. J. Pennington Potter would have classed them as "Preposterous!" Dunn would have taken notes and written an editorial on the passing of Nordic supremacy. Merrit would have chuckled inwardly with glee.

"Who's the scrawny neophyte with the J. Popeyed Potters?" from the reputedly wealthy Cornelia, who was tall and regal in bearing and thoroughly, beautifully Ethiopian in appearance.

"There are two," said Hernie. "Which one?"

"Where's the two?" demanded Cornelia.

"One's off dancing with Nora Byle."

"Nothing scrawny about *him*," said Sarah Long.

"No," agreed Cornelia, "and nothing dumb. The way he's learning, it won't be long now—that Nora Byle is a dog."

"Jealous!" grinned Hernie. "After the way you extracted Jimmie Polio from her clutches?"

"Don't be a damn fool, Hernie. Wonder where Jimmy ran off to, come to think of it? Hasn't reported to headquarters for an hour—Sarah"—to Mrs. Long, "I want you and that bad-haired husband of yours over to a little stomp-down Saturday night. Consider yourselves flattered—Con and Betty'll be the only other shines present." Her eye fell again on Miss Agatha Cramp. "That's the homeliest woman in the world, bar none," she avowed.

Peter Long, who was "tight," rose and sang in a loud voice:

"Oh her face was sharp as a butcher's cleaber, But dat did not seem to grieb 'er—"

"Yes," said Cornelia, "and I bet ten dollars she's saying 'Beautiful savage' or 'So primitive.'"

Conrad said, "Potter's got a sense of humor any bow. Hooking her up with Gloria Dunn and Nora Byle. I'll bet Gloria snubbed her."

"No, Con. You're the only fay I know that draws the color line on other fays."

"It's natural. Downtown I'm only passing. These," he waved grandiloquently, "are my people."

"Yea—so you seem to think, the way you sell 'em for cash," said Cornelia.

"They enjoy being sold," returned Con.

Betty said, "Don't you think that Nora Byle has the most beautiful hands in the world?"

"I never pay much attention to her—hands," grinned Con.

"All the girls I know in Harlem have beautiful hands," Betty complained.

"You don't know many, then," Cornelia remarked.

"Just look at mine," Betty went on. "Pudgy as a poodle's paw. This Caucasian superiority stuff is a lot of bunk."

"Don't let your liquor out-talk you, Betty."

"No danger." said Betty. Then, "Say—do you know what I'm going to do?"

"Commit suicide," suggested Cornelia.

"In a way. I'm going to write a novel much better than anything Con has done—"

"Not much of an ambition—"

"—and present it as the work of a Negro."

"Negress," corrected Hernie with irony.

"Well," said Con, "you can be sure of two things."

"What?"

"You can be sure some critic will call it the best thing ever done by a Negro."

"Yes," said Cornelia, "as if that's paying you a hell of a compliment."

"And," Con continued, "you can be sure that me fay will insist that it should have been more African."

Rabinowitch."

A tall, very blond young man with rosy cheeks, whose eyelids were ptotic with alcohol, came clambering into the box as if he had six pairs of feet.

"Where's my Ethiopian?" he cried at the top of his lungs, peering about myopically and waving his arms like antennæ. "Hey!—Where's my Ethiopian queen?"

"Jimmy!" called Cornelia. "Bottle that racket. Come here and sit down, you imp."

"Where?" pleaded Jimmy Polio. "Can't see you at all, really. Can't seem to get my silly eyes open—"

"Look, Con," said Betty, indicating Miss Agatha Cramp, who had heard Jimmy's cry and was now observing from a distance. "Look at the horror on that poor woman's face. She's just about ready to die."

Together they looked at the wide-eyed Miss Cramp and together they chuckled with merriment.

"Well," sighed Miss Cramp, "Mr. Potter told me that this would be an excellent chance to observe different types of Negroes."

"It seems to be an excellent chance to observe different types of Caucasians, also," said Merrit.

"Disgusting, isn't it?" I can't understand why people of apparently our own kind, Mr. Merrit—it's humiliating, isn't it?"

"They out-Herod the Romans, don't they?"

"Unpardonable. How can we hope to help these others if we set so poor an example ourselves?"

"An excellent point. If we are not careful, instead of helping them, we will find them helping us."

"Helping us?"

"Yes. Or more. Transforming us. If things go on like this, one of these days this country's going to wake up with dark brown skin and kinky hair."

"Horrible!"

"Horrible? Why?"

"Oh, Mr. Merrit!"

country would enjoy it."

"Well—I for one shouldn't."

"But think, Miss Cramp," he prodded, "how much better off our country would be—"

"With dark brown skin? I can't imagine—"

"No. Figuratively of course. With a spiritual attitude—an emotional makeup like the Negro's."

"Just what do you mean?"

"This tropic nonchalance, as Locke calls it. This acceptance of circumstance not with a shrug, like the Oriental, but with a characteristic grin. Nobody laughs at the miseries of life like the Negro. He laughs at himself, at his own pains and dangers and disappointments and oppressions. He accepts things, not with resignation but with amusement. That, it seems to me, should be a most alarming thing for his enemy to see."

"I don't understand at all."

"No? Suppose you were fighting somebody, and at every blow you delivered, your antagonist simply grinned and came on. Wouldn't you soon get scared? Wouldn't you begin to lose your nerve? Would you begin wondering if maybe the other fellow wasn't grinning at the futility of your blows—if maybe he wasn't just biding his time in the certainty of his power? How could you wound a fellow who simply laughed? How could you be sure what he was laughing at? Himself? Maybe. But I know I'd begin to think he might be laughing at *me*."

"It isn't easy to follow you, Mr. Merrit. But it seems to me that the Negro would be far better off if he didn't laugh so much, no matter at whom. He doesn't take anything seriously. If he did, if he worried more, I think he'd be far better off today."

"Well—maybe today, Miss Cramp. But what about tomorrow?"

"What *can* you mean?"

"Wouldn't it be funny, Miss Cramp, if the Negro let his fair-skinned brother—or cousin, to be a trifle more exact—do all the so-called serious work? Build bridges, dig canals, capture natural forces, fly airplanes, amass wealth, evolve if the Negro let others worry their brains out devising and developing the civilized luxuries of life—while he spent time simply living, developing nothing but his capacity for enjoyment; and then when the job was finished, stepped in and took complete possession? Suppose—just suppose, for one can never know—that this irrepressible laughter, this resiliency, is caused by the confidence that he will reap what his oppressors have sown?"

"But that's impossible. Where will he ever get the power to take complete possession?"

"Power? Sheer force of numbers—the overhelming majority of dark skins in the earth. Together with the—er—the effect of climate. If the climate keeps changing, or if people keep exposing themselves to changes in climate, the time will eventually come when there won't be but a few pure skins left—now won't it be positively uproarious if the serious achievements reach their height about then?"

"Well," she said after a moment, "I don't think either you or I need worry over that, Mr. Merrit. It's altogether too remote. If I can't see that far, I doubt that any Negro can. It need not worry you at all."

"Quite right. Nobody needs worry over any of it—past, present, or future. Its course is unchangeable by anything so futile as people's worry. That's the joker in this very occasion, Miss Cramp. Uplift the Negro? Why, his position is the most profoundly strategic on earth."

"You really think so?"

"He that is last shall be first."

"Well, that would certainly be awful, wouldn't it?"

There was silence between them.

Presently Miss Cramp remembered that Merrit had been presented to her as an inured bachelor. She said:

"Mr. Merrit, these are serious questions. We must thresh them out sometime."

"I should like nothing better," he said.

"Do you spend the summer in town?"

of the summer."

"Then you must come and see me on your return. We shall have so much to discuss."

"Nothing would give me greater pleasure," he said, and she saw from the present pleasure in his eyes that he must mean what he was saying.

It gave her a thrill. "Summers," she sighed, "are so long, aren't they?"

"MY MAID," SAID MISS CRAMP, "is a Negress. The first one I have ever had, and I must say, the best. She is very pretty, too. She is so different from what one thinks of on hearing the term, Negress. Extremely pretty, really."

"And she remains a maid?"

"Why not? It's honest work and very good pay."

"The pretty ones usually prefer to go on the stage."

"Oh, Linda wouldn't think of any such thing. You see she was raised in an Episcopal Orphanage and seems to be rather religious—I was quite glad to learn how many Negroes are Episcopalian. I didn't know there were any, did you?"

"Are there?"

"A large number, from what this girl says. And what do you think Mr. Merrit? Religious as she is, she never sings spirituals!"

"No? I can't believe it. But she must have some vices?"

"Her only recreation is dancing. Her rector seems to be a very up-to-date person. There are weekly affairs at her church community center and she always goes."

"Must be an awfully dull person."

"On the contrary, extremely interesting. It was through her that I learned of the General Improvement Association. No doubt she is here tonight. In fact, I thought I saw her once just now, down there on the floor, dancing."

She looked sharply for a prolonged moment, then suddenly exclaimed, "I did too! There she is, there. That tall one in the gypsy costume—isn't she unusual?"

"The one just starting to dance with the big chap in gray?"

Merrit too looked sharply. Appreciation of unfamiliar features at that distance in a crowd was dificult, but—

"I've seen that girl somewhere. You say she's your maid?"

"I'm positive that's Linda."

A moment's rumination; then he remembered. Slowly over his face came an expression of elation far more than commensurate with the recognition.

"Miss Cramp," he said, "do you by any chance live on Court Avenue?"

"Yes, I do." She was extremely well pleased.

"I was about to give you my address. However did you know?"

"Why, Miss Cramp," there was no mistaking his joy, "we're neighbors!"

"Really? Why, Mr. Merrit!"

"You live at three hundred nine, don't you?"

"Yes!"

"And I live at three thirteen—that is I will when I come back to town."

"How lovely! But—how—?"

"I saw that girl go into your house one morning when I was having some things moved in. She had her own key."

"Well, isn't this nice, Mr. Merrit." She laughed. "I suppose when you saw Linda come in like that, with her own key, you thought you might even have got into a Negro neighborhood?"

"I admit, I wondered."

"That would have been tragic." She lowered her voice. "I can imagine nothing more awful. To help them is quite all right. To live beside them is quite another matter."

"It is indeed, Miss Cramp. It is indeed."

"You need never have any fear of that in Court Avenue. Frankly, we are rather exclusive, you know."

"I had that in mind when I purchased."

"And to think we are next door neighbors, Mr.Merrit."

They beamed at each other, each in the delight of his own withheld motive, his own private anticipations; a tableau that was soon interrupted by the noisy return of the two couples that had decided that he must leave. He rose to go.

"I shall look forward to your call," she reminded.

"If I could only be sure you were doing that," said he, "you've no idea the pleasure 'twould give me."

"You can be sure," she said.

As he left, he chuckled and chided himself:

"Damn shame to worry that woman like that—she'll die before the night's over. Somebody'll tell her sure."

He had hardly gone when Tony called attention to an odd commotion on the floor below.

"What's going on there?"

Dunn forgot his gallantries to Nora Byle in his eagerness to reach the front of the box. Everyone else pressed forward also to see, Miss Cramp bewilderedly, Gloria Dunn eagerly, Nora Byle amusedly, J. Pennington Potter apprehensively.

"The big guy in gray—" explained Tony. "Girl—yes, the gypsy costume—suddenly pulled away and he wouldn't let her go. Don't blame him, she's a peach. Look—she jerked away so hard she upset everybody around. They're all stopping to look."

"See—he's apologizing," observed Dunn. "Elaborately. Drunk, I suppose. Drawing quite a crowd, aren't they?"

"Look!" Gloria cried. "Over on the side—that one—he's starting for them! God—he's big!"

"This looks like a fight," Dunn said. "See him move over that floor—why, he actually leaves a wake!"

"There'll be a wake somewhere else if those two big boys meet."

"That's Linda!" exclaimed Miss Cramp.

"Who?"

"Linda—my maid—!"

"Who? The gypsy?"

"Yes. Oh—however did she ?"

"Poor kid can't get out of the crowd. Graysuit's right on her heels, protesting. Some sheik."

A suppressed cry of "Fight!" went about. There were gasps and quick searching looks of alarm. The orchestra, distant, oblivious, struck up: "Take Yo' Fingers Off It."

Then those who from above focused attention on the little crowd of dancers around Patmore and Linda, saw Shine succeed in breaking through to meet Linda as she endeavored to escape; saw Patmore look up, draw back, shrink, stand for a moment uncertain, as if both eager and loath to flee; saw Shine and Linda halt, facing each other, the girl distressed and surprised, the man him, uttering an inaudible but obvious plea; saw him catch her, thrust her behind him, and turn back—to find Patmore gone; saw Patmore, already out of the crowd, moving with surreptitious speed toward one of the lateral exits.

Then they saw the collection of observers disperse, Shine and Linda moving off together. Couples casually resumed dancing, and the stream, as if undisturbed, resumed its course.

Everyone in J. Pennington Potter's box sighed prodigiously.

"Marvelous!" commented Mr. Dunn.

"Marvelous!" echoed Mrs. Dunn.

And after a moment, "Marvelous!" cried J. Pennington Potter, like one who at last sees the light.

MISS CRAMP FOUND THAT NORA Byle had dropped into the chair beside her, and that insistent questions in her own head clamored for utterance at this opportunity. She was however quite unprepared to make the most of this opportunity, because she had never considered that certain methods of approach might be useless. She thought she had only to ask, and it would be given.

Between members of opposed races, however, the subject of race is difficult, almost indeed delicate. Neither party quite wholly sacrifices his illusions about his own people nor admits his ignorances about the other. The conversation, therefore, becomes a series of unwitting affronts, mistrusts, and suppressed indignations increasingly harder to bear, till at last it futilely breaks off with both parties ready to burst—each inwardly smoldering at the other's unforgivable ignorance and tactlessness. Here is the hedonistic paradox if anywhere, that one best learns the facts of a race by ignoring the fact of race. If Nordic and Negro wish truly to know each other, let them discuss not Negroes and Nordics; let them discuss Greek lyric poets of the fourth century, B.C.

Wise observers sense this and avoid the crassly obvious. But Miss Cramp was too deeply sincere and too genuinely curious to exercise tact. She ventured the usual opening:

"Your people seem to enjoy themselves so."

"They do seem to," agreed Nora with slightly different emphasis.

"Well, some folks laugh to keep from crying, you know."

Miss Cramp thought she saw in this a personal confession. This exquisite creature of blended blood must indeed be very unhappy. The personal implication surely invited intimacy. She said sympathetically:

"I suppose you speak from experience, my dear. How much white blood have you?"

Nora suppressed a gasp; then said too, too gently, "I don't quite know, Miss Cramp." And added sweetly as if returning a greeting, "How much black have you?"

Miss Cramp did not suppress her gasp; she merely prolonged it into a sputtering little laugh and exclaimed, "What a sense of humor you have, Mrs. Byle!"

"Yes, haven't I?"

"I was just saying to Mr. Merrit," Miss Cramp persevered, "that so much can be done for your people. Not for you, of course. Or Mr. Potter. But the great majority. You have heard that remark of somebody's, no doubt, that most Negroes are just three jumps ahead of the monkeys?"

"White monkeys?" smiled Nora.

"Oh, Mrs. Byle—how amusing—! But seriously. I think there is much to be done, don't you?"

"Oh, yes indeed—"

"I was telling Mr. Merrit about my maid, Linda. The girl we were watching down there just now—I must scold her severely for that. But—why, do you know, I had no idea what really marvelous servants they make. After having Linda I wouldn't think of having any other kind of maid. I've had Irish and French and German, but none of them were nearly so good as Linda."

"The best maid I ever had," disagreed Mrs. Byle, "was a German girl."

That Mrs. Byle should have had a maid at all seemed to come as a shock to Miss Cramp, a shock unrelieved by the casual reference to the maid's Nordicity. "You had a—a German maid?"

"Yes. A wonderful worker. But I had to let her go finally. I simply couldn't endure her English."

girls to any of the others."

"Perhaps because they're American."

"American? Oh—well, yes, they are—in a way."

Nora bit her lip.

"I'm so int'rested in the Negro problem, genuinely int'rested, you know," Miss Cramp continued.

"How do you plan to solve it?"

"Well there is the labor aspect of it. As I said before they make excellent servants. Why not have more Negro servants?"

"Porters and scullions and chamber maids?"

"Exactly. It may be possible to increase the numbers of such workers."

"I don't see how increasing the numbers helps solve any problem."

"Well—"

"Why not try to change them over into governesses and secretaries?"

"Oh, my dear—who would want a colored secretary?"

There was an awkward silence between them which neither the beating of tom-toms nor the rain falling on banana leaves seemed to relieve. Eventually Miss Cramp said:

"You met Mr. Merrit, of course?"

"Met him?"

"Didn't you, my dear? A fine type of American gentleman—"

"Why, I've known Fred Merrit for years." The familiarity in this remark struck Miss Cramp as unseemly.

"Yes," remarked she. "He said he'd worked among Negroes all his life."

Nora experienced first resentment at the implication of this supremely thoughtless comment, then, conflicting with it, amusement at the realization that Fred had evidently been masquerading at this lady's expense.

"Is there any reason," she said, "why he shouldn't work all his life among his own people?"

The statement transfixed Miss Cramp like a lance, and the swift change of mien from complacency to unbelieving

RUDOLPH FISHER

occasioned it.

"What!" Miss Cramp managed a faint little squeal.

"You weren't under the impression that Mr. Merrit was *not* a Negro, were you?"

"Why—I—I didn't know. I thought—"

"I'm sure he wouldn't have deceived you intentionally."

"But Mrs. Byle—his complexion—his skin is so fair—"

"Yes. He even has green eyes."

"I should never have thought—"

"You ought to have noticed his hair, 'my dear.'"

"His hair?"

"It's all that betrays him and you have to look close to see that it really is kinky."

At this point the irate Buckram Byle made his presence felt. No one had been paying much attention to Mr. Byle. And so, as much to attract notice as to punish his wife, he now called loudly to her that he had long since indicated his intention to go home and had no idea of letting her ignore it. Nora, having topped off an excellent evening, raised no objection.

"I must go," she said to Miss Cramp. "It's really so very nice knowing you—er—my dear"

Miss Cramp sat staring about with eyes that comprehended nothing, the turbulence in her own mind confusing every perception: eddies and currents of heads swirling about in the stream below her; constantly shifting, insane patterns of color, coming and going; wanton cries, prodigal jests, abandoned Negro laughter; and the orchestra, remotely dominant, sustaining it all with a ceaseless rhythm like the pulse of a pounding heart.

All this the mad accompaniment of a pitiless cycle of reflections:

"A Negro on Court Avenue and I asked him to call—they'll blame *me*—A Negro on Court Avenue—"

JIVE

Despite the genial atmosphere of Pat's pool room, the substantial good will of the table over which the vari-colored ivory balls rolled, the cozy cheer of the green-shaded low-hung light, Jinx and Bubber could not discuss even the weather in agreement.

"Sho is hot," Bubber had commented, missing a shot and wiping a glistening brow on his arm.

"Don' blame d' weather jes' 'cause you can't shoot pool," returned Jinx. "I likes warm weather like this."

"Can't see what fo'."

"Well—we got to work outdoors, ain't we?"

"Yea—in d' heat."

"Aw right. In warm weather you kin find some place outdoors to cool off, but when it's cold, damn if you kin find any place outdoors to git warm."

"Cold weather fo' mine," disagreed Bubber, "Shuh!"

"Yas *suh*. We got to wear clo'es, ain't we?"

"Uh-huh."

"Well, when it's cold you kin put on enough to git warm, but when it's hot, damn if you kin take off enough to git cool!"

Jinx pretended to ignore this unanswerable point by bending far and low over a long corner shot.

"Number eight," he called, signifying his intention to pocket the black ball. "Sho loves to make this eight-ball—jes' like punchin' you in d'nose." And he made it, cueing the ball with exaggerated vehemence.

Henry Patmore sauntered up. "Where's yo' boy?" he inquired.

"What you mean—Shine?"

"Don' mean his brother."

"Hell," said Bubber. "Ain' see 'at boogy a single night sence d' dance."

"Jivin' a dickty gal now," explained Jinx, regarding the table critically, with a sidewise twist of his head. "Bringin' me mud."

"Yea?" said Pat.

"Ev'ything," said Jinx preparing to try a difficult combination, "—compared to him."

"Mean the gal he picked up at the Casino th' other night?" asked Pat.

"Don' mean her sister," assented Bubber. "She ain' nobody's dicky, though. Powerful easy to look at but jes' ordinary K.M. right on."

"She may be a K.M." conceded Jinx, "but if they's anything ordinary 'bout her, I ain' seen it."

"Got the big boy goin', huh?" grinned Pat.

"Goin' and comin'," said Bubber; then to Jinx, "How long you go'n' look at that ball, man? Go on—shoot!"

"Who d' hell's makin' this shot?"

"Ain' nobody makin' it, far as I kin see."

Pat smiled metallically and moved off. Jinx called and shot, dispersing a cluster of balls, of which not one found its way into a pocket. Whereupon Bubber echoed their cackling laughter, revealing his stretch of bare upper gum between the two lateral stumps.

"One of these times when you laff like that," prophesied Jinx with great ill-humour, "I'm gon' bus' you in d' mouth so hard you'll grow yo'self some teeth."

Bubber's scorn was superlative. "You might stick out a fis'," he warned, "but you won't draw nothin' back but a nub." He busily chalked his cue, surveying the pattern of balls with enormous gravity.

"Yo' laigs is so bowed," Jinx observed, "that you wear yo' shoes out on d' sides. Better stop laffin' at me like that. One of these times I bet I'm go'n' run you knock-kneed."

"I wouldn' run that fas'," returned Bubber, squatting to squint over the table, "after nobody."

"Ain' talkin' 'bout after-talkin' 'bout from."

"From?" Bubber stood erect. "Me run from you?"

"You do have bright moments, dark as you is."

"Brother, let me tell you sump'm. If it ever even looks like I'm runnin' from you, they won't be but one explanation fo' it." Bubber paused oratorically.

wid me ag'in." Wherewith he made his shot.

Jinx solemnly shook his head. "It sho' would be awful hard," he said.

"What?"

"Awful hard on old man Isaacs."

"What you talkin' 'bout?"

"To lose two good men at once."

"Boy, you done gone crazy?"

"No. I was jes' thinkin—"

"Oh. Thass different."

"—I'm go'n' have to kill you sooner or later—only way to git along with y'. And that gal is jes' 'bout ruint Shine—he ain' never go'n' be no mo good."

"Shuh!" scoffed the other. "She might scratch 'im a little, but ain' no gal go'n' put no deep dents in that jasper. He ain't got no place soft enough."

"The hell he ain't. Know where I seen 'im goin' tonight, dressed up like a monkey-back?"

"Where?"

"Seen 'im goin' in 'at 'Piscopal church."

Bubber stared a moment, then proceeded disgustedly with his sighting. "What d'hell you 'speck a man to believe?" he commented.

"Swear I did. Not d' main door. You know that side door—'nuther buildin' it is, where they have dances and basketball and ev'ything else they scared to do in d' church itself. Call it d' immunity-house or sump'm like that."

"Yea?" Bubber dropped his stick. So long as Shine hadn't entered the main door of the church, the matter was credible enough to be startling.

"I sho did."

Bubber slowly shook his head. "Bye-bye, blackbird." Then, still somewhat suspicious, "Where was you when you saw 'im?"

"Followin' 'im. Thought he might need some help if he was out sheikin'."

imponderable a moment, slowly recovering his stick and most of his incredulity. "Aw, don' be no fool. That jigaboo's jes' jivin'."

"Maybe. But, same time, ain' nuthin' to hinder her from jivin', too. And when two folks gits M to jivin' each other, first thing y' know sump'm happens."

"Sump'm go'n' happen awright, 'tain' go'n' happen to *him*." Bubber resumed his survey of the balls scattered widely by Jinx's miss. "Bet I'm go'n' run off all the res'," he wagered.

Jinx, however, had become philosophical. "Jes' goes to show y' see? There's a guy what's so big and hard he can't be had. Mos' these gals 'round bych tries they damnedest to make him—but he jes' don' fall. No mo'n he fell that time Spider Webb cut at him and missed and nearly got broke in two. So hard. So hard his spit bounces. Says to me—say, 'Jinx you speckled-hide awstrich you, women ain' no different from men—only worse. You gotta be tough and tight, boy. Once they see you slippin', it's yo' hiney from then on—they'll put d' locks on you and throw d' key away. But if you be hard with 'em, they ain' no trouble 'tall.' Yea. And then this one come along. She's diff'runt, see? Act all dickty 'n ev'ything. High-hats 'im. K.M. awright—but not jes' ordinary K.M.—*Dickty* K.M., see? That jes' 'bout gits 'im. He gives up without a struggle."

"How do you know he's give' up?" Bubber's doubt persisted.

"Went in d' damn church after 'er, didn' he?"

"That ain't nothin'. I've seen women I'd go in worse places 'n that after."

"Yea?"

"No lie. And they wasn't near as easy to gaze on as that sister, either. Dickty—shuh—that ain't got nothin' to do with it. It's that ball-bearin' movement, thass what."

"Damn if it makes *him* run any smoother. One day he's good natured as a puppy-dawg, 'nother he's evil as a black cat. Never seen a man change so. She done put it on 'im all right."

"Bet he go'n' put sump'm on her, too."

"Damn 'f I believe it. She'll have 'im goin' in d' *main* door nex'. This is serious."

balls, unnoticed. Thereupon, mimicking perfectly, he duplicated the shot which Jinx had made earlier with such exaggerated vehemence. The ball was the last on the table, and it sped to an already full pocket eagerly, greeting its fellows with a cheerful "clack!"

Bubber looked at his victim with a grin. Jinx frowned unbelievingly at the clean green table top and, as Bubber broke into his customary guffaw, stood scowling malevolence at him, as if undecided whether to dispose of him at once or let him live a little time longer.

B aby—" Began Shine.
       "Don't call me baby!" exploded Linda.

"'Smatter? Don't you like children?"

"It sounds so—common."

"I couldn' mean it that way—you know that."

"How do I know what you could mean?"

"Couldn' ever say nothin' common 'bout you. Couldn' even think it. 'Baby's' a nice name."

"Think so? Well, save it for your sweetheart."

"I did," he grinned.

"Wrong number," she said, but she smiled.

"That was my lucky day," he mused. "What did Pat say to you that night? Why wouldn't you ever tell me?"

Thus, while Bubber and Jinx discussed them over a pool table, Shine and Linda strolled slowly along the west walk of Riverside Drive. A few blocks east lay Harlem, black and sullen, too uncomfortable by far for dancing this hot August MM night, even the distant and circumspect dancing permitted in a parish hall. Nearer was Court Ave nor, whither the present roundabout walk led.

Here on the Drive it was cool. Occasional me couples passed arm in arm, and on the long benches that rimmed the walk, facing the Hudson, still others made love, oblivious and unashamed.

"Huh?" insisted Shine.

"Nothing to tell," murmured Linda.

"Must be. Saw enough myself to know that."

"What 'd you see?"

"Well, I'm lookin' for Pat myself, see? He's jes' pulled a crooked deal on me a minute before, and I'm askin' for 'im. Well, you know the crowd—only people you can find is them ain't lookin' for. I'm standin' at the foot o' the stairs lookin' for that gray suit. Finally I sees it 'way across the floor-and damn if the sleeves ain't 'round *your* waist."

"Stop swearing—"

in anything. But I got to have some o' Patmore. So I'm standin' there wonderin' what the top card is and lookin' at you. Then I see you don' look so good—kinda like a kitten some rough kid won't turn loose. Turnin' y' head this way and d' other way and sorter pullin' 'way from this bird even though y' keep on dancin'. And I *smoke* him over, and he's grinnin' like a Chess-cat with a mouse—a nice young tender mouse, see what I mean? Well, I've seen that grin before, and I know it like I know my landlady's. Only, anytime I see a guy grin like that before, I jes' feel kinda sorry for 'im f' bein' such a sap. This time I ain't sorry. That same grin turns me cold."

He paused so long that she urged him on. "You didn't stay cold long."

"No—and why? Because the next thing I know you stop dancin' right in the middle of a step and look at him like you didn't know anybody's breath could smell so bad—"

"Oh!—"

"But it don' worry Mr. Patmore none. He jes' pushes his face on out at y', and makes another crack. That's the one I want to know about, because that's the time you jerks away from him like as if be your fingers. Meantime the kacks is closin in and you can't make a quick getaway. And when I come to, I'm down on the floor haulin' it through the crowd."

"There's an empty bench under that tree," discovered Linda. They sat down, deep in the shadow of foliage, and during a moment's silence, looked out over the river. Directly opposite loomed the Palisades, like a wide and gloomy black fortress, clear-limned against a sky dimly pale with an adolescent moon. Below, the dark water glittered a smile that derided the callow moon's wooing.

"Well, I don' know jes' what happens then," Shine presently continued, "but when I reach for Pat, he's breezed. Never see a man catch so much air so fas'. Then you looked like you was gonna cry and said you wanted to go home or some place—so I took you."

"I didn't know what I was saying."

"Seen 'im since?" she asked.

"No. That's why I want the dope. When I crown 'im I want to tell 'im exactly what he's king of."

"You mustn't bother 'im—let 'im alone."

"I got a picture o' myself lettin' any guy alone that gets fly with my girl."

"Your *what*?"

"You ain' blind."

"Well of all the nerve!"

"Hit me," he invited contritely, exposing a rugged cheek.

"Your—" She was overcome. "Well what do you know about that?"

He answered her literally. "Nothin', but I'm willin' to learn."

She averted her face to hide her smile. "I couldn't have been your—anything—anyway, then. Didn't even know your name."

"Well," he said with elaborate innuendo, "maybe I *was* jes' a little bit previous." "What do you mean!"

"Nothin' lady—nothin'. Don't get so excited. I jes' mean to say, you know my name now, thass all."

"Well, you needn't think—"

"And now *that* storm is over, how 'bout the dope?"

"What dope?"

"What'd Pat say?"

She was silent a long time. The lights of a home ward bound excursion boat broke through the river's moonlit smile, but when the ship had passed, the smile was still ironically there. Wraiths of music and laughter drifted shoreward.

"If you promise not to get in trouble over it—"

"Promise anything. Spill it."

"You know he had said there were prizes for the best costumes."

"Yea—and he was a judge."

"Yes. Well, I believed it. When he came back for the second dance, he was lit. I'd asked someother folks about it—"

"The Sunday School boys you was dancin' with?"

"No! The girls I came with. I asked them about the prizes and nobody knew anything about 'em. But I wasn't sure and I didn't him right out, I said, 'I thought you told me there were going to be prizes,' just as if I'd already found out there wasn't. And all he did was to grin with all those brass teeth of his. That made me mad, and I told him what I thought of anybody that would do anything like that—and—"

"Yea?"

"Well, finally when I saw he really had been lying, I stopped dancing and tried to walk off but he held me and people began to look. Then he said—"

"Said what?"

"He said I needn't act so disappointed over losin' twenty-five dollars-that he was a judge, all right—and—"

Her voice became low and hard. Unconsciously they drew closer together. "And what?" he said after a moment.

"Well—he offered me twenty-five dollars."

Silence enfolded them, deeper than the shadow. It seemed an endless period before laughed in the darkness a distance away. There upon the leaves of the tree overhead heaved a gentle, prolonged sigh.

They sat for a long time wordless, looking across the sardonic Hudson.

It happened the next morning that Linda ran out of sugar, discovering her predicament only a few minutes before Miss Cramp's breakfast was to be served. There were, of course, no grocery stores within three blocks of exclusive Court Avenue, and while ordinarily Miss Cramp would have waited without complaint till the errand was run, today the situation was awkward: Miss Cramp had company, a lady from Baltimore, Maryland; a friend, to be sure, but a friend whose breakfast must not be delayed by the delinquencies of a colored maid.

Linda, therefore, following professional tradition, resolved to borrow sufficient from her next-door neighbor to tide over the temporary lack, and was already on the kitchen-porch going to the Irish girl next door, when she saw a Negro woman beating rugs in the backyard of the second house. She had her own curiosity about that particular house, because she had overheard Miss Cramp and the present guest discussing it, and she decided that this was her chance at an opening that would satisfy that curiosity. She would borrow the sugar from the colored woman.

It was thus that she made the acquaintance of Fred Merrit's housekeeper, Mrs. Arabella Fuller.

"Drop in anytime," invited Mrs. Fuller, who was a genial, lonesome soul, not too insistent on the social distinctions between housekeepers and maids, and who would apparently have had more to say had Linda been less obviously pressed for time.

"Thanks," smiled Linda. "This afternoon. My folks are going to a show."

And so that afternoon found her and Mrs. Fuller conversing in the Merrit kitchen with all the ease and confidence of a much more extended friendship.

Without conscious effort Mrs. Arabella Fuller would have arrested any cartoonist's attention. Her profile was a series of adjoining semicircles—a large one for the bulbous forehead, then a succession of smaller, approximately equal ones, forming from above downward nose, upper lip, lower lip, first chin, and unanimously rearward, so that the forehead bulged and the chins receded, and the general attitude was that of one caught in the act of swallowing half a banana.

This profile only stated the motif on which Mrs. Fuller as a whole was composed. Every outline of every part was a perfect semicircle, and so on integration she naturally became a cluster of hemispheres. There were, to be sure, unanticipatedly sudden constrictions about her at points: between chins, for example, at wrists, at waist, and at ankles. But these repressions were futile, for on either side of each constriction the flesh triumphantly bulged. They simply heightened the lady's agglomerate bulbosity.

Out of the midst of this there escaped on occasion, an asthmatic wheeze. This confab was such an occasion, and it revealed at once that the asthma in no wise discouraged Mrs. Fuller's flow of language.

"Yes, indeed, chile. Anytime you want anything like that jes' come right on over and get it—we always has plenty ev'ything on hand. Thass one thing about Mr. Merrit—he sho believes in eatin'. Reckon thass why he so thin. And it makes him mad as a wet hen to run out'n anything and thass why I always has plenty ev'ything on hand. So anytime you run out, jes' come on over and I'll trust you to keep 'count o' ev'ything you get." She fanned her shining round brown face with a limp dishcloth and smiled as she paused for breath. The smile revealed a shining row of white teeth, each of them just half a circle.

"It's nice here," Linda observed, looking about.

"'Deed it is. And Mr. Merrit's such a nice man to work fo'. 'Cose he have his big times and so on, and he like his toddy now'n then a little too good, and ev'y once in a while he gets tied with up some woman 'nother, but 'cose thass natural, him bein' a bachelor and havin' so much money. I jes shets my eyes and says nothin', 'cause 'tain't none my business, and he ain' never said nothin' out the way to *me*, y' understand, so I jes' do my work and go on. You know how 'tis—you mus' see and don' see." There was another reluctant pause.

at the conflict in Mrs. Fuller's speech. It appeared that while Mrs. Fuller's labored respiration sought to shorten her sentences, her sentences had a will of their own and simply refused to be shortened. Linda already found herself drawing deep sympathetic, but wholly useless breaths.

"'Cose there's a lot o' folks what don' like to work fo' colored, I understand that, and I don' know as I would myse'f if it had to be some these uppity colored women what ain' never been used to nothin' and jes' now got sump'n and think they so much mo' n' eve'ybody else. Take fo' 'n instant that Sarah Bell Long, what's always ridin' 'round in Cornelia Bond's auto. I knowed her when she was a baby—knowed her father and mother before 'er. Neither one of 'em wasn't nothin'. Ole man Bell run a saloon in Augusta till he made enough to buy up half the black belt; then he retired, got religious, gave d' church a lot o' money and got hisse'f preached into d' kingdom and his wife along with 'im. Then this Sarah gal married this young doctor—least, he was then—and set him up in business, and when they got tired livin' down there 'cause some them women liked his treatment too well, why they up and comes to New York. And havin' plenty money natchelly they starts right out at the top. But I always say the top ain' but a little way from the bottom—can't be—'tain' been risin' long enough. And ain' none of us so much better'n the rest of us that we can afford to get uppity 'bout it—and thass why I jes' couldn' stand workin' 'round nobody that act that way. Ain' no sense in it. But Mr. Fred ain' like that. Ain' nobody in Harlem got no better things 'n Mr. Fred is, and some them things up in the country he brought back with 'im all the way from Europe and France and them places 'way yonder 'cross the water. You'll see 'em when they get hyeh—he always have 'em sent in town fo' the winter. An ain' nobody in New York got nothin' no better, but it don't turn his head none. Look like he jes' buy things to spend his money and when he get 'em that ends it. All 'ceptin' one thing—a picture of his mother. Least, I think it mus' be his mother, though he ain' never tole me so, but he stands and looks at that picture fo' hours at a time, seems like. I b'lieve 'twould near 'bout kill 'im to lose

RUDOLPH FISHER

'bout nothin'."

Linda decided it would be less exhausting to do some of the talking herself. She hastened to inject at this pause, "I should think it would be nice, working for a man, anyhow. Bet he isn't fussy 'n' everything like an old woman—specially an old maid. Gee!"

"Yo' madam ain' never had a husband of her own?"

"Uh—uh."

"How come she ain't?"

"Guess she never knew whether a man wanted her or her money."

"What diff'runce that make?"

"Well, I guess she figured if he *did* want it, she didn't want *him*, and if he *didn't* want it, there must be something wrong with him. That just made the whole thing sorter hopeless."

"She nice to work fo'?"

Linda saw that the way to prevent Mrs. Fuller from talking herself to death was to keep her asking questions. "Well," she answered, "she could be worse. Nicest part is she lives all alone and that makes the work light. But she get sick over the least little thing and she spends a lot o' time in bed. She just got over a three weeks' spell yesterday—only reason she got up was because this friend from Baltimore was coming last night. You can't imagine what made her sick this time."

"Is this visitor a gen'leman friend?"

"Nope."

"Then what?" Linda could sense that Mrs. Fuller was merely nosing for an opening through which she could break for a long unobstructed run of speech.

"She found out that your boss was a jig, and it put her in bed for three weeks. I didn't know what the trouble was till last night and I heard her talking to this Baltimore woman. The way she's carrying on you'd think the house had turned to a hospital for smallpox. 'Deed it wouldn't surprise me to see it burnt down anytime."

"What you mean, chile?"

door to 'em."

"Deed I do. I remember years ago—"

"Specially if it's a nice neighborhood. They'd do most anything to get 'em out. Look at what they did to that man in Staten Island last fall. KuKluxed him. It was even in the fay papers, how they burnt the man's house down while he was out. I believe Miss Cramp is wild enough to do the self—same thing or have it done."

"Have it done—how you mean?"

"*Pay* somebody to do it."

"No!"

"Bet she'd offer to pay *you* to do it."

"And I bet I'd smack her from hyeh to yonder, too!"

"Well, there's plenty of fay toughs around here—not right on this street but near enough—and I bet she could get somebody to get *them*. Then she wouldn't be suspected. Everybody'd think it was like that house on One Hundred Forty-Ninth Street somebody put dynamite under."

"What!"

"Didn't you read about it?"

"No!"

"It was in The Black Issue—oh, a long time ago now. Man bought a house on One Hundred Forty-Ninth Street and they dared him to move in. Sent letters and all. But he went on in. And less'n a week after he moved in, they blew him outbajooey!—Just like that."

"Well I never in all my life!"

"'Deed they did. And Miss Cramp is worried and mad and everything. You ought to 've heard her last night talking to this southern woman."

Linda decidedly had the floor now and she did not intend to relinquish it.

"She's from some little dump in Maryland, but she swears she lives in Baltimore—as if even that was anything to brag about. She's just like Miss Cramp, only more so. Well, you know one time Miss Cramp asked me a lot o' dumb questions about shines

G.I.A. to find out for herself. And for doing it!"

"Say what?"

"Last night she was telling this other one all about it, and I mean they just carried on. Miss Cramp says, 'My dear, I'm in the most awful trouble—you simply must tell me what to do."

"This other one is the funniest thing—talks like a jig fresh from down home. First time I ever heard a fay talk like a shine—I was never so surprised She says, 'Deed, honey, with all yo' money Ah cain't imagine what could worry you.'

"Then Miss Cramp says, 'If something isn't done pretty quick this whole neighborhood's going black!

"'What!' says this Mrs. Parmalee—that's the other one.

"And that isn't the worst of it,' Miss Cramp sniffles. "The worst of it is that *I'll* get the *blame* for it.'

"'You'll get the blame fo' it?'

"'I'm not responsible, really. But I got int'rested in the welfare of Negroes and joined a mixed organization for the improvement of conditions among them, you know. Well, naturally, I had to go about among them—'

"'Ah've always tole yuh yo' cha'ity'd get y' in trouble.'

"'Well it certainly has. I went, on a friend's advice too, to see how they acted in their own surroundings and there were both white and colored people in the box with me—'

"'What!'

"'And one of them was the man that has bought a house almost next *door* to me here on Court Avenue and Irene, he intends to *live* in it!'

"And Irene says, just like a jig for the world—'Well, bless mah soul!'

"'But my dear,' Miss Cramp, 'that isn't the worst of it. You can't imagine. My dear, I asked him to call!'

""You what!'

"'I thought he was white. He looked like it. He's blonder than I am.'

""How'd you find out he wasn't?' says Irene.

"'Someone else told me after he'd gone.'

to invite a strange man to call—'

"'But he was so nice, Irene—'

"'Agatha!'

"'I mean—you wouldn't have suspected, yourself. And, Irene, he swore he was coming, too.'

"'You don' mean you ackshally think he will?'

"'Why won't he?'

"'A nigger ought to know better.'

"'Well, this is New York, you know.'

"'Ah don' care what this is—'

"'Anyway, suppose neighbors of mine see my name on the literature of this organization. As soon as this man moves in, I'll be accused.'

"Then Mrs. Parmalee looks real evil and says, 'He wouldn' move in down in Balt'mo' City, I bet y'.'

"'He will here though,' Miss Cramp says. 'And if he does, I declare I'll move out. I couldn't bear the shame.'

"'Thought you so anxious t' uplift 'em?' Irene says, and I nearly split.

"'Well,' answers Agatha, 'it's one thing to help them and quite another to live beside them as equals. And to have everyone in the street *blaming* me—I simply couldn't bear it.'

"'Mean to move?'

"'What else?'

"'Move all these hyeh beautiful old things you've accumulated and yo' daddy befo' yuh? Leave this house he left yuh, where you've lived all yo' life? Mean to jes' get up and walk out and do nothin' else at all?'

"'But that's why I'm telling *you*, Irene. What else *can* I do?'

"'Ah'll tell yuh what else you can do. You can—.' Then she stops a minute and says in a lower voice, 'That maid o' yours likely to be eavesdroppin'—?'

"So of course then I had to catch air. Certainly wish I knew what she told her to do."

The oppression of Mrs. Fuller's compulsory silence together with the emotions excited by what she had heard by this time

Linda paused to look on with curiosity and some alarm. The girl's apprehension cost her the floor.

"Know what you ought to do?" Mrs. Fuller managed to get in; to which there was but one thing to say:

"What?"

"You ought to refuse to stay in that woman's house another minute. You ought to up and leave."

"And go where?"

"Ain't you got—" Mrs. Fuller stopped short, struck with a notion. The notion flowered into an idea. She grinned a half-moon grin, scalloped with tiny lesser half-moons, drew breath prodigiously, and delivered herself:

"Chile, I'm go'n' need a maid right hyeh. I done told Mr. Merrit already, and he say soon's he come in town it'd be all right. Y'see we been livin' in a 'partment all along and 'twasn' but six rooms and I could take care of everything with a little day help, but now with all this house it's go'n' be too much fo' me and I don' feel none too good nohow Mr. Merrit say it'll be fine and to get a good girl and make sho' she ain't too ugly 'cause he didn' want his stomach turned, and bless my soul if I ain't forgot all about it till this very minute. Now if you ain' got no objection to workin' fo y'own people, he's a fine man to work fo' and 'll never give you no trouble—least, not about yo' work. Cose you kinda pretty fo' a maid, but I reckon you can take good care o' yo'se'f, and any how he's a gen'leman. So hyeh's a job ready and waitin' fo' you if you want it."

"How much?" said Linda. "I'm getting eighteen—that's pretty good, you know."

"Shuh, chile, he'd give you twenty—jes' to be givin' you mo'n you been gettin'. He pays me twenty-five—and says it's a heap cheaper'n marryin', but I jes' tells 'im he needn' hint at me like that 'cause they's some things he couldn' pay me to do—"

"Twenty dollars!"

"Sho, chile. All I got to do is tell 'im—"

Linda jumped up. "You mean it?"

"Mean ev'y word of it and you'd have lots mo time to yo'se'f, too."

"Do you think maybe I could go to night school sometimes and learn to run a typewriter?"

This time Mrs. Fuller stopped breathing altogether. "Do which?"

"I don't want to be a K.M. all my life."

"Aimin' to better yo'se'f, huh?"

Linda was afraid she had made the wrong move here, but it was too late to change. She nodded with exaggerated vigor.

"Glory be!" was Mrs. Fuller's surprising com ment. "Glad to see it, chile, glad to see it. Does me good to see one our young girls what wants to better herself. Our girls ain't got no ambition, no ambition 'tall, 'ceptin' to go on the stage or dance in a cabaret or some such thing as that."

There followed a lengthy dissertation on the laziness of "our" girls, to which Linda listened, eagerly impatient. Finally Mrs. Fuller perorated with:

"Deed, chile, thass fine and I'm glad to see it and I'll help you all I can—you can get off mos' every night—and I bet Mr. Fred'll give you all the encouragement in the world—and maybe one them typewritin' things to boot. Well, want to try it? You can start soon's he get back. How 'bout it?"

"How 'bout it?" Linda exulted. "How 'bout it? Oh boy!"

While he couldn't compare it with the Lafayette Theater of course, still Joshua Jones considered it a pretty good show. At least it would have been if the dumb-bells hadn't jumped up and down so often.

It began with music, a chorus singing far away behind the audience—outside the church, it seemed. The singing came nearer and entered at the rear, and Shine obeyed the impulse to turn and look; but before he could determine what the trick in it was, Linda pinched his arm sharply and brought him about, puzzled and resentful, to see her shaking her bowed head with ill-concealed vigor. There upon he noticed that everyone else stood like Linda, motionless, with lowered head, as if it wasn't proper to look; and he wondered what manner of performance this was, which one might attend, but on which one might not gaze.

Into his surreptitious sidewise vision first came two kids carrying enormous lighted candles. The kids wore black bordered white robes and seemed to have an awfully hard time waiting for the rest of the procession to catch up. Then came the leading man, distinguished by his sedate bearing and singular position, also in a flowing white robe; Shine saw the lean face with its sharp profile and pallid skin and concluded that this guy didn't much enjoy his job.

There passed, following the leading man, a countless succession of increasingly taller couples, all in robes, all singing lustily without ever once consulting the books they carried before them: not much of a chorus, since the costumes made it al most impossible to distinguish the chorines from the chorats. Good singing though, funny, slow, no pep, but something about it—

Eventually they all found their places up front. There followed fifteen minutes of many and mysterious diversions: The two kids playing a game with the candles-lighting a lot more candles arched over the stage, seeing who could light the most. That ended in a draw. The leading man singing a solo with the whole chorus coming to his rescue everytime he paused for breath or seemed to falter. The this was better—with the audience joining tardily in. Much jumping up and down on the part of everybody. And now the taking up of admission—Shine exhibited a quarter to Linda questioningly. She nodded and presently he dropped the coin into the proffered box, murmuring—"Well, y'can't go wrong for a quarter."

This marked the end of the first act. The leading man rose in his place at one side of the stage and began to talk. His deep-set black eyes seemed to fasten themselves on Shine, who soon found himself watching and listening intently. If ever as a youngster he had heard this tale at the Orphanage Sunday School, it had been in so different a guise that now it appeared brand new.

He told it to Jinx and Bubber later, and told it with great accuracy:

"It was all about a bird named Joshua—a great battler some years back. A general, see? Led his own army, and how! This bunch could lick anything that marked time, see?

"Well, this Joshua thought he was the owl's bowels, till one day he run up against a town named Jericho. Town—this place was a flock o' towns. It was the same thing to that part o' the country that New York is to this. It was the works. With out it the rest of the outfit jes' simply couldn't go 'round.

"But try and get in. This burg has walls around it so thick that the gals could have their jazzhouses on top—not a bad idea at all: if a tight Oscar held out on 'em, they could jes' let him out on the wrong side o' the wall. And here this red hot papa, Joshua, who's never had his damper turned down yet—here he is up against that much wall—and the damn thing don't budge.

"Now comes the castor oil—the part that's hard to swaller but that does you good if y' do. Joshua asks the Lord what the hell to do about this wall. And the Lord says, 'Josh, you're my boy, see? You do jes' what I tell you and them walls 'll fall so hard they'll make a hole in the ground.' 'Spill it,' agrees Josh, and the schemes is un-schum.

"Take it or leave it, this crack army o' Joshua's don't do a damn thing but walk around that wall once a day for a week—Monday, around, blowin' horns. On Sunday they walk around seven times and on the last go 'round, the way they blow on them horns is too bad, Jim. Sounds like a flock of steamboats lost in a fog.

"Then every son-of-a-gun and his brother unhitches a hell of a whoop—and—take it or leave it—that wall comes tumblin' down same as if it was trained. Dynamite couldn't a done it no better. The birds on the inside have been laffin' at Joshua for a week-damn fool tryin' to blow a wall down, tootin' a few horns. The brass-band army. Huh—but now they ain't even got time to pull up their pants, and what happens to their hinies is a sad, sad story, no lie."

BUT SHINE DID NOT REPEAT what Tod Bruce said from this point on. Enough to admit that you'd been in a church, without further confessing a genuine interest in the meaning of a sermon—especially if the meaning was a little too deep for you anyhow.

BRUCE SPOKE QUIETLY, WITHOUT SHOW but with impassioned conviction; and though many of his hearers no more grasped his message than did Shine, there was none who felt the same when Bruce ended as when he began. His honesty and sincerity were contagious and the very defects in his imperfect analogy revealed a convincing absence of artifice, a contempt for trifling disparities, an impressive disregard of minor obstacles in conveying a major idea.

"Many a man laughs," said he, his voice penetrating like his eyes, "at the preposterousness of this Hebrew fairytale. Some of you perhaps are laughing now. For your sake I am going to say something that a minister of the Gospel is not expected to say. I am going to say this: that I don't care the least little bit whether this thing ever happened or not. To us it does not matter. Consider it a Jewish legend—a parable of Paradise, if you will—a myth, without any basis of factual truth. Even so, the spiritual value of the story looms and remains tremendous.

"You, my friend, are Joshua. You have advanced through a life of battle. Your enemies have fallen before you. On you march till find yourself face to face with a solid blank wall—a wall beyond which lies the only goal that matters—the land of promise.

"Do know what that goal is? It is the knowlyou edge of man's own self. Do you know what that blank wall is? It is the self-illusion which circumstance has thrown around a man's own self. And so he thinks himself a giant when in reality he is a child, or considers himself a weakling when truly he is strong, or more often judges himself the one or the other when he is actually both. There are still subtler contrasts: he may consider himself irreligious when at heart he is devout. Atheists and agnostics—this may be heresy, but it's true—are likely to be the most profoundly religious of all men, and clergymen, with whom it is all so routine, the least. A man may think he is black when he is white; boast that he is evil and merciless and hard when all this is but a crust, shielding and hiding a spirit that is kindly, compassionate, and gentle; may pledge himself to a religion when he is by nature a pagan, thus robbing himself and his generation of all that might come out of honest self-expression.

"There is no better advice, I think, than that of the ruffian on the street, whose motto is 'Don't kid yourself.' But we can't help kidding ourselves sometimes, and we almost always kid ourselves about our Self. And what is our Self, our knowledge of ourself, if not Jericho—chief city of every man's spiritual Canaan? And how can we strip off illusion and take possession of our own soul save by battle? No man knows himself till he comes to an impasse; to some strange set of conditions that reveals to him his ignorance of the workings of his spirit; to some disrupting impact that shatters the wall of self-illusion. This, I believe, is the greatest spiritual battle of a man's life, the battle with his own idea of himself.

"Far more incredible than this tale of the Israelite warrior are the circumstances under which you and I engage in a similar battle today. It is easier to believe, I think, that the blast of rams' horns and the shouting of a mob could cause a stone wall to crumble than that you and I should hope to find ourselves—to take our Jericho—by some brief event that shatters in a moment

But it is true. It is not only possible—it must happen to all who would see things as they are. Self-revelation is the supreme experience, the chief victory, of a man's life. In all the realm of the spirit, in all the Canaan of the soul, no conquest yields so miraculous a reward.

"I urge you therefore to besiege yourselves; to take honest counsel with the little fraction of God, of Truth, that dwells in us all. To follow the counsel of that Truth and beset the wall of self-deception. So will towering illusion tumble. So will you enter triumphant into the promised land."

A casual visitor to Seventh Avenue that a bright Sunday noontime might have thought, on seeing the released congregations, that many had already entered triumphant into the promised land.

This weekly promenade is characterized not only by an extravagant and competitive elegance but also by an all pervading air of criticism. Hither come self-satisfied, vari-colored flocks from every fold in Harlem, to mingle and browse, to inspect and sniff, to display and observe and censure.

It must be explained that of Manhattan's two most famous streets, neither Broadway nor Fifth Avenue reaches Harlem in proper guise. Fifth Avenue reverts to a jungle trail, trod almost exclusively by primitive man; while Broadway, seeing its fellow's fate, veers off to the west as it travels north, avoiding the dark kingdom from afar. A futile dodge, since the continued westward spread of the kingdom threatens to force the sidestepping Broadway any moment into the Hudson; but, for the present, successful escape.

And so Seventh Avenue, most versatile of thoroughfares, becomes Harlem's Broadway during the week and its Fifth Avenue on Sunday; remains for six days a walk for deliberate shoppers, a lane for tumultuous traffic, the avenue of a thousand enterprises and the scene of a thousand hairbreadth escapes; remains for six nights a carnival, bright with the lights of theaters and night clubs, alive with darting cabs, with couples moving from house party to cabaret, with loiterers idling and ogling on the curb, with music wafted from mysterious sources, with gay talk and loud Afric laughter. Then comes Sunday, and for a few hours Seventh Avenue becomes the highway to heaven; reflects that air of quiet, satisfied self-righteousness peculiar to chronic churchgoers. Indeed, even Fifth Avenue on Easter never quite attains to this; practice makes perfect, and Harlem's Seventh Avenue boasts fifty-two Easters a year.

Shine and Linda, released from church with the others, might have overheard much critical comment as they walked along Seventh Avenue:

"Hot you, baby—!"

"—'co'se it's a home-made dress-can't you see that crooked hem?"

"Wonder where the fire sale was?"

"What is these young folks comin' to—dat gal's dress ain' nuthin' but a sash!"

"Now you know a man that black ain' got no business in no white linen suit—"

But Shine and Linda had issues of their own to decide.

"How'd you like it?" she asked.

"He's a smart guy, that dude," Shine passed judgment. "After he got through tellin' 'bout that bird, Joshua, I didn't know what the—what it was all about. Where's he get that stuff 'bout knowin' y'self? How's a guy go'n' help knowin' hisself? What's the grand secret?"

"It's easy," said Linda. "S'pose a girl thinks she likes a fellow. Likes better than anyone else. Then s'pose somebody else comes along and she falls head over heels in love with *him*. Well, see? She didn't know herself the first time."

He grinned. "Who was the guy ahead o' me?"

And she answered with merry eyes, "There wasn't any. You're the first one. I'm talking 'bout the one that'll come next."

"Hope I don' have to spank nobody 'bout you," he said gravely.

"You make me tired," she declared. "Just be cause you're big you've got the idea that nobody can lick you. You think muscle's everything." "It's all that ever done me any good."

"*Did*."

"I mean did."

"Well, why don't you say what you mean?"

"Aw right—listen. Here's what I mean. I ain' never yet hurt nobody as much as I could've, see? But, what I mean, the first bird gets in between me and my girl—"

"Oh—you didn't tell me you had a girl."

"Well I have—and she's the owl's—feathers."

"Really?"

"Yes?"

"Yea. She looks like an angel, but talk about one evermore hard woman to get along with—"

"I am not!"

"Who's talkin' 'bout you? Girl I mean ain' nothin' like you. This girl likes to go to church a lot and it's near 'bout ruint her. She's jes' as evil and tight and hard to get along with as all d' other church folks."

"That isn't true!"

"What isn't?"

"That about church folks. They're the best peoples on earth. Kind and nice and—everything They're the only ones that even make believe doin' to others as they'd have others do to them."

"Make believe is right. Look at my landlady. My landlady lives in church—all day Sunday and mos' every night in the week. Yea. But jes' let me miss a week's room rent—jes' one, all."

"Is she the girl you were talking about?"

"Girl! Shuh—that woman's got a grandson in the old men's home."

"Do you mean you don't believe in church?"

"Ain' talkin' 'bout church. Talkin' 'bout folks. Tain't the church that makes the folks, it's the folks that makes the church. Only trouble with church is, folks ain' no 'count. All time kiddin' themselves, jes' like the man said this mornin'. He's right. Take my girl. My girl kids herself sump'm terrible. She thinks she's the hardheartedest Hannah that ever poured water on a drownin' man. But she ain't. Naw. Say, she's soft as a baby."

"Is that so?"

"Yea. She ain' foolin' nobody but herself. Say—that's what that guy meant, huh?"

Linda sniffed and changed the subject. "I'm going to change my job."

"No!"

"Uh-huh. Got a new job starting next week—pays twenty dollars a week."

ain't in some show. Make lots mo' money."

"Never tried—haven't had a chance. I was in the Home till I was sixteen and I've been in service these other two years."

"Well you're lucky. Where you go'n' work now?"

"Right on the same street. For a man named Merrit."

"Merrit!"

"He's a jig."

"Don' do it."

"What?"

"I said don' do it."

"Why not?"

"Well, I know that bird. I done—I did a job for him once. He's funny."

"What's wrong with him?"

"First thing is, he's a jig. Jigs is bad to work for."

"*He* isn't. He's a—"

"Nex' thing he's too doggone yaller. Yaller men ain' no good."

"No good! Huh—he's got money enough to—"

"Nex' thing is, he's a big-time dickty. Dickties is evil—don' never trust no dickty."

"Well—is that all?"

"No. Worst thing is, he drinks too much licker."

"Really?"

"Patmore was crazy to get his trade a while back—claimed it was enough by itself to support him. I don' think you ought t' have no licker-head for a boss."

"Huh! I can take care of myself."

"Maybe. But where you're at now, you don't have to take care o' yourself. Th' extra money ain' worth th' extra worry."

They had turned west, leaving Seventh Avenue, and were now entering progressively quieter neighborhoods.

"But I've got to take it. I talked with his housekeeper, and she said I could probably go to night school 'n everything. In a little while I could get a job in an office."

"And turn dickty."

"Well, you don't think I want to be a K.M. all my life?"

these days. Long distance movin'. Good money."

"Really?" The sarcasm was ignored. "You won't have to be nobody's K.M. then."

"You mean nobody else's."

"Well, jes' since you get what I mean."

"Well, I don't. And even if I did I'd take that job."

"Why?"

"Because if I do I'll learn to typewrite."

"You sure are the hard-headest woman—"

"Hush—and if I learn to typewrite you can give me a job in your office when you get one."

In astonishment he stopped to stare at her. The expression of mingled amusement, decision, and tenderness with which she returned his look gave him a sudden overwhelming happiness. It almost upset him.

"Gee!" he said, his face shining. "Gee—Lindy—"

He had an impulse to catch her up and kiss her right there on the street corner oblivious to broad daylight and possible observation. Had he done so, spontaneously, on crest of that emotional wave, the result would doubtless have been different. But the old habit of hardness, which for the instant he had almost escaped, promptly clamped itself down on his exuberance and distorted his natural impulse into a presumably safer substitute. Every act must be sentimentally airtight. The device he adopted to make this one so, lost for them both that surging moment to which the girl would have responded.

"Ain't it somewhere in the Bible sump'm 'bout turnin' th' other cheek?"

Puzzled, her own spell broken, she answered, "You mean—if a man smite you on one cheek, turn him the other also?"

Before she sensed his intention, he had pinioned her arms and kissed her on one cheek. "Well, turn me th' other one, then," he grinned.

But Linda could play as safe as he. For answer she snatched herself away, and the sounding smack that met his face must have made the girl's palm burn.

without, Shine stood rubbing his cheek and watching her stride indignantly away.

What he eventually said was: "Now ain't she a hell of a Christian?"

WALLS

O n the night when shine told Jinx and Bubber the story of the battle of Jericho, he had no sooner left Pat's than another argument was on. Hitherto, Jinx and Bubber's nocturnal enmity had always ended at least without catastrophe; tonight catastrophe descended upon them, and the thing which each sought to divert by the very extravagance of his quarrel was by the same extravagance rendered inevitable. Tonight they came to blows.

Jinx started it.

"There now, you dumb Oscar," he said to Bubber with great relish, in a voice that carried throughout Pat's barroom. "There now whut, jackass?"

"Didn' I tell y'?"

"You ain' tole me nuthin'—and if you did, it 'twasn' nuthin' nohow."

"I tole you—Jinx spaced his words for emphasis, "that nex' thing we knowed she'd have "im goin' in d' main door of d' church— and whut 'd you say? 'Aw no. Ain' no gal go'n' do nuthin' like that to *that* boogy. Hard boogy, he is.' Thass whut you said. Yea. And look. He comes in and tells us ev'ything d' damn preacher said. Don' leave out nuthin'."

"That don' prove he went in d' main door," argued Bubber with overacted patience. "He could 'a' come down through d' skylight f' all I know."

"Like a big black angel, I s'pose?" said Jinx and grinned with surrounding laughter.

"Yea—or a long-laigged, speckle-face giraffe," retorted Bubber, swelling.

Jinx grew sombre. "That's d' trouble with a li'l round black hippo like you. All give and no take. When you kid me I kin take it. When I kid you you can't."

"You don' seem to be taken' that so good," said Bubber.

"Don' nobody git no madder'n you do."

"No?—Look at y' now. 'Bout to bus' open and spatter d' whole bar room with ink."

nobody's long lost brother. Never will fo'get that night you got so mad you started slippin' me in d' dozens."

This was approaching dangerous ground, this reference to their own reactions. To quarrel over subjects in general was bad enough; to quarrel over each other might be disastrous. It brought them closer to the truth about themselves, yet not quite close enough; it did not reach the actual sore, it only lifted off the scab.

"Well you oughter been slipped," Jinx said. "Any bird can't take kiddin' no better'n that needs to be kidded and kidded hard."

The customary comments accompanied this discourse:

"Tell 'em 'bout it!"

"That means fight in my home."

"Grease us twice!"

"They jes' foolin'. If they meant it they'd both be daid by now."

"Me, I'm bettin' on Long Boy. He'll wrap hisself 'round Squatty and squeeze all th' ambition out'n 'im."

Bubber challenged, "Well—you better not slip me ag'in."

"No?" said Jinx like a small boy who has been dared to knock off the chip. "No? Well—yo' granddaddy was a mule Now—what you got to say 'bout that?"

Bubber said nothing. Instead he moved toward Jinx with surprising ease and mysterious rapidity and suddenly Jinx doubled forward from the force of an almost invisible blow to the midriff. "What *you* go'n' say 'bout *that*?" Bubber asked, looking belligerently up into Jinx's astounded face.

Not quite certain whether this was serious or make-believe, Jinx reached mechanically forward and gathered Bubber's neck and shoulders in an embrace usually reserved for pianos. Failing to twist himself free, Bubber began swinging away at the other's kidneys, and in a moment the tussle removed from the atmosphere all suggestion of possible jest.

"Look a yeh!" somebody gasped.

"They ain't roughin' sho' nuff, is they?"

"They ain' playin' hop-scotch."

"Well, ain't this sump'm?"

excellent manager and always at the spot that needed him most, had heard the commotion from the next room and hurried to the scene. Pat was not bad with his hands himself, and it is significant that with apparent ease he managed quickly to separate them.

"What the hell you think this is?" he inquired, as for a moment they stood off from each other glaring.

"Jes' git out d' way, thass all," said one.

"He been cryin' fo' it—now he go'n' git it," vowed the other.

"Not here he ain't," Pat decided. "Look," he pointed. "Y'all see that door? All right. I told y' once before the nex' time you wanted to settle sump'n I was go'n put you in the cellar and let the best man come up." He strode to the door, unlocked and opened it, and pressed a button. "Come on, if you mean it—come on."

Neither was willing to admit that he did not mean it, and in another moment the gaping bystanders saw them disappear through the cellar door, which Pat promptly closed behind them.

"Well, what do y' know 'bout that?"

"Ain't this a dog?"

"Salty dog, I mean."

"Damn if d' worm ain' turned."

"Yea—but which a one is d' worm?"

THE BYSTANDERS CROWDED ABOUT THE door, listening. Pat, grinning, kept his hand on the knob, his ear against the panel. The others pressed forward: a lean black boy as tall as Pat, with tight slick skin and wide, white, shifting eyes; a thin, short tan-skinned lad of twenty, with a sharp face half hidden by a voluminous, lopsided cap; a paunchy old brown fellow in shirt sleeves and suspenders, with puffed cheeks and rolling pop-eyes; a long, thin, senilely crouching grandad with the complexion of a mummy and a gloating, toothless grin; a parchment-covered gambler, a tea-colored card-shark, a khaki-skinned pick-pocket easing one hand into a pompous racing-man's pocket, a donen others, all surging forward, all listening with arched brows or grins of relish. This was gonna be good, this was. Them two guys meant blood.

commenting:

"Bet on the long boy!"

"Give you odds."

"Don' tell *me*—that jasper can *fight*."

"Squatty'll wear him down, though."

"I knowed they'd ask f' each other sooner or later—"

"Too bad now."

"Thass the reason I never kid nobody—might have to *make* him take it, see?"

"Wonder if they'll cut?"

"Can't tell what a guy'll do when he's losin'."

"Who'll move pianers tomorrer?"

"Better git yo' mop out, Pat."

"Anybody sent for the ambulance?"

"Ain' got a chance in the world—"

"Five bucks says he *is*—"

"Who—String-bean?"

"Put yo' money wha' yo' mouth is—"

It seemed an endless time, but nobody's eyes left the door for long. Stories suggested by the present affair began to be told, sudden gusts and flurries of laughter swept the room. Argument es sued over the nature of the quarrel—how had it begun? So The hell it had—it was like this Good thing: those two were a constant pain in the what's-a-name with their continuous quarrel. Over a woman, hey? Huh-jes' goes to show y'—

Pat was called away from his post by some duty in the pool room. He made sure the cellar door was locked and went about his business, promising to return in time for the rest of the fun.

Another long wait followed—hear anything? Not a damn thing. Fools must'a gone down there and kill each other. Remember the night Sam Tyler and Joe West got hooked up? Yea. Waitin', they was, in the same hotel. The head waiter give Sam a check that should 'a' been Joe's, so Joe was sore to start with. Well the man ordered Washington pie, see? You know—that white stuff with whoop' cream all over it. And Sam brought *chocolate* pie by mistake. So the fay man looked up at Sam, he did, and turned up me Booker." Well, Joe heard it and when he got through kiddin' Sam 'bout it, 'twasn't nothin' left for 'em to do but fight. Brother, I mean, neither one of 'em ever got over that scrap—Judas Priest— it's been three-quarters of an hour! Nary a sound. Better get Pat— thought he was coming back so soon? He was, but he got in a argument with Boody Mullins over a protection-fee. Well, let's go get him for Chris' sake—them two damn fools may be tricklin' all over the floor by now. . .

PATMORE CAME HURRIEDLY IN FROM the pool room, flanked by the two who'd summoned him. He paused a moment to listen, his ear against the door. "I hear sump'n," he said. "Wonder is—?" and at once unlocked and opened the door.

Everyone had pressed forward behind Pat, but now they all fell back, and as a lane opened through their midst, Jinx was seen framed in the doorway. He was swaying a little from side to side even though he attempted to steady himself against the door frame, and there was a far-off vacancy in his eyes that made him seem completely unaware of those who stood and stared at him. No one said anything, no one moved to help him, as he relinquished his support and started uncertainly forward.

He took four or five grotesque tottering steps, then his legs and feet seemed to get all tangled like those of a fly trying to escape sticky paper, and rather slowly, he sank to the floor and lay crumpled in a twisted, senseless heap.

Pat, who alone of all the onlookers could afford to take an active hand in this matter, started toward that crumpled heap. A sound behind him brought him up short and he turned with the others to see the short broad form of Bubber come into and through the doorway.

Bubber looked decidedly dazed, yet not so much so as had Jinx, and the unsteadiness of his bearing was somewhat modified by his rotundity. His progress through the crowd toward his prone enemy resembled that of a pool ball through a scattered field of its fellows, kissing first this one then that and accordingly zig-zagging forward from side to side; like the other balls, his extending a supporting hand or revealing a sympathetic impulse. Even Pat did not offer to catch him when he reached Jinx's figure, tripped over Jinx's feet, and fell across Jinx's body.

Then curious things happened.

Jinx, roused by the jolt of Bubber's fall, stirred drowsily with a movement that rolled Bubber off to one side, and Bubber was heard to murmur stupidly, "Ain' nuthin' to fight about, boogy. Ain't you my boy?"

Pat called abruptly to a bystander for help, and together they reached down and raised Jinx to his feet. He opened his eyes for a moment, then, as if realizing the futility of trying to see anything, allowed his heavy lids to drop again. They got him on to a chair and his head sagged limply forward.

As they were in the act of turning to render similar assistance to Bubber something halted them half-about and they exchanged puzzled and appre hensive looks. Everyone exchanged similar glances with his neighbor, gazed at Jinx's sagging form in a fear that grew into conviction; for in that moment the something happened again, as if to substantiate itself by repetition: A shudder took hold on Jinx's body, shook it from below upwards, halted in his throat with a little choking sound that seemed almost to break his neck.

"Death rattle—Jesus—!" somebody muttered. One or two peripheral observers near the door eased stealthily out. 'Ain' go'n' be no witness in no murder case—no *suh*."

Scowling, Pat stepped forward, seized Jinx's shoulder, shook him, called him, pushed up his lids with a thumb. Each lid, released, drooped slowly resolutely shut. Pat frisked Jinx's clothing, palpated him, searched swiftly but futilely for the wound that must have been dealt; swung around to find Bubber on hands and knees trying to rise, laid hold and yanked him to his feet. Bubber stood teetering like an exercising ball, stared sleepily about, said, "Where-my-boy?" and unceremoniously sat down unanswered. Pat strode through the cellar door and disappeared down the stairs.

Somebody now searched Bubber for a weapon, and somebody else said Pat had gone to find it. Periodically a spasmodic shudder do, everyone was helpless.

"Must a strangled 'im, huh?"

"Seem like it—chokes off his breath."

"Jes' goes to show y'—"

Presently Pat returned and came into the circle with ominous deliberateness. He stood for a moment looking down on the helpless pair, nodding his head in mingled conviction and disgust. Then he held up what he had found downstairs, a round quart bottle with perhaps a half-inch of whiskey left in its bottom.

"Give it to Jinx," urged stop that rattle yet—"

"Rattle, hell," said Pat. "That jigaboo ain't got a thing but the hiccoughs." He set the bottle on the bar counter with a sarcastic thump. "That," he growled glumly, "is the only damn thing they hit. They found a case."

The fact that Linda had taken the job in Fred Fred Merrit's house as soon as it was available seemed to Shine, like the slap, a mere gesture of defiance, as a matter of fact rather complimentary and encouraging. But the fact that she stubbornly withheld her company and had done so now for two weeks seemed an unnecessary emphasis of her already defined position.

And because it was for him an entirely new experience, for which his knowledge of women contained no therapy, his own futile resentment rendered him daily more and more violent. He worked harder and played harder and knew that nothing ailed him; but with a stubbornness greater than Linda's he refused to admit to himself that the girl had anything at all to do with the change. No mamma in this man's world was tight enough to put it on *him*.

Bess, the great van, became a willing mistress, and from her he derived a sort of unconfessed con solation; took to driving her at top speed when ever conditions permitted: when traffic was light and fast and Bess was empty; literally hurled her, roaring like a fire truck, along Seventh Avenue's asphalt; and when opportunity presented, took her over to the Speedway for a rattling headlong romp. On such occasions if Jinx and Bubber were present, they would exchange wise looks and apprehensive grimaces, and Bubber invited annihilation one day when, on narrowly missing a coal truck, he asserted that it just wasn't good arithmetic for no three men to commit suicide over one woman.

BUT THE ZEST WITH WHICH Shine drove Bess did not give him sufficient relief, left him still unsatisfied, like the deep but ineffectual breathing of a man suffering acute air-hunger. Hence his whole behavior took on a reckless vehemence, and whether he laughed or cursed, worked, drank, or gambled, he did so to excess.

Ordinarily he used two belts around an upright piano to be hoisted; two belts surrounding the treacherous instrument near ring. When the tackle was hooked into this ring and raised, the two short cables became the legs of an isosceles triangle, the apex of which was the ring and the base the top of the piano. This arrangement was absolutely proof against tilting and slipping.

Now however he decided, jes' for meanness, to dispense with approximately half of this apparatus and used only a single belt about the middle of the piano. It pleased him then to stand off and dare the blam-blam thing to slip.

Ordinarily when he drank it was with a modicum of caution. No sense getting drunk down. The way to lick liquor was to hit it and run-no man was lined with copper. Drop in on one of these new young doctors that had to write "scrips" to make it; or go to one of these drugstores that had prescriptions already written and could sell you the best rye right off at five or six bucks a pint. On thirty-five bucks you wouldn't be able to do that but once a week, and so you'd be pretty sure to take it easy.

Now, however, he told himself he could drink anything anybody else could drink, and drink as much of it, too; sought out the venders of synthetic corn and gin and drowned himself in the pale stuff; and cursed to find that he awoke the morn ings afterward without even so much as a headache.

Ordinarily, when he played blackjack in Pat's back room, he played with a definite system: started with the minimum stake, doubled three rounds, then passed. Above all he never hit seventeen.

Now he played with no regard for rules or the laws of chance; doubled often five times straight, "stopped" the bank at every opportunity, and invariably hit a soft seventeen and usually a hard one as well.

None of these devices satisfied. Not a piano slipped, none of the liquor proved to be poison, and at the end of a week his blackjack stood him eighty-six berries to the good.

In the midst of these exaggerated reflexes, an order came to the office of Isaacs' Transportation Company for the removal of one load of valuable furniture from Fred Merrit's country house to his residence on Court Avenue. Old man Isaacs was off duty, boss appoint a new foreman. Finding this impossible, he told himself that no girl's presence was going to make him dodge a job any damn how.

There was, nevertheless, an unmistakable reluctance in his piloting of Bess this morning. Merrit's place was only a dozen miles north of New York, but it took Bess two hours to get there. Once arrived, there was much palaver about the best way to negotiate the terrain.

"This place jes' sprawls all over this hill," observed Bubber. "Looks like a flock o' hencoops. How we gon' git up yonder?"

The question was settled by uproarious but careful navigation of a steep side road which led to a plateau behind the flock of hencoops. Here they were greeted by Mrs. Arabella Fuller, who began at once to wheeze interminable directions. Eventually, in spite of all Mrs. Fuller said, the load was on, each piece swaddled partly in quilting, and partly in that lady's verbiage, which seemed to hover about it long after Bess was headed back townward:

"Yes—that goes—thass a picture of his mother—the onliest one he's got, so be awful careful. I know he'd die if he lost it. Take care o' that if you lose all the rest. Now be careful—y'all never care how you handle things and them table laigs'll snap off if you sneeze at 'em—that's a genuine redwood table and you know them's expensive look out f' that vase!—The way y'all handle things anybody'd know they wasn't yourn. Chile, that vase cost mo' 'n yo' foot—if it break yo' foot yo' foot'll git well, but if yo' foot break *it*—yes—them's chests and y' needn't think they ain't valuable and that you can scrape 'em up bad as you please jes' because they ain't go not paint on 'em and got the hinges on th' outside; they come from Siam or some them places Mr. Fred was where the folks is all colored but won't admit it and you carry 'em by puttin' two broomsticks through the sides, but deed I ain't got no broomsticks f' y'all to scratch up and break—they have their own kings and queens and ev'ything jes' like in the Bible, only I say colored folks ain't got no business tryin' to act white 'cause it always gets 'em into troublewhere's that other boy—that big one come with y'all? Why don't he turn in and help?—He's work—Ain't we been had the worst summer rainin' ev'y day and look like it always had to ketch me outdoors with nothin' on my head and you know what happens to this kind o' hair when it gets wet—"

"Whew-ee!" heaved Bubber. "Damn 'f that woman can't talk d' spots off d' dice."

"No lie. I ain't got my breath back yet—jes' listenin' to 'uh."

"Yea—and you tellin' 'uh she could ride back with us if she wanted."

"Who?"

"You?"

"When?"

"Didn' you stop and tell 'uh to come on, less go—we was finished?"

"Oh yea. But I swear I thought I was talkin' to you. Y'all look like sisters. If you and her didn' have d' same grandaddy, somebody played a awful dirty joke on y' both."

The inevitable quarrel ensued, and this somewhat took their minds off Bess' unusual jogtrot. If the trip out had been slow, the trip back was endless. For out of all that had reached his ears, Shine remembered only one part of Arabella Fuller's dyspozic discourse, and this hummed in his mind as persistent and unvarying as the rumble of Bess' innards:

"Go where, chile? Back to town with y'all? Deed I'll have to stay out hych mos' another week packin' things f' the winter. Y'all go right ahead, though—Linda's there and I done told 'er where to tell y'all to put ev'ything—"

Linda living alone in the house with Fred Merrit, toper and dickty.

A piano is a malicious thing, the temporary dwelling of some evil spirit that follows you from one instrument to the next. Sooner or later that spirit catches you off guard and, using the instrument as its weapon, swiftly, viciously strikes. Either it gets you then and there or is itself permanently defeated.

Every man who enters this work thereby invites this pursuit. Both Jinx and Bubber had escaped for a time, but finally each had been crushed, leaving a permanent deformity. These injuries, however, did not materially hamper their work, and so Jinx and Bubber considered themselves fortunate; for, as the superstition had it, they now enjoyed immunity.

Shine had so far gone without a scratch, had never been caught off guard. It was Jinx and Bubber's belief that he would probably go on escaping. What chance did any piano have at a steel man lined with cast iron? Shine was just as hard toward things as toward people, no more vulnerable in the one case than the other, and though ordinarily he could afford to be more generous and genial than most men, who dared not thus risk imposition, still in a pinch he was known to be more unyielding than bedrock. Nothing fazed Shine. "Remember how he held on to that piano the day the roof broke?"

But today for the first time Shine's preoccupation put him quite off guard; and so today his evil pursuer struck.

THE PIANO WAS AN ELDERLY upright which Merrit kept because it had been his first luxury. It was to go to the front room on the third floor of the house, a room which had been set apart as a remote and private playground—a combination of den, poker room and too-bad-party resort. The instrument stood alone and sullen at the edge of the cluttered sidewalk, aloof, superior, apart, permitting the lesser pieces to go first.

Shine likewise aloof and apart, refused to enter the house with the others. He saw Linda only once, when first she gave Jinx admittance, and although he did not allow himself to make frank observations, he was aware from many a covert glance that the girl had withdrawn into the inner regions, evidently as intent upon avoiding him as was he upon avoiding her.

The time soon came, however, when all but the piano had been removed. Shine's active partici pation had so far consisted only in handing things down from the van. Now he must direct the hoisting and so lend a more active hand.

It was now that his brooding inadvertence combined with his recently assumed recklessness to make him do an unprecedented had not once trusted either of them to anchor hoisting tackle. But now, instead of going to the roof of the house to anchor the tackle himself, he ordered Bubber to do so in his place. He'd be damned if Linda should think he was trying to see her.

"Well—what the hell's holdin' y'?" he inquired as Bubber hesitated, doubting that he had heard aright. Bubber turned slowly, shaking his head and meditating aloud:

"When that boogy gits evil he gits *so* evil. They's so damn much of 'im."

"Then come down and unsash that winder,"

Shine commanded balefully, "and stand by to pull in, see?"

Jinx would have followed to check up on his confrère's technic, but Shine halted him to give further orders.

"You keep them flat feet o' yours right on the sidewalk and hold on to this guide rope. I'll do the pullin'. When Squatty pulls in up there you can go up and help him take it down."

So it was arranged, and presently Bubber, directed to the roof by the red-hottest mamma that had ever smiled upon him, was casting about for anchorage. A cylindrical airduct presented itself as the most likely object to use; it was well away from the front ledge of the roof, giving good purchase, it was of ample height and diameter, and it was apparently constructed of heavy cast-iron, cold, black, and shiny. As a matter of fact it was made of glazed mortar and had a hidden joint just below the roof.

To this duct Bubber made his major attachments, using many windings of line and an intricate system of knots; and for double security he carried the line ten feet further rearward to a chimney and around this wound the rest of it, fastening it uncompromisingly with a second complex of knots. When he tossed his tackle line over the edge, it was with the air of one who is sure that at least his end of the job has been well done.

Shine, on the sidewalk, had surrounded the uncovered piano with a girdle of quilting, and about this, somewhat loosely, had adjusted a single belt. Now he hooked the block into a ring fastened to the top of this belt. Then, with quite unnecessary the guide rope. The piano began to rise.

It rose in a succession of small, upward jerks, each epitomizing the vehement force that Shine imparted to the pulley line. That force, increased by the piano's weight, extended to the anchorage on the roof, and the joint of the airduct in the floor of the roof felt and responded to each impulse from Joshua Jones' inner conflict, heard and answered each wanton effort to vent through muscle what could not escape through mind. An even ascent that joint might have borne, a jerky one it could not; there was no question of whether it would snap, but simply of when.

Shine's malevolent pursuer chose to decide this important question: the piano was just short of the end of its journey when the break came. Shine, getting a sort of satisfaction out of prodigious effort, gave an especially tremendous tug—to find resistance vanish so suddenly that he pitched forward on his face still holding the line. He heard Jinx utter a terrified "Jesus!" and as he rolled over, instinctively attempting to clear the pathway of the falling instrument, he glimpsed it swaying above, knew that a second "safety" anchoring was all that gave him that instant's doubtful grace, and heard a girl scream, "It's slipping out—! Quick—it's slipping out!"

The second anchorage held, but the initial drop had been enough to displace the soft girdle and belt from the center toward one end of the instrument. There was an instant's hesitancy, as if to give direction, and abruptly the belt released the piano, which dropped like a live thing freed; plunged with a drive to crush and kill, like a beast pouncing on witless prey. The crash was like no other sound on earth—explosion, groan, and whine—thick wood, coarse metal, taut wires—a noise that struck and shattered itself, then rose, spread, and hovered. It was as if a corner of hell had been blasted off and a thousand souls swarmed out, wailing.

Shine stood erect, looking dazedly about, touching an abrasion over one eye with exploratory fingers. And miraculous as a vision, Linda was before him, breathless with horror, apprehension, relief, with the effort of reaching him so quickly.

"Honey—" she said, and found that nothing more would come.

"Oh—" she managed, "I was at the window—upstairs—" and stood there a while in silence. Then because words failed, because something pinioned her arms that wanted to reach out to him, and because her eyes and throat mysteriously and ridiculously filled, she had a blank moment in which to realize how silly and impetuous she and another in which to be ashamed and take swift refuge in the house.

Shine on one side, Jinx on the other, looked down upon the wreckage. The piano lay half supine in a grotesque angular posture, its row of white keys gleaming like teeth, the lid of its key board back and fixed, like the retracted sprung upper lip of a creature that has died in agony.

Jinx gave forth a prayer of thanksgiving:

"It sho' as hell meant to get y'—but it's long gone now."

Shine remained silent and contemplative. Bubber came down. He and Jinx exclaimed comments.

Bubber came over to palpate Shine and ask how the hell he ever missed it. A small crowd was gathering. People were looking out of windows.

"Crazy as hell," Shine muttered absently.

"Honey'—well, I'll be john-browned—"

His hand again touched the raw place over his eye. "Little cold water wouldn't do it no harm—" and following in Linda's wake, he too entered the house.

That Shine should visit a hospital when he felt almost perfectly well meant that some decided difference had come about in him. The scramble which had delivered him from grave injury had had no more serious visible effect than to abrade his hands and forehead against the cement, but it marked a conscious internal change which first came to light when he followed Linda into the house. Shine, the disciple of hardness, not in any imaginable situation have been guilty of a surrender like that. Now again the change appeared when he decided that maybe he'd better go on 'round to the man's clinic and let one them doctors look him over—might even be some bones broke, who could tell?

He sat at one end of a white metal pew, an article of hospital furniture as uncomfortable in fact as it is in suggestion, and awaited his turn. Funny kid, Linda. Come runnin' out there yesterday, scared clean white, then didn' do a damn thing but turn around and go back. But "Honey—yea. He fell for that. And when he went in the house for water—huh—she was like as if nothing had happened. Showed him the sink and let him wash his head and gave him a towel—but not another word. Honey. Yea. When he had stalled around as long as he could, he too said, "Well, honey—and all she answered didn't need to be so tight about it, either—was, "You better go see a doctor and make sure you're all right." Damned if he would. But here he was a whole day late, but here.

Since Harlem Hospital was in a state of transition, it happened that, of the two internes on the service, one was white with brown angora goathair and the other brown with black sheep's wool. A blank white door opened, a patient was ejected and the white interne beckoned summarily to Shine. Shine looked at him a moment then said:

"I'll wait for th' other doctor."

He settled back in his pew. Sweet kid, though, no lie. All women are funny, but can over look that—if they're good-looking enough. And Lindy was sure good to gaze on. Skin like

RUDOLPH FISHER

light behind it. You could almost see through it—you could see through it—you could see red flowers behind it; and when she got excited over anything it seemed that somebody waved the flow ers back and forth. Like in the Casino that night, or that Sunday on the corner of Court Avenue. Gee!—Eyes, too. Talk about eyes! Looking into her eyes was like looking into the sky at night—looking from the bottom of an airshaft: deep, soft, and awfully black, with bright little stars twinkling away off—that night on the Drive—Judas Priest!

"Next!" called the brown interne cheerfully from a different blank white door, and Shine found himself in a clinical dressing room with tables and screens about and a little bed on wheels in one corner. There were mysterious varicolored bottles and jars and wickedly gleaming instruments everywhere, and the odor of phenol and iodoform took all the humor out of the air.

Not, however, for the interne nor the dressing nurse who assisted him, a little round, stiffly starched brown doll-baby who should have been in a toy-shop window.

"Yes, *sir*," said the interne to the nurse, watching as she soaped and dried Shine's forehead. "Best looking girl that's been in this place since the man said, 'Let's have Harlem.' Came in last night late. Ward VII. I sure mean to see her again."

"Ward VII—oh Doctor—not Ward VII!"

"What difference does it make? She can be cured."

"Find out her name?"

"I didn't miss. Young. Linda Young. And as soon as dressing clinic's over, the doctor—ahem!—is going to take Miss Linda's history. This fellow's my last case. Oh boy—how I love to take histories: Did you ever have measles, chicken-pox, whooping cough, mumps, scarlet fever? How many children? Oh no—of course not—I meant brothers and sisters? How many nights a work d you have to yourself, and how? When were you last out with the boyfriend? And now you have a pain in the bottom of your stomach—?"

The interne dabbed iodin on the denuded area of Shine's forehead. An abrasion, haring the most sensitive nerve-ends, is might have been anesthetized for all the pain he felt. Linda in this hospital? Linda?—What the—? Linda?"

The interne finished his dressing after a fashion and bustled the dazed Shine out, hurrying on past him. The interne was on the way to more pleasant duties.

Shine, numbly incredulous, followed slowly in the same direction. The white uniform was soon lost in a tangle of other white uniforms. Shine wandered on. Ward VII. Oh yes, you want the G. Y. N. service? Down that way, turn left then right—looking for some place, mister? Ward VII? Second floor north. Ward VII? Right around the corner—yes, you'll see the sign—if you look—

Ward VII. Yes, this is Ward VII. Whom do you wish to see? Linda Young—yes, a new patient Have you a card? She's a ward case you know, and visiting hours are over. I'm sorry, but you'll have to go back and get a card.

He went back to get a card. Miss Linda Young on Ward VII. Was it a relative? No. Just a friend? Sorry. Couldn't be issuing cards all day. Come at visiting hour tomorrow—two to three P.M. Very sorry, but it was really against the rules. Find out how she is for you, if you like. Click. . . G.Y.N.? How is Linda Young? . . . Yes. Resting comfortably? . . . Click. Resting comfortably.

Scarcely able to sense direction, Shine wandered away through a labyrinth of hallways. Linda resting comfortably—what kind of a joke, for Pete's sake—he was completely lost when, after a long time, he met a familiar figure, the interne who had dressed his wound and gone off to consult Linda Young. He caught the interne by the arm—had a crazy impulse to laugh at the way in which the interne shrank from that apparent attack. The interne had quite forgotten him.

"Listen, doc—Linda Young—Ward VII—I want to know about her."

"You want to know about her? Know what?"

"Is it really her?"

"Really her? What the—do you know her?"

"Oh so you're the guy?" There was untold scorn in the intern's voice.

"Me? What guy? Is she hurt?"

The interne looked him over cynically. "You ought to know."

"Know? Know what, doc? I didn' even know she was sick. I saw her yesterday. She was all right yesterday."

"What time yesterday did you see her?"

"Early afternoon."

"Early afternoon. Oh. Well—she came in late last night. You didn't see her last night?"

"No. Why? What's wrong with her?"

"Nothing much. Only some guy ought to get his block knocked off."

"What you talkin' 'bout, doc?"

"Tell me is this your girl?"

"She ain't nobody else's?"

"Well then, you ought to know this. Some guy found her alone last night where she works, see, and tried to show her a deep point. He couldn't make her listen to reason, so he tried caveman stuff. There was quite a scuffle. The girl got loose and out of the house, but she keeled over on the sidewalk before she got two blocks away. Scared dumb. She was brought in with a diagnosis of assault with intent—"

The change that distorted Shine's face told the interne he had gone far enough. The features writhed, the bronze skin seemed to have suddenly been dusted with ashes, and there was unquestionable intent to kill in his eyes and the whole attitude of his body. The interne, too late as he now realized, tried to mitigate his story:

"It's all right of course he didn't succeed. She's just got a sprained ankle and a little shock—"

But Shine brushed past and moved away in huge, infuriate strides. Even far down the corridor he looked the size of ten men.

The interne watched him swing out of sight, then shrugged his shoulders helplessly. "I wonder," he asked himself, "when I'll learn some sense?"

BATTLE

Overnight Fred Merrit's court avenue house had become a ghastly ruin. Every pane had been bashed in with flood, every window frame charred with fire, each of the gray stone window margins frayed and blackened with smoke. Yesterday these windows had surveyed the world serenely, bright and alive. Today they looked like the deep, dark-circled orbits of sunken blind eyes.

The place had been gutted, heart and bowels. Its vitals, whatever things had given it substance, circulation, and life, all had been hopelessly battered and crushed till they'd shrunken out of sight: One could stand on the sidewalk and see the sunset through and beyond the rear wall—a hard broad grin of a sunset, which transilluminated the flame sacked dwelling, mocking its emptiness without pity, deriding its devastation. When eventually the sun's grin faded out, it was as if a contemptuous, amused observer had at last turned aside and gone off on more important business.

The house stood stark as a corpse in the shrouding dusk.

IT WAS UPON THIS SCENE that Shine came, less frantic now, but no less grim than when he had left the hospital earlier in the day. Even then he had realized that Merrit would not be found at home during the day, and had finished his afternoon's work in a silent turmoil. Added delay had not subdued his fury—had merely stored up a greater potential violence, like added tension on a spring. Now, when he unexpectedly came upon this ruin, it was as if the spring suddenly cracked.

He stood on the sidewalk looking up at the looming gray carcass of a house. For a moment it took his breath. Twilight made it the more indistinct—he craned his neck and stared; looked all about him to verify the neighborhood, walked forward to a point where he could discern the number on the house next door–315–came back, stood in a stupor of unbelief; and after a while heaved a great sigh of reluctant, bitter conviction:

For the time being his present mission of vengeance was submerged in the onrush of a greater hatred, a hatred more deeply ingrained and of far longer standing; for the moment he glared insanely around at the cool, still, empty street and at the rows of serene gray houses standing side by side. They gave forth a maddening impression of distance and unconcern. They looked quite satisfied. This catastrophe was for them the answer to all their prayers. Now that it was done, they could go on as they always had. The ruined dwelling had simply earned and received the wages of sin—if Shine could have trampled and crushed them all in that moment, he would surely have done so.

But as this tide of hatred fell and receded, his original murderous intent emerged like a spire through abating flood. What if they had got Merrit? A guy like Merrit deserved everything he got. And he hadn't got half what was coming to him yet—not if he could be found—Linda resting fortably the dickty liquor-head—

He knew it. Merrit had meant to put it on he ever since that first morning here on Court Avenue—the morning she strode past like a million dollars, ignoring Jinx and Bubber's comments "Figgerin' on a jive already—the doggone dickty hound. Why the hell can't dickties stick to their own women, 'stead o' messin' 'round some honest workin' girl?" That was the thought he had gt from the way Merrit looked at her that morning—well—it wouldn't be long now—let him get one hand on that yellow throat-just let him sink the fingers of one hand into it-just let him take the bastard's ankle in his hands and twist it off—

But this house—hell a'mighty—what a wreck—

His turbulent emotions strangely dominated by curiosity, he slowly, almost fearfully made his way up the front stoop of the house. Shattered glass, strewn over the steps, crunched dryly under his feet. The doorways bounding the vestibule were open; the outer door a mere frame to which angular fragments of glass still clung like monstrous teeth; the inner a fallen barrier, shattered and blackened, prone on the floor.

He explored the front room, stepping cautiously over obstructing wreckage, just able to perceive in the dimness the soaked, woodwork a burnt-cork caricature, patches of plaster fallen away baring the carbonized understructure.

"Whoever done this sho' knew his business—the—"

The floor was a clutter of water-soaked pieces, some still wrapped in burlap. A cabinet lay on its side in a corner, its upper half bared and blackened, its lower still embraced in a scorched, wet covering. Little puddles glistened here and there; a rug protested under Shine's step with the squish of a full sponge, compressed. A besooted prism chandelier still hung from the channeled ceiling, against the gray of which it was silhouetted like a shadow of itself. To the rim of the broad doorway leading from this room, there still hung traces of what had yesterday been portieres of m brocade, now shreds of gray lace woven of cobwebs, the greater part fallen about the threshold, a scum of soft wet ash.

"This ain't a damn thing compared to what I do to him—"

Shine moved through the foyer past a crumbled charcoal staircase, and on thence into the back room. This room, equally demolished, was nar rower than the front, and presented at one side a doorless doorway leading into a small side room. Disregarding the settling darkness, Shine went over to this doorway, then suddenly halted, stood quite motionless, intent on an unexpected sight within that room.

The rear wall was almost entirely occupied by a tall broad window. There was a table before this window, and seated at the table, a man. Looking obliquely through the doorway, Shine saw that the man did not sit wholly erect, but slumped down in his chair as limply as if his backbone had melted, drooped there almost double, his head bowed forward on his chest. Despite this lifeless posture, it was possible to recognize the figure by the gray dusk of the window against which it was outlined. Shine knew that he was looking upon Fred Merrit.

He stared scowling a moment, bent forward a bit to catch some sign of life, and was on the point of approaching the figure when it moved in a curious way: shook like a man with a chill— slumped quiet—violently shook again. Slowly it dawned on Shine that maybe the bird was crying. And as he continued to stare and grasped in one of Merrit's extended hands: a fairly large picture frame, out of which the canvas had been burnt, leaving only a frayed, singed, marginal rim. Shine belabored his brain to catch an elusive memory of that frame, till it broke upon him that this was the one that had contained the likeness of Merrit's mother; the one about which Mrs. Fuller had warned, "He'd die if he ever lost it."

For what seemed a long time Shine stood look ing, things romping through his brain. Linda strug gling—no—resting comfortably. The God-damned dickty—what happened? Fays got him—dirty sneaks—I mean they got him—look at this place. Merrit. There he is—what the hell—crying—Jesus—that picture of his mother—

Then Shine did what would have seemed to his associates an amazing, an unpardonable thing. There with the man he'd set out to punish alone, within his grasp, he stood silent, apparently undecided, made not a single move to strike. And after a while, slowly turned about and found his way out of the house.

It amazed Shine himself—amazed him and chagrined him. He felt rather glad of the darkness outside it was a sort of balm for his shame. Hard boogy he was—yea—awful hard—the hardest boogy in Harlem. There he was, this dickty, this guy that—right there, crying to be crowned. And what does the hard guy do-the hardest boogy in Harlem? He gets a seasick feeling in the belly and turns around and sneaks out!

He mumbled excuses to himself as he wandered away down the street: "Hell—I'll get 'im later gee—y' can't hit a guy when he's down—"

He was the first visitor to arrive on Ward VII the next afternoon. The odor of phenol and iodoform that had pervaded the clinic hovered here also. The beds were repellently white and orderly. There were only a few scattered patients ugly women in bath robes and mules.

He found Linda seated beside a bed; a profusion of cotton and gauze was piled at one end of the bed, and from these Linda, with great concentration and delicate, mysterious precision was fashioning oblong pads which she stacked at the opposite end. Her back was toward him, and he stood for a moment behind her, looking; and if yesterday he had had strange emotions watching the unaware Merrit, today his feelings were past understanding watching the unaware Linda. Nothing seemed to be wrong with her, yet the sight of her sitting there in that clean, sparse, terrible place, bending so intently over her task, made his breath stop in his throat, so that he had to swallow it deliberately before he could speak.

"Hello, Lindy."

She turned and looked up, half rose, sank back; the stars came out in her eyes, which consumed him in unbelieving astonishment, and she gave a little catching laugh. "Why—how'd you know I was here?"

He appropriated the chair beside the next bed and sat down.

"Didn't you tell me to go to the hospital?"

She quickly sought the iodin stained place on his forehead, reached impulsively toward it, checked the motion. "No—'tisn't s'posed to be touched, is it?"

"You—all right, Lindy?"

"Great. Going home today. Wasn't any sense in them bringing me here anyhow, I wasn't—I was only scared—I guess."

"That all?"

"Well—I hurt my ankle—see?" She displayed a bandaged joint. "Not bad. Strapped. They'd transfer me to another ward if I wasn't leaving so you soon. How'd you know?"

silence. To relieve her embarras ment, evident by her averted face, he assured her, "He won't pull nothin' like that anymore, Lindy."

She was alarmed.

"You didn't—didn't?"

"Nope. Not yet."

"Don't!"

"Don't? Don't what?"

"Don't you know. It's all right. Really. You'll get into trouble—"

"Trouble?"

"Please—"

"Listen, baby. Trouble ain't half what I'd get into if—"

"But what's the use? What good will it do?"

"He's got it comin' to him."

"He'll get it—without you gettin' into trouble."

"I ain't go'n' get in no trouble. It's him that's go'n' get in trouble."

She was silently distressed, and this reinforced his vengefulness as if he were witnessing her original pain instead of this that he himself was causing. He too was silent, far in the depths of a thwarted and now redoubled malevolence. Just let him get his hands on that half-white dickty cake-eater—he'd tear him apart slowly—he'd rip his yellow arms out-just let him get that close again—

But the vision of Merrit as he'd last seen him, limp and shuddering amid devastation, grew clear, whereupon, in spite of himself, this redoubled malevolence sagged.

Linda said, "Remember that morning in church what Father Tod said 'bout Joshua and the battle of Jericho? 'Bout people kidding themselves?"

"Yea. I can see that story all right 'bout the walls; that's a good one. And I can see how people kid themselves. That's easy. But I never did get the connection. Little too deep for me."

"You're the connection."

"Me?"

"Uh-huh. There's a wall around you. A thick stone wall. You're outside, looking. You think you see yourself. You don't. You only loose. Always get the other guy. That's the wall."

"Mean you don't really b'lieve I'm gon' this bird for what he done to you—?"

"No—no—no. He didn't do anything. I mean—"

"Gee, Lindy—what'd you think of a guy the claim' to be likin' you and let a bird get away with anything like that?"

"He didn't get away with anything, I keep telling you."

"He didn' miss tryin'."

"I'm not talking about just him. I mean all the time. Everything. You're kidding yourself. You're not hard."

"What?" His eyes dilated as if that explicit remark were a sort of doom.

"You're not hard or mean or tough or any those of things. You're just scared."

"Scared?"

"Scared. Scared to admit you're not hard. Scared you'll be found out. So scared, you take every chance you can to prove how hard you are. I don't believe you'd ever do anything really cruel. Don't believe it's in you."

Again that vision of Merrit stricken and of himself paralyzed, strangely unable to strike. Linda kept on:

"You're just big. You can lick everybody. So you get away with it. All you have to do is let folks think you're hard. That's all right. Let them think so if that's any fun. But when you think so yourself—well, you're kidding yourself, that's all."

He grasped vaguely for comprehension and captured only excuse:

"Well, you kid yourself too sometimes, Lindy."

That seemed to kindle something in her that flared and persisted like fire. "I know it—and I'll never be happy while I do. Oh, I see what he meant all right-I tell myself things, things about you. I tell myself I don't even want to see you anymore— that you can't be really liking me after I let you pick me up—yes, that's what it was, a pick-up—that night in Manhattan Casino. I tell myself I hate you for grabbing me up on the street that Sunday. Lies—all of 'em. I liked it. I've been wild to see you. And the only thing I hate about you is the thing that keeps you from telling me what I'd give both ears to hear. But no—you wouldn't do that, because"—her voice was all scorn—"just because you're hard and it's soft to fall for a girl." Her eyes filled, and she turned her face away, biting her lip.

To save his life, he could not utter a word.

"And now look at me," she said, her face still averted. "Making believe I'm ashamed when I'm not a doggone thing but mad. Oh you're right. I kid myself, too." There was a long pause. Then, "But I know I'm doing it—you don't."

"But listen, Lindy. The only time I tried to tell you, you hauled off and bat me one."

"Of course I did."

"But now you're sayin' you liked it."

"I didn't say I liked the way you did it. Playing safe. Making me quote the Bible—giving yourself protection. Scared. Scared to be yourself. That's what I—that's what I hit at."

For a while there seemed to be nothing to say. When at last Shine spoke it was to make a quite irrelevant statement:

"Lindy—I'm crazy 'bout you."

Still she did not look at him, but she said:

"That's how I know about you. That's how I know you're not really hard. That's why I don't want you to bother—him. You say you'd be doing it for me—but you could kill him and it wouldn't give me any satisfaction—just make me unhappy because you'd done it and kept us apart—maybe for life—so if you bother him now, knowing I don't want you to, knowing it won't give me any satisfaction and 'll only make me unhappy, why then you'll just be doing it for your own satisfaction. You'll just be proving again to yourself how tough and tight you are. It won't be because you're crazy about me that'll just be the excuse."

He went through a good deal of figuring before he answered that. What he eventually said was:

"Well—I'm crazy 'bout you, Linda."

Only then did she look fully at him, and again there were stars in her eyes, and color deep in the honey of her skin. She gave him that little halting laugh and said, "The walls must be tumblin' down."

RUDOLPH FISHER

He wated to tell her how completely she had dominated him these past days, all the newly realized illusion about himself that now was crumbling. He wanted to say "Walls? Tumblin'? You said it, baby," but habit sealed his lips.

It did not however close all avenues of communication. He reached out, not fully aware of his gesture and placed his great hand over hers on the bed. She placed her other hand on top of his. It was the closing of a switch, the making of a circuit through which leaped new, strange, shat tering impulses. Not a thousand dances all in one with Lottie Buttsby could have moved him so, not a thousand of Babe Merrimac's entreaties and avowals. For one brief, eternal moment that mere contact of hands as completely obliterated the surroundings as if their whole bodies had been fused in passionate, tender embrace. When eventually the white beds came back into the picture, they might have been billowy clouds, the ugly women in their bathrobes and mules might have been winged angels, and the odors of phenol and iodoform might have been the fragrance of roses.

Shine smiled. He thought yet again of his strange behavior yesterday which now through her, he was beginning to understand; and the self disgust he had felt as he spared and left Merrit within his ruin, began curiously to give way to a sense of tremendous relief.

A familiar sound came from outside. Bess had been parked in the street below. Jinx and Bubber had grown impatient and were "laying" on the horn, by way of suggesting that the driver hurry and return. The sound came faint but clear through the open windows.

"Know that is?" Shine asked her. She smiled and answered, "I guess that must be the ram's horn."

I n the Small Back Room of Pat's Place, the regular evening black-jack game was in session green shaded electric light hung low over an A oval dining room table covered with a dishonorably discharged brown army blanket. Around it a dozen players sat and around them a dozen side-betters stood. The room was full of men, and smoke and low talk.

The dealer, standing, taunted the players in a soft, half plaintive voice:

"What's your contribution, friend? Only a half? Can't buy the sweet mamma shoes on four-bit bets. How much to you, dumb-and-ugly? One buck, right. Next? A dollar and a dime to Jinx, the freckle-face wonder—dime's for luck—my luck. How 'bout you, Squatty? Make it light on y'self. Two-dollar bills is bad luck, you know. Wha' d' y' say, Stud? The rest of it? Nineteen bucks four bits to you. Deal it? Consider it doled. Perfect, gentlemen, perfect."

He had dealt each player a card as he spoke. Now he dealt them each another, renoting the amounts of their bets as the second card fell. He put down the rest of the deck, picked up his own two cards and, holding them close to his chest to prevent his neighbors' seeing them, studied them long and hard. Suddenly he warned with exaggerated malignancy—"Don't a man move!—Knew I'd turn the bug on you dinkies this time!" And he threw down an ace and a jack, the supreme combination.

He was collecting his winnings when Shine came in, edging sidewise through the crowd. Finding no place available at the table, Shine would have ordinarily lifted some player out by the collar, thanked him with a grin, and assumed his place. Tonight he simply looked on. Had anyone else appropriated valuable space just to look on without betting, there would have been trouble; first gentle hints about how crowded it was, then less gentle hints about the value of fresh air to kibitzers, and finally, if the offender was especially dense, an ultimatum suggesting that he try the pool room or the roof. Nobody however, manifested a trace of annoyance at Shine's profitless presence.

As for Shine, he felt tonight a new exhilaration, a satisfying ability to fill his lungs, a conscious, pitying superiority over these companions of his. For to him, through Linda and after considerable meditation, had come a new outlook on old things. He had finally been able to phrase it for himself in terms that brought it home to him, terms that made it ridiculous to feel shame for having let Merrit off unpunished. He put it thus:

"The guy that's really hard is the guy that's hard enough to be soft."

That about got it. That covered him. That made him unafraid to do what he damned pleased in any situation. If he felt like letting a bird off, he was big enough to do it. Hitherto he'd been like a little shrimp that dares not go without a gun or a knife, only his size and strength had taken the place of the weapon. Sort of coward, sure 'nough—no wonder it made Lindy sore. She sure had got him told, too. Sure had—some kid, no lie. Funny he never could see it before-the walls of Jericho. Lindy—Judas Priest—he'd forgotten to ask where she was going from the hospital. Dumbbell. Well he'd find out. Gee, what a feeling! Boy! Like a port-wine drunk—

He saw the men 'round about anew-lean and long bodies, thick and short, round heads, egg heads, bullet heads, steeple heads, thick lips stuck out, thin lips drawn in, skins black, brown, tan, yellow. He picked out two or three strangers, conjectured about their occupations. This lopsided one was undoubtedly a waiter, that plump cocoa one a porter, the bald, custard one whose cheeks had been left in the oven a trifle too long a—well, what the hell else were boogies but waiters and porters?

In this superior frame of mind, he was not at all prepared for what he was now to learn.

WEARYING OF THE TURN OF cards, the stereotyped comments of players, the occasional deft, furtive exchanges between collaborating cheaters, Shine waded out into the pool room, where the air was a trifle less thick. Here the talk was loud and thump of cue sticks, the eager shuffle of players' feet, freed this room of the covert atmosphere oppressing the other.

As Shine abandoned the game room he encountered Patmore who was coming toward it; and he was a little surprised to observe Patmore quite so drunk. A slick coat of sweat made Pat's face shine as though it had been greased; his eyes, also, were unusually bright and his manner a trifle too genial.

"Hello, Mr. Jones!" he greeted Shine. "What's Mr. Jones gonna say tonight?" And Shine felt a vague disproportionate annoyance at the ironic form of address. He brushed past with a noncommittal response, while Pat stood back, turned to watch him pass, and grinned derisively: "Must be turnin' dickty."

Shine ignored this as he had ignored Pat himself ever since the dance. He found a cue stick and an empty table and proceeded to amuse himself solitaire. He had hardly racked-'em-up when Bubber appeared at his side.

"Come 'eh," Bubber said, "Come listen to this." And Joshua Jones went and listened.

PAT WAS PROCLAIMING TO ALL his friends in the game room:
"Yassir. Fair and square, that's Henry Patmore. Anything you do for him, he's gonna do for you. Good or bad, don't make no difference. You know what the man says—as ye sow so shall ye reap. You see me go—I'll see you go. You put it on me, I'll put it on you. Sooner or later. Don't make no difference—sooner or later, thass all. Five years ago, I tell y', this dickty—dickty, mind y'—put it on me, see? Cost me damn near all I had. Ten thousand Got-damn dollars. Cost me that to stay out o' jail. Yassir—ten thousand berries. Well—thass aw right. Jes' go up on Court Avenue and look at his house now. Huh. Thought I'd forgot it, see? So damn smart, movin' in 'mongst d' fays. Fay nigger. Movin' in 'mongst d' white folks. Well, d' white folks sho' give 'im a welcome. Jes' go up on Court Avenue and see what d' white folks done. White folks. Yea. Henry Patmore—white folks Hah!—Damn if this ain't d' first in my life I ever passed for white."

had heard such proclamations before, and no particular example of any of Pat's special excellences could be expected wholly to detract them from their game. But at this moment the dealer, who was still standing, caught sight of Shine looming in the doorway; and the dealer became fixed as suddenly as a figure in a cinema when the projector abruptly stops; fixed in the act of dealing, with his thumb at his lip and the deck in his hand, his eyes wide, set, unmoving.

All the men turned and looked. What they saw affected them differently. The dealer, now like an actor in a slow motion picture, his eyes still set on Shine, put the deck down on the table, gathered up the bank without looking at it, and retreated toward the far door of the room, which led into the saloon. Those nearest him seized their piles and moved in the same direction, as if the dealer were attached to them, drawing them along by strings. The lopsided waiter backed terrified against the wall and stood there as if stuck, while the plump cocoa porter, his eyes on Shine, clawed absently and futilely at the place on the blanket where his pile should have been, and made no effort to rise. Some pushed back their chairs and yet seemed too fascinated to get out of them, some jumped up and elbowed their way through the midst of their slowly retreating comrades, while a few sat quite still as if aware that the effort to get clear of danger was useless. All this because of what even the blindest of them saw in the face of Shine.

Not slowly, first with doubt, then with mounting conviction, had revelation come to Shine this time; not as in the case of the ruined house, nor of the sobbing Merrit, nor of Linda's analysis of his hardness. Not so, but instantaneously, like something revealed by lightning in the dark—the moment he heard Patmore's words he knew all of what had happened; knew who had craftily sent Merrit that fake warning the day before the lawyer moved in; knew who had thus established an alibi, awaiting an opportune moment to strike safely when suspicion would fall elsewhere. Knew who, finding Linda alone, had renewed the advances which had been interrupted at the Man hattan Casino dance; knew all months ago to enlist his own aid as an "agent" to this last vicious spiteful snap at himself through Linda. And it seemed that all the hatred he had ever felt for anybody welled up within him to be concentrated now on Henry Patmore alone: his hatred of the asylum superintendent, of the fay who had called him Shine, of all fays, of the evil thing he'd escaped in pianos, of dickties in general and the blameless dickty Merrit in particular—all these now gathered in one single wave, advanced in one tidal onrush. And all that he knew and felt gleamed in his bronze face.

Patmore saw it there and confessed everything by reaching for his gun. Jinx, one of those who had not moved from his seat at the table, was neat enough to strike at Pat's arm as the weapon went off. Shine felt his left hand go numb, felt his hatred break into action. All of a sudden he became madman with no notion of what he was doing, with no sustained consciousness, only a succession of fragments that thumped in his head.

Linda resting comfortably. Merrit crying like a baby. Picture of his mother. Fays sure got him. Fays? Fays hell—Patmore got 'im. Wonder how many kinds of a jackass that guy thinks I am—? Never seen a man catch air so fast. Walls tumblin'—damn if they ain't. Offered me twenty-five dollars—no—Linda. Fly guy, passing for white. Assault with intent—not Merrit—Patmore, Patmore done it did it. Not the fays—Patmore. Patmore put it on Merrit. Like *this*—walls—haw!—Damn right, walls—look at 'em fall—let 'em raise hell when they fall—like that God-damn piano—

From the saloon room a few observers, some of them those who'd escaped the game room but had in intention of sacrificing the spectacle of a good fight, watched the tumult grow. The game room door had been shut tight behind them, but the wide passage between the saloon and the pool parlor revealed a part view of the latter; and presently forms came into sight, were framed in the doorway, vanished, returned for brief moments. The field of vision was maddeningly small, but it showed that more men than Pat and Shine had become involved in the battle.

Pat's gun out of line, an adjacent friend of Pat's had seized Jinx and retaliatively yanked him back; that Bubber had cheerfully kicked the shins of another interferer who would otherwise have tripped Shine at his first move; an interferer who resented interference and so promptly turned on Bubber; that from such small beginnings the conflict had grown to a come-one-come-all fracas, and that Jinx and Bubber were gleefully trouncing some of those who would have enjoyed seeing them trounce each other not long since.

Unintelligible, fragmentary glimpses came through the too narrow doorway—Bubber ducking a cue stick, swung butt-end—to in a villainous are—somebody reaching for a pool ball in a corner of the one visible table—a figure pitching forward headlong out of sight—Jinx with a pianohold, vehemently bending his particular adversary back across the edge of the table—wild swings of bodiless arms, senseless twist and tangle of disjoined legs and feet. Accompanying these glimpses, noise, a strident yet muffled tumult: shuffle of feet, grunts, curses, thumps, thwacks, hisses, stifled cries; a deep background of sound against which stood out an occasional wooden crash.

And now there swept into the doorway, framed as if by stage design, that pair of antagonists from whom all the others derived their energies, the two whose bitterness reduced the rest of the conflict to mere friendly tiff. Patmore, ordinarily no mean combatant, now gin-mighty and frantic with fright; and Shine, a gigantic madman, himself heedless of what everyone else saw: that his useless left hand was an impediment to himself and a decided advantage to Pat, a more than equalizing damage and all that had prolonged the battle.

They had lost their coats and clawed each other's shirts into shreds, and though Pat had been shiny at first, he now glistened no more than Shine. Shine however, maintaining himself with one an gave the superior impression: blocked knee-jabs anticipated kicks, foiled elbow-thrusts, invalidated all the other man's rough-and-tumble skill. Even in the short time and brief space of this doorway view, one could see that all of Pat's effort be decisive; while Shine's every move only anticipated some future stroke that he knew would be wholly crushing. Every instant, every buffet seemed to enlargen his ominous intent; his purpose mounted visibly, so that those who watched saw in him not merely one crippled yet splendid in battle, but a towering, inescapable instrument of vengeance.

The end came suddenly. Had Pat been less of a toper and less of a jiver, it might have been different; but in a prolonged encounter these handicaps of his were far more telling than Shine's. A thrust from the latter's bare left shoulder sent Pat's head back like a blow from a fist. It snapped away the last of his reserve, and of a sudden his whole body sagged as if his spine were broken. Clinging to Shine like a man slipping down a tree trunk, he sank to the floor on his knees, and his head remained sprung back like the open lid of a box. This was the moment that Shine had seemed to be awaiting; his fist hip-high, he deliberately drew back his right arm to strike the exposed throat. Every observer knew that if that blow should land Pat's neck would be broken.

It did not land. Some friend of Pat's in the room beyond hurled a pool ball at the imminent victor. The heavy ivory sphere missed its mark, sped through the doorway and over the observers' heads, shattering the great bar mirror behind them.

The crash and jangle of the falling glass wall was all that snatched out of madness. The sound transfixed him as if all the walls of the place had tumbled instead of just one. He stood set, motionless, blinked once or twice and stared a long moment at Pat.

Only then, perhaps, did he actually see him, on his knees, gasping, helpless. Presently the poised, retracted arm began to relax; the tension went out of Shine's frame. His head sank a litle forward, and his good arm slowly dropped to his side, as limp as its useless fellow.

RUDOLPH FISHER

JERICHO

Whenever a caller told Fred Merrit an wunanticipated story, he whirled about in his swivel chair, jumped up and walked to the window. This he did now, as soon as Shine stopped talking. For a long time he stood looking down on the Avenue.

"Well," he said at last, "I'll be tarred and feathered if that isn't the damnedest—"

His office commanded a corner. On the curb two portly well dressed idlers stood in leisurely conversation; they proclaimed their important opinions to all and sundry. A thin, hunched, hungryeyed vagabond nearby watched them in ominous silence. A boy with yellow hair and the fairest of skin came slowly up the street, leading an aged, black, gray-bearded blind beggar.

"Can you imagine it? A Negro—using white prejudice to cover what he wanted to do—putting the blame in the most likely spot—almost getting away with it, too—can you beat that?"

Merrit came back, sat down in his chair and shook his head. "So it wasn't Miss Cramp after all—I swear I thought it was she. Well—" he showed himself true to his race hate—"it isn't because she wouldn't have done it if she could." He banged his fist on the desk. "I'd bet the insurance on that house that Patmore just beat her to it."

"Insurance?"

"Yes sir."

"Mean the house had life insurance on it?"

Merrit laughed. "Yes. Not a bad name for it."

"Mean you didn' lose nothin'?"

"Well, not as much as you'd think to look at the place."

"Well—but when I seen you in there—"

"Yes—I know. I had been out of town overnight—just got back that afternoon. It was quite a shock—but it wasn't the house. Not altogether. That is the picture, you see, wasn't insured—can't replace that."

"That's too bad," said Shine.

those warnings. Wise. Rather admire that chap really. And I swear I'm sorry it wasn't the fays."

"Well—" Shine rose—"jes' thought you'd like to know the whole story."

"Wait a minute where you going?"

"Goin' to look for a job," Shine grinned. "Old man Isaacs bumped off this time. Business for sale."

"Sit down. Let's have a drink." Merrit produced part of a pint and they drank, rat and dickty, as equals.

The drink gave Merrit a thought: "You know what killed old man what's-his-name? Your boss?"

"Bad heart."

"Yea. And bad news: when he heard you busted my piano. You're a hell of a mover."

"No lie," Shine admitted. "But the next guy won't know nothin' about that."

"Yes, he will."

"Huh?"

"Keep your jumper on—I'm the next guy."

"Say, it gets you quick, don't it?"

"What?"

"The liquor."

"I'll be on my feet when they haul you out, my boy. This isn't whiskey talk. Listen."

Shine listened. He owed Merrit a piano, so it was to Merrit's advantage to get him employed. On the other hand, Merrit owed him—or the girl, maybe something more. Nothing but the grace of God had stayed Shine's hand the evening he stood behind him, intent on murder. All right. Here was the idea: Here was a business. Shine knew that business, didn't he? Been in it five years now. Why the hell couldn't he run it, then? He ran it when the old man was sick, didn't he? Suppose Merrit bought it— easy—only a one-truck moving business—and turned it over to Shine to run? Fiftyfifty on the profits with an option to purchase outright in due time. That's what we Negroes need, a business class, an economic backbone. What kind of a social structure on one end and doctors on the other. Nothing in between. No substance. Everybody wants to quit waiting table and start writing prescriptions right away. Well, here's a chance for you and a good investment for me. Race proposition, too. How 'bout it?

Shine had no word to say, so suddenly had this thing come.

"All you put up is experience," Merrit said. "You've got your own hoisting license, haven't you? You and that girl can hit it off sooner, maybe—she's out to the country place now, by the way. And there you are. Well, what's the hold up? How about it?"

Even now that Shine saw Merrit meant it, all he could manage to utter was "Gee—!"

The thrill and terror of a house afire so uncomfortably close by had been a little too much for Miss Agatha Cramp. Even now, a week after the night of the uproar, she was still having breakfast in bed. Everytime she thought of the excitement—the smoke, filling the quiet neighborbood before anyone suspected its origin, the long wait for the engines while the flames gained headway, the shriek, roar and clangor of arriving fire trucks, men shouting, thumping her own front door, yelling for admittance, dragging hose line through her house to the roof—she had to suppress shudders and draw deep breaths. It was a shattering ordeal.

She said as much this morning over her tray to her new Irish maid, Mary. Mary, an extremely acquiescent person, answered solidly, "Yes'm."

"I feel so badly," Miss Cramp went on, "about such a great loss of property. It must be extremely discouraging. The poor man never had a chance to take up his residence in the place, you know."

"No. You see, he was a Negro."

"Yes 'm."

"And I shouldn't be surprised if someone weren't guilty of arson in this case."

"Y' nivver kin tell, mum," said Mary wondering what in limbo arson was.

"There is so much hatred between races," sighed Miss Cramp. "Still, it is all that can be expected. Now Negroes, for instance are most extremely deceitful."

"Is 'at so, mum?"

"Indeed it is. Why, this man Merrit, who owned the house that burnt up—he was always practicing some sort of deceit. Do you know what he did, Mary?"

"No mum."

"Of course you don't. Well, he was extremely fair of skin, you see, so that you wouldn't ordinarily have noticed that there was

RUDOLPH FISHER

you understand. But he was always posing as a white man."

"Y' don't say, mum."

"He certainly was. He posed as white when he purchased that house—otherwise he'd never have gotten it. And, Mary, you can't imagine what else he did."

"No, mum."

"He even went so far as to deceive white women in order to get into their homes—God knows for what purpose."

"Is that so, mum?"

"Yes. So you see, after all, some disaster like this was all that he could expect. It was simply poetic justice, that's all."

"Justice of the peace," amended Mary.

"I once had a colored maid. She was very deceitful, also."

"Is that so, mum?"

"Very. She used to go out at night without letting me know, and finally she left on only three days' notice."

"Y' don't say, mum."

"So you see, everything considered, ther is some basis for race-distrust after all."

"Like England and Ireland," suggested Mary.

"Exactly, Mary. Exactly what I was thinking. And that reminds me, Mary."

"Yes'm."

"Who is the president of your country now?"

"Feller named Coolidge," said Mary.

"No, no, Mary. I do not mean the United States. I mean the Irish Republic, your native land."

"I sorter fergit, mum," Mary apologized. "Y' see, when I come away, sure there wasn't no Irish Republic."

"Isn't it a man named De Valera?"

"Yes—I believe it is, mum."

"Now there is something I can't understand—how a Spaniard—he is a Spaniard isn't he—how a Spaniard could become a native son of Ireland?"

"Well," said Mary philosophically, "them things will happen, mum."

Look at the way that McRey starved to death. Something ought to be done. I' there some organization that takes care of such matters?"

"I think his family buried him all right," Mary reassured her.

"No—no, Mary. You do not understand at all. What I mean is this. Here is a young and inex perienced newborn nation, planted on a little isle of the sea, and left quite alone, helpless. It does seem to me that those of us who are in a position to do so should contribute all we can toward their welfare."

"Yes'm."

"Indeed there should be some organization having that as its purpose. Are you sure there isn't?"

"Well—there's what they call the Irish Free State Association, mum."

"There!" said Miss Cramp triumphantly. "I knew it. Exactly what I thought, Mary. I must get in touch with them at once. Have they a phone, do you suppose?"

"Wouldn't be surprised if they did, mum."

"Very well, then. That will do, Mary. That's all. When you come for the tray, bring the phone book, will you, Mary?"

When Shine, en route upstate with Bess, drew up at the driveway that led into Merrit's country place, he had no idea that the sound of Bess's voice would awaken even the dog. It was barely daybreak, and though Merrit had promised yesterday to be up in time to greet him as he passed, Shine had no faith in the possibility of getting a dickty out of bed in the cool gray dawn. It surprised him therefore to see, before a minute had elapsed, a dim figure at the head of the driveway coming quickly toward him.

It surprised him a good deal more, however, when the figure came near enough for recognition. It was Linda, bareheaded, wrapped in a coat, smiling at his astonishment.

"Heard you were coming," she said. "Got up early and waited."

It seemed to Shine that the sky turned from gray to gold in the twinkling of an eye.

"When you coming back?" she asked.

"Tonight."

"Tonight?"

"Yea. Barrin' accident. Only a fifty mile trip. Got to go pick up a load and bring it back."

"Where's your gang?"

"Still gettin' over the fight—I'll pick up a couple o' guys to load on up there."

"And you'll only be gone till tonight?"

"Be back by bedtime easy."

"And you're going up alone and coming back alone?"

"Sure."

Linda made up her impetuous mind. "You're doing no such thing, Mr. Jones." And she circled Bess' nose and clambered into the cab from the opposite side. While Shine regained his breath, she casually herself; stretched out her legs, rested her head back, hunched up her coat, stifled a yawn and murmured with great unconcern:

"'S chilly—huh?"

the cab. Before he reached the road, Bess, with a joyous roar, carried them off. Too amazed to call out, Merrit went on down, out into the middle of the road, and having confirmed his vision, grinned and told the world he'd be damned.

He stood there smiling and watching in the middle of the road, one hand absently plucking at his throat where the soft, open collar of his shirt left it bare. He had preposterous feelings, far too absurd to admit: an impulse to run after the departing Bess, crying, "Wait—for God's sake—" as if she were carrying off some chance of his own; a terrifying sense of some slow crushing futility, allowing them to escape, but holding him captive, surrounding, insulating, oppressing him, like the haze of this morning's mist, beyond which he could perceive but out of which he could not emerge; as if he moved and must always move in a dismal, broad, gray cloud, outside of which were clear blue skies that he could know of but never reach.

Strangely irrelevant people and things flashed into and out of his mind: a fleeting glimpse of his brown mother's picture—Patmore in court shaking his fist-Tod Bruce in his pulpit drawing some remote and ridiculous analogy—Shine in the office explaining unintelligibly why he "let him out"—Miss Cramp inviting him to call—why in hell couldn't it have been Miss Cramp instead of Patmore? All wrong, the way it actually happened. Should've been Miss Cramp. Should've been the fays—damn it—fays were supposed to do such things. Well of course—Patmore had just beaten 'em to it-just beaten 'em to it, that was all. Bright boogy, Patmore, figuring it all out like that—bright jig-walker—knew how to do things. Perfect alibi—perfect. . . Jigs had a future, really—jigs were inherently smart. . .

He stood and watched and smiled. The road led up and over a crest beyond which spread sunrise like a promise. Away for a time, then up moved Bess, straight into the kindling sky. With distance the engine roar grew dim and the van seemed to stand and shrink. Against that far background of light he saw it hang black and still a moment—then drop abruptly out of vision, into another land.

Ain't Got 'Em
Possesses no virtues—is no good.

Ask For
Challenge to battle in terms that don't mean maybe.

Belly Rub
An indelicate but accurate designation of any sexy dance, the *bump* being the popular current example.

Biggy
Saronstic abbreviation of *big boy*.

Boogy
Negro. A contraction of *Booke*, used only of and by members of the race. My own favorite among all the synonyms of Negro, of which the following are current: *Cloud, crowe, darky, dinge, dinky, eight-ball, hunk, hunky, ink, jap, jasper, jie, jigaboo, jigwalker, joker, kack, Mose, race-man, race-woman, Sam, shade, shine, smoke, spade, aigabeo.*

Boy
Friend and ally. Buddy.

Bring Mud
To fall below expectations, disappoint. He who escorts a homely *sheba to a dickty shout brings mud*.

Brother
A form of address, usually ironie. A bystander, witnessing the arrest of some offender, may observe; "It's *too bad now, brother*."

Bump
Bumpty-Bump

Bump-The-Bump
A shout characterized by a forward and backward swaying of the hips. Said to be an excellent aphrodisiae. Also said to be the despair of *fays*.

BUTT
  Buttocks.

CAN
  Buttocks.

CATCH AIR
  To take leave, usually under urgent pressure.

CHOKE
  To defeat. To turn *one's damper down*.

CHORINE
  A chorus girl.

CHORAT
  A chorus man.

CLOUD
  See *boogy*.

CROW
  See *boogy*.

DADDY
  Provider of affection and other more tangible delights

DARKEY
  See *boogy*.

DICKTY
  Adj.—Swell.
  Noun—High-toned person.

DINCE
  See *boogy*.

DINKY
  See *boogy*.

DOG
  Any extraordinary person, thing, or event. *"Ain't this a dog?"* is
  a comment on anything unusual.

Do That Thing!

Do Your Stuff!
"More power to ye!"

Down The Way
Designation of some place familiar to both parties talking.

Do One's Stuff
Exhibit one's best. Show off.

Drunk Down
Plumbing the nadir of inebriation. Soused to helplessness.

Eight-Ball
The number 8 pool ball is black.

Evermore
Extremely, as an evermore red-hot mamma.

Fay
Ofay
A person who, so far as is known, is white. *Fay* is said to be the original term and *ofay* a contraction of "old" and "fay."

Freeby
Something for nothing, as complimentary tickets to a theater.

From Way Back
Of extraordinary experience and skill.

Get Away
i. e., with something. Escape unpunished for audacity; to triumph, as does the successful *jiver* or the winner at blackjack.

Give One Air
To dismiss one with finality. To "give one the gate."

Gravy
Unearned increment. *Freeby*.

Great Day in the Morning!
Exclamation of wonder.

Haul hiney. Depart in great haste. *Catch air*. It, without an obvious antecedent, usually has pelvic significance. "Put it in the chair" means "Sit down."

High

Enjoying the elevated spirits of moderately advanced inebriation. "Tight" in the usual slang sense. Cf. *tight* in the Harlemese sense.

Hiney

Affectionate diminutive for hind-quarters. "It's your hiney" means "It will cost you your hiney," i.e., "You are undone."

Hot

Kindling admiration. As overdone among jigs as is "marvelous" among fays.

Hot You!

Pronounced hot-choo. Equivalent to *Oh no, now*! q.v.

How Come?

Why?

Hunk, Hunky

See *boogy*.

I Mean

"You said it." Ex. "Some *sheba*, huh?"—"I *mean*."

Ink

See *boogy*.

Jap

See *boogy*.

Jasper

See *boogy*.

Jazz

1. The modern American musical idiom, of course.
2. Sometimes synonymous with *jive*, q. v.

See *boogy*.

JIVE

1. Pursuit in love or any device thereof. Usually flattery with intent to win.

2. Capture

In either sense this word implies passing fancy, hence, deceit.

JIVER

One who *jives*.

JOHN-BROWN

Dog-gone.

JOKER

See *boogy*.

KACK

Extreme sarcasm for *dickty*, q. v.

K.M.

Kitchen mechanic, i.e., cook, girl, scullion, menial.

LONG-GONE

Lost. State in which *it's one's hiney*.

LORD TODAY!

Exclamation of wonder.

MAMMA

Potential or actual sweetheart.

MARTIN

Jocose designation of death. Derived from Bert Williams story: *Wait Till Martin Comes*.

MISS

Fail. A question is characteristically answered by use of *miss* or some equivalent expression. Ex. "Did you win money?"—"I didn't miss" or "Nothing different." "Do you mean me?"—"I don't mean your brother" and so on.

Dude.

MONKEY-MAN
"Cake-eater."

MOSE
See *boogy*.

MISS ANNE

MR. CHARLIE
Non-specific designation of "swell" whites. Ex. "Boy, bootlegging pays. That boogy's got a straight-eight just like *Mr. Charlie's*."—"Yea, and his *mamma's* got a fur coat just like *Miss Anne's* too."

MUD
See *bring mud*.

NO LIE
You said it. *I mean*.

OFAY
See *fay*.

OH, NO, NOW!
Exclamation of admiration.

OSCAR
Dumb-bell

OUT (OF) THIS WORLD
Beyond mortal experience or belief.

PAPA
1. See *daddy*.
2. Equivalent to *brother*.

PLAY THAT
i.e, play that game, hence, to countenance or tolerate.

POKE OUT
Be distinguished, excel.

Premature, hence, presumptuous. He who tries to break into a ticket-line is likely to be warned, "Don't get too *previous, brother.*"

PUT ONE IN
To report one to some enemy or authority in order to have one punished.

PUT (GET, HAVE) THE LOCKS ON
To handcuff. Hence to render helpless. Most frequently heard in reference to some form of gambling, such as card games and love affairs.

PUT IT ON ONE
To injure one deliberately.

RACE-MAN (WOMAN)
See *boogy.*

RED-HOT
Somewhat hotter than hot, Extremely striking.

RIGHT
Somewhat in excess of perfection.

RIGHT ON
Nevertheless.

RAT
Antithesis of *dickty.*

SALTY DOG
Stronger than *dog.*

SAM
See *boogy.*

SEE ONE GO
Give one aid. "*See me go for* breakfast?" means "Pay for my breakfast?" It is the answerer's privilege to interpret the query literally, thus: "See you go—to hell."

Striking "Keen." A beautifully dressed woman is "*sharp out this world*."

Sheba
Queen. Frail. Broad.

Shout
1. Ball. Prom.
2. A slow one-step in which all the company gets happy.

Slip
1. To kid.
2. *To slip in the dozens, to disparage one's family*.

Smoke
See *boogy*.

Smoke Over
"Give the once over." Observe critically.

Smoothe
Verb—To calm, to quell anger. What *sweet mamma* does to *cruel papa* when he gets *tight*, q.v.
Adj.—1. Cunning. "alick," as a *smoothe jiver*. 2. Faultless, as a *smoothe brown*.

Strut One's Stuff
See *do one's stuff*.

Stuff
1. Talent, as above.
2. Hokum. Boloney. Banana oil. Ex. "They tell me that *sheba* tried to
commit suicide over her *daddy*."—"Huh. That's a lot o' *stuff*."

Tell 'em!

Tell 'em 'Bout It!
Exclamation of agreement and approval.

Designation of abstract authority. He who trespasses where a sign forbids is asked: "Say, biggy, can't you read *the man's* sign?"

There Ain't Nothing to That
This signifies complete agreement with a previous assertion. It is equivalent to saying, "That is beyond question."

Tight
Tough. Redoubtable. Hard. Not "drunk" in the usual sense, for which the Harlemese is *high*.

To Be Had
To be bested.

To Be On
To bear actual or pretended malice against.

Too Bad
1. Marvelous.
2. Extremely unfortunate.

Tootin'
Right. Unquestionable. Full remark is "You are doggone tootin'."

Turn 'Em On
Strut one's stuff.

Turn One's Damper Down
To reduce the temperature of one who is *hot*, q. v. Hence, to *choke*.

Uh-Huh
Yes.

Ur-Uh
No.

Uppity
High-hat.

How do you do?

Can't Say It
  No complaint.

Zicaboo
  See *boogy*.

Said by Langston Hughes to be the "wittiest of these New Negroes of Harlem," Rudolph Fisher (1897–1934) was a Black physician, novelist, musician and orator. Born in Washington D.C., Fisher had shown himself to be studious from a young age. He graduated from high school with honors at the age of eighteen and immediately pursued higher education at Brown University. Within ten years, Fisher would obtain a bachelor and master of the arts from Brown and take up his medical studies at Howard University. Not one to be singularly focused, Fisher would entertain all three of his interests—medicine, writing and jazz—during his college years and upon graduation built a steady career in the medical field as a radiologist while using his medical experiences as inspiration for his mystery novel. Fisher would also compose musical scores and spent the first summer after college touring the East Coast in a two-man band. Much like his contemporaries Wallace Thurman and Langston Hughes, Fisher would be moved to write about Black life as it *was* and not as it was idealized to be, with his first novel, *The Walls of Jericho* (1928), exploring themes of colorism, intra-community prejudice, and class inequality. He would make literary history just four years later with the publication of his mystery novel, *The Conjure Man Dies* (1932). Set in Harlem, the novel was one of the first mystery stories published by a Black author (preceded by Pauline E. Hopkins with her short story "Talma Gordon" in 1900), the second novel to have a Black detective (preceded by John Edward Bruce's *The Black Sleuth*) and the first mystery novel to be written *by* a Black author, feature a Black detective and have all Black characters. During the course of his literary career, he would also produce several short stories in 1925 and an influential essay, "The Caucasian Storms Harlem" (1927). Fisher died at the unfortunate age of thirty-seven in New York City, leaving behind his wife, Jane Ryder, and their son, Hugh "The New Negro" Fisher.

bookfinity & MINT EDITIONS

Enjoy more of your favorite classics with Bookfinity, a new search and discovery experience for readers. With Bookfinity, you can discover more vintage literature for your collection, find your Reader Type, track books you've read or want to read, and add reviews to your favorite books. Visit www.bookfinity.com, and click on Take the Quiz to get started.

Don't forget to follow us @bookfinityofficial and @mint_editions

9 798888 970713

THE BLACK TREE ATOP THE HILL

KARLA YVETTE

CL◢SH

For my parents, who taught me how to wander.

"A longing to wander tears my heart when I hear trees rustling in the wind at evening."

— HERMAN HESSE

CHAPTER
ONE

The tree appears during the calving season's first storm.

Marisol spots it through the barn window, and sneaks out to look as soon as Luis and Jack Boyd are distracted. This morning, the ranch lands had been quiet beneath a field of marigolds that released so much pollen the air was as yellow as their petals.

Now, the sky is silver and white. Marisol thinks a funnel cloud must have snuck through while they were distracted with the heifers and churned up enough mud to hide the flowers completely.

The wind sends raindrops flying into her face like buckshot. The storm has a taste Marisol can't quite identify—something metallic that aches in the back of her teeth. She listens to cows breathing hard in the pasture and the distant grunts of panicked antelope, and stares at the enormous tree on the horizon that certainly had not been there this morning.

"Damn witch," Jack Boyd calls from the barn door, "Best get back here *now*."

Jack Boyd doesn't raise his voice often. Marisol has learned to read his moods through the slant of his hat or the way he rearranges rocks with a boot tip while staring into open country. But tonight's birthing has not gone well, and Jack Boyd's forearms are covered in blood that looks colorless in the storm light.

"That tree," Marisol says, gesturing toward the horizon as she jogs back to the barn. She can feel heat radiating from inside. The rain dissolves as it gets close, enveloping the building in a sphere of fog. Shapes move through the calving pasture like enormous ghosts.

Jack Boyd retreats inside, shaking his head.

On the ranch, cattle always come first. Marisol can worry about the tree later.

CHAPTER
TWO

Jack Boyd hired Marisol because every ranch needs a magician from the Lodge, and because Jack could not afford one, he got a witch instead. But, Marisol is certain her talent for witchwork is only secondary to Jack—more importantly to him, Marisol is *not* a conversationalist.

Even if Marisol wanted to speak now, she would not have the words. Three births in one evening, and not one of the calves had taken more than a few halting breaths.

"You ever seen anything like this?" Luis asks. There is a whistle in his voice, like his lungs have got too much air or too little.

Luis has worked this ranch for two seasons longer than Marisol. He was a cattle driver who'd made it to Kansas City, and was struck with such fevered momentum he'd continued west until his horse collapsed from exhaustion a quarter mile from Jack Boyd's ranch.

Marisol has seen Luis drag calves out of a landslide with his bare hands, but right now, he looks ill.

"This some sort of witchwork?" Luis asks, as he and Jack Boyd stare at the creatures strewn across the barn floor, covering their mouths with handkerchiefs.

The large ranches on the other side of the hills are wealthy enough to hire a proper Lodgeman from Pomona or San Francisco, but Jack Boyd's operation only pays for itself on a good year. Marisol's duties mostly revolve around distilling tinctures for sick cows or shooing away spirits that drift in from the hanging tree three miles south. And, of course, there's also the matter of breaking curses.

"Could be," Marisol says, and pauses. Jack Boyd seems satisfied enough with this assessment, but Luis urges her on by raising his eyebrows.

"I did hear about a Lodgeman who put a curse on a shepherd's favorite horse. It gave birth to a grown wolf that ate through half the flock before they could put enough bullets in it. That sort of magic would take the whole of a Lodge to pull off —what kind of enemies you been making in town, Jack Boyd?"

Water leaks through gaps in the roof, but the storm has mostly moved on. Marisol can see the glowing white bellies of geese passing overhead.

She remembers the tree, but does not mention

it. Neither Jack nor Luis has shown a tolerance for anything other than herbalism and weather omens, and anyway, Jack doesn't answer.

There are three stillborn calves. One, with an extra set of legs jutting out of its chest. Another whose head looks as though it has been split down the middle, with three quarters of a face on each end. The last, Marisol can hardly make sense of— there are hooves and tails and limbs, but none in the right place, and all in odd numbers.

"I'll prepare a heart," Marisol says, wiping sweat and blood onto her skirts. She does not look up from the calves, but can sense Luis watching her from beneath the handkerchief pressed against his forehead.

The air is still wet and heavy from the storm, and Marisol's thoughts drag like they're moving through sap. The ranch sits atop a low mound and faces a wide empty valley, flat until it meets distant foothills, visible only on the clearest of days.

Surely, Jack Boyd or Luis would have noticed a new tree too.

"Use a chicken heart," Jack Boyd says, "We don't have any others to spare. Luis, get rid of these things."

Marisol nods, and Luis searches for a shovel among other tools in the shed.

THREE

Marisol builds a campfire out of ironwood, into which she tosses a chicken heart punctured with a sewing needle. A horse's heart and an iron nail would be better, but Marisol's Witchmother had insisted there was nothing inherently magical about any single item. A pebble was just as valuable as a gold nugget if what you need is a hard object to throw at someone's head.

The great Knot that connects the physical world with that of the unseen could be accessed without any tools at all, of course, but that sort of magic was wild, tricky, and often imbued with an intention the spellcaster was not themselves aware they had. Marisol prefers to focus herself with objects she can touch.

She watches firelight reflecting off damp grass. This spring has been wet and mean, and the smoke cannot completely mask the scent of uprooted sage in the valley below. Marisol feels no indication that the counter curse has worked—no snap, no fizzle, only the itch of mayflies hatched in the rain, zipping past her nose and eyelashes.

She turns her attention to the tree instead, just as she hears Luis's boots squelching in the mud behind her.

There is no such thing as privacy on the ranch, though the property stretches for acres, and is only home to three living humans and one dead.

Jack Boyd's late wife, Lena, is buried beneath an overgrown catclaw bush, and her appearances are sweet and quiet. Marisol often finds her own lost buttons placed atop the kitchen table, or a whistling kettle moved off the stove before it can overflow.

Luis is in his late thirties, a few years older than Marisol, with an accent that tracks his route across the country—a bit of Laredo, and Kansas City, and the barely concealed exhaustion of anyone living closer to the Pacific than the Mississippi. Luis's skin is the color of driftwood. There is a permanent, attentive look on his face, like he is aiming a rifle.

Marisol is as decent a shot as anyone who'd grown up in cougar country, but she rarely carries the revolver she'd been gifted on her second week in Jack's employ. She's never seen so much as a salesman approach the ranch. The folks of Starcross have rumors of their own, and all seem to revolve around a blue ghost that smells of singed hair and hay smoke.

This suits Marisol just fine. Jack Boyd and Luis are excellent company; the type that let Marisol keep her thoughts to herself and would rather watch the sun go down through the kitchen window than converse over dinner.

Luis stands silently next to Marisol, brushing tufts of cottonwood off his shirtsleeves. Coyotes yip at each other across the valley. Luis always treats Marisol with careful kindness. They have kissed several times while searching for missing cattle at the property's edge, but Marisol knows they exist in two separate worlds that only happen to occupy the same space.

"The curse?" he asks. Luis does not like to talk about witchwork any more than is necessary.

"Broken, I suppose, if there was one to begin with. Don't mention this to Jack Boyd just yet, but I'm more concerned with that tree."

Luis squints into the distance. The storm has left streaks of violet in the sky, and swallows appear to pluck mayflies off the breeze. The tree is distant enough to remain entirely in silhouette, but now that the rain has cleared, Marisol can get a sense of just how large it really is.

"*What* tree?" Luis says, moving to warm his hands over Marisol's fire. He thinks better of it when he sees the smoke is black and hissing.

"The giant one, right there. Some kind of pine, I think. How did it spring up overnight?" Marisol says, pointing.

"Your spell backfire, Mari? That old fir has always been there. Least as long as I've been at the ranch, and probably for a hundred years before that."

"Huh," Marisol says, but does not attempt to contradict him. She can see the orange smudges of other campfires on the far horizon. The birdsong has silenced with the appearance of a barn owl, watching from a rotten fence post.

Marisol's Witchmother had also told her that magic was often just seeing things other people didn't.

"I'm going to cook up that chicken," Luis says. "You coming?"

"I'll be in soon as this fire burns out. Say, Luis— can I borrow Fiona tomorrow? Jack Boyd asked me to go into town for groceries."

Marisol brushes hair out of her eyes. It is dark and kept in a long braid that won't stay neat no matter how tightly she binds it. Marisol is short, but her legs and shoulders have grown strong from two years of ranch work. There is a permanent freckled sunburn across her cheeks and the bridge of her nose, but right now, her complexion is awash in golden firelight.

Luis gives her a narrow-eyed look that says *I don't believe you, but also, I don't want to know the truth.*

"Sure thing, Mari. Just don't forget to pick up coffee beans. Lena keeps knocking over the tin to remind us we're low."

"Of course," Marisol says, but does not look up from the campfire. It's bad luck to snuff a spell out before it's been fully cast. She'll be here for some time, staring into the space where the tree was visible only a few minutes ago.

CHAPTER
FOUR

There are three horses on the ranch—Gerard, Molly, and Fiona.

Gerard is old as the ranch itself and seems to stay alive through sheer stubbornness. Fiona is their newest addition. Luis won her in a game of High Dice, but Jack Boyd does not approve of gambling. Marisol has not bothered to keep track of whatever story Luis has spun to justify her appearance.

And Molly. Well.

Marisol does not like to say Molly's name aloud, for fear the word itself might become an unintentional curse.

Molly had been Lena's horse, but Jack Boyd has never clarified whether the mare had been born with an ounce of hellfire in her stomach, or if that'd been lit after Lena's death. Either way, Molly is not an option, and Gerard is useless without the promise of a strong drink to ease the way. It will have to be Fiona.

Fiona is a chestnut quarter horse with a white streak on her forehead the shape of an oak tree. Like most working horses in the country, she has the sigil Sahep branded into her flank. Sahep means *swift*, and when applied by a proper Lodgeman, a horse can outrun sparks from its own shoes.

As a girl, Marisol had been kicked in the head by her father's stallion. A part of Marisol wonders if this is the moment she became a witch—magic requires a bit of madness, as her Witchmother used to say—but the fear of horses has never entirely left her.

Fiona has always made it quite clear that the distrust extends both ways, and Marisol's palms ache from how tightly she grips the reins.

It is late afternoon before she is able to set off. The air traveling eastward from the mountains smells of sea salt. The sun flickers wildly behind rolling clouds.

She keeps her eyes on the tree, squinting into the cool winds. Summer will begin properly soon. Fiona's hooves startle thrushes in the sagebrush, and they erupt from the ground with screaming bluster.

Marisol follows the faint line of cattle trails, and dismounts at twilight to let Fiona drink from the creek that marks the property's edge. The water is gold with high desert soil. Signs of human activity this far from the ranch are scarce—a shotgun shell gleaming amongst river rock or twists of wire and railroad nails, carried downhill by a flood many years ago.

She eats a handful of dried apples from her satchel, stares at the tree, and thinks: *I haven't gotten any closer.*

Fiona sneezes and paws at the ground, shaking her massive head. A rattlesnake passes through wet grass and disappears into a patch of wildflowers.

Marisol had tucked a bedroll into her saddle, but truly hadn't thought she'd need it. It won't be the first time she's unexpectedly left the ranch overnight, but never when there was a job only she could do.

She thinks of last night's calves and their painfully twisted limbs.

"Well, you certainly won't like this—but, a witch has many duties, and running toward problems before they can catch you unawares is one of them," Marisol says to Fiona. She's always found it easier to speak to animals. Even horses, despite the calculating meanness in their eyes.

She feels a trail of dust rattling in her throat. "I suppose you can keep a secret, can't you?"

Fiona only snorts.

CHAPTER FIVE

Marisol builds a small fire, shares the rest of her apples with Fiona, and eventually, she curls into the bedroll but does not sleep. They'd ridden until twilight through scattered patches of rain, and, for a while, alongside an elk herd dotted with nervous yearlings.

The drop in temperature has cleared the sky, and the spring constellations look bright and low to the earth. Marisol keeps her eyes on the base of the fire and thinks.

She'd ridden through most of the afternoon. The tree had gotten no closer.

Marisol hears Witchmother June's voice, half-hidden in the sound of the fire. *Sometimes the only thing that makes a witch special, is she notices things nobody else does.*

Marisol had always been a fine student.

Perfectly mediocre in every subject and so obedient that, at times, she suspected it made Witchmother June resentful.

Before Marisol had come to work for Jack Boyd, she'd been employed by one of the larger ranches nestled in good grazing territory up north. They already received regular visits from Lodge magicians, so she hadn't been treated as anything more than an herbalist.

It hadn't been all bad, at first. The long days gathering yarrow and black sage meant Marisol didn't have to speak with anyone other than the ranch hands, who reported which cows had infections or needed sedation. But, all the same, there'd been anger growing slowly inside her.

She'd felt it in her stomach and the base of her spine, and in the nicks on her hands where the whiskey she used to make tinctures seeped in. It frightened Marisol that she'd been a host to this anger for so long without noticing. It had reminded her of ranch dogs, so adept at hiding their illnesses that by the time anyone discovered something was wrong, she'd be sent out to gather foxglove for the culling tea.

Marisol twists in her bedroll and tries to listen for a pattern in the sound of grass creaking as it dries. She's still angry, sometimes, at the wagon trains dragging homesteaders into the valley, and the railroad tracks chipping through the mountains, but she cannot say why.

She tries to think of the tree instead, but in this

darkness, the anger seems to travel through her freely and forcefully, like a spring river clinking with ice, somewhere up north, very far away.

CHAPTER
SIX

When Marisol wakes, she is underneath the tree.

The sky is rose pink, and Marisol can smell distant chimney smoke and the warm musk of cattle trodding sleepily into the valley. Fiona is standing over Marisol's bedroll, blinking gnats out of her eyelashes.

Marisol scrambles up, searching for her hat in the grass.

She takes stock of everything but the tree. The creek is to her right, and Marisol can see the distant lump of Jack Boyd's ranch to the east. Fiona is still saddled, and the tracks they'd made last night— shallow and unhurried—are solidifying in dried mud.

Marisol takes a deep breath. She brushes dirt off her trousers and does not rush to face the tree. This is not something her Witchmother had taught her, but rather Jack Boyd the first time wolves had travelled through their pastures in the night.

Their gray shadows had been long and slender on the shorn grass, and their eyes shined like embers drifting off a bonfire. Jack Boyd had said, "Don't cry out. Don't make a sound. They are waiting for something that is afraid of them."

When Marisol finally turns to look, she does it slowly. She forces her fists to unclench. Fiona paws at the ground, frightening a prairie dog that had approached to investigate their dinner crumbs.

The tree is tall enough to scrape against low morning clouds. It is a pine tree—or at least, shaped like a pine tree.

Witchmother June's cabin had been nestled in spruce forests of the northern territory. This tree's silhouette is no different from the ones in those woods, a side pummeled half-bare by wind.

But it is much larger than even the redwoods Marisol had seen from the window of a stagecoach in California. It is darker too, with pine needles so black the entire tree looks like a torn piece of mourning clothes, rippling against the sky.

Another flock of snow geese pass overhead. Their V splits as they approach the tree, and they pass in two parallel lines before rejoining near the horizon. Marisol rolls her shoulders beneath her shawl and tries to list the facts in a way that will restart her mind.

Trees do not spring up out of nowhere, and even if they did, they did not travel miles in the middle of the night. But, this one did.

Trees can be green or brown or any of the thousand hues of autumn, but they are never black—true black—so black that Marisol's eyes ache to look at it.

When she blinks, the tree's shape is still pressed against her eyelids.

"Alright," Marisol says aloud. "You're not technically on Jack Boyd's land, so I suppose it isn't within my rights to tell you to leave, but I would like to know—"

Marisol pauses. She isn't quite certain what she's meant to say.

Now that she can fully perceive the tree's size, speaking to it seems as futile as speaking to a mountain. The mountain can't hear you shouting or stamping your feet any more than it can hear the sound of rustling leaves.

Witchmother June had taught Marisol a secret word to calm horses and dogs, how to command an apple tree to ripen or rot, and how to extract a lucky stone from the belly of a toad. Marisol knows that when a family member dies, you must inform not only their neighbors and lenders, but also the bees that shared their homestead.

The tree *will* speak to her, she just needs to find a language it can understand.

A breeze whips pollen up from a patch of milkweed, and both Marisol and Fiona sneeze. A nearby crowd of meadowlarks scream back in annoyance. There is a distant patter like hailstones clinking against rock, but clouds have only just begun to gather on the far horizon.

Marisol searches her saddlebags for a satchel of loose tobacco and a chicken skull wrapped in linen. She also gathers a handful of smooth, gray rocks from the creek. The cold water makes her fingers go numb, but she suspects there is a different reason for the tingling in her scalp as she arranges the rocks in a circle.

She keeps her distance, careful to avoid the tree's cross-hatched shadow, though Marisol isn't quite sure why. The tree is *beautiful*, after all, and even though its height and color are jarring against the landscape, it seems to belong.

Hm, Marisol thinks, catching herself. Strange thoughts. Better to try and have none at all.

Marisol is silent as she works, but the valley is not. Fiona's teeth grind as she grazes, and wild barley shakes in the wind, but the tree is absolutely still.

When the rocks have been arranged, Marisol places a pile of loose tobacco at the eastern curve of the circle and the chicken skull at the west. They're simple tools and if the situation were different, Marisol might wonder if they were not specialized enough to counter Lodge-magic. But, there is no time for that worry now.

Worry could weave itself dangerously into a spell like a braid that was two parts rope and one part snake.

This is a simple spell, the same Marisol might use to find the path of bewitched cattle heading for another rancher's pastures. The words make her throat itch, but fill her mouth with the honey sweetness of persimmon. Fiona glances up at Marisol's voice, but decides it is not more interesting than the patch of ryegrass she has found growing by an ancient hitch rail.

Marisol searches for a response. Magic can show itself in many ways—a dust devil tracing words as it moves or a swallow flying backwards overhead. Marisol has learned not to expect how an answer will come, but to accept it when it does.

Right now though, there is nothing.

The tree is still giant, and dark, and completely silent.

It's not right, Marisol thinks. Everything speaks, in one way or another, if you know how to listen.

The wind changes direction, rippling the ponds from last night's storm and dragging in fresh clouds. The puddles react to the sky by turning a matching silver, as if they are reaching for one another, longing to be connected by a bridge of rain.

Jack Boyd will tolerate Marisol's secrecy to a point, but not when there are pregnant heifers, and certainly not in capricious spring weather mean enough to leave their little ranch stranded like an island in a flood.

"Fine," Marisol says, standing. A cool raindrop hits the back of her neck and slides beneath her shirt collar.

Marisol draws her hunting knife, but it seems

too heavy in her hand. There is an itching in her legs that usually only happens when the goldenrod blooms in late summer—it is a furious sensation, one that makes Marisol want to turn and sprint down the hill, so she can drop into mud on the banks of the shallow creek.

She grinds her toes inside her boots. There is plenty of magic in the world that wants to stay hidden, but Marisol couldn't call herself a witch if she turned tail every time a stray spell made her feel like she'd swallowed a centipede.

She carefully steps over her stone ring and uses the hunting knife to slice off a thin branch near to the tree's base.

She expects some other reaction to this, but again, nothing comes. She is only struck once more by the loveliness of the tree, standing like an ancient monolith. Once she removes the branch, Marisol resists an odd urge to jab it into the earth. Let its roots take hold. Restore the forest that must have been here once, but was so decimated, only this lone ruin remains.

More strange thoughts, she realizes. Best be going.

Marisol feels the last of the day's sun hitting her shoulders. By the time she has secured the branch in her saddlebag and nudged Fiona into a gallop, the rain has arrived, then turned to hail. For a while, they are joined by two young foxes that twist their bodies and snap into the air, crushing ice with their teeth, but they eventually grow tired of dodging Fiona's kicks.

Luis waits for them on the ridge, arms crossed. Hail is collecting in his hat brim, but Marisol can tell he'd rather be there to show his disapproval than head into the safety of the barn.

CHAPTER
SEVEN

There are no births that evening, so Marisol is forced to endure irritated silence from both Luis and Jack Boyd over a dinner of warm chicken and kidney beans. Lena's pale blue outline stirs the empty pots on the countertop.

Ghosts always seem fond of unfilled jars, burnt food, broken glasses, things that are no longer fulfilling their purpose.

Lena's old knitting needles are set on the end table where she'd left them the evening before she died. They're attached to a yellow tangle of yarn that Marisol supposes would've become a scarf. Jack Boyd has never touched any of it, and the needles have sat far too long for Marisol to consider moving them now. Not all magic is intentional. Some objects acquire power on their own, and these needles have absorbed too many of a widower's mournful glances. Only Jack Boyd can break their spell, and Marisol does not think he is ready to.

The storm has passed and left behind an orange sunset that beats so brightly against the windows one could think the valley was on fire.

Marisol positions herself at the table so she can keep an eye on the tree's silhouette, swaying beyond the window. It seems no closer now than when she'd first spotted it.

Maybe the tree hadn't moved. Maybe the tree had been camouflaged by twilight shadows, and she'd slept beneath it without realizing.

But, the best magic—magic at its most beautiful and terrible—was like that, wasn't it? Magic that stitched itself so precisely into reality no one noticed something had been torn in the first place.

Marisol feels that old anger tickling her stomach and drops her fork to the table more forcefully than she means to.

"Jack Boyd, when you hired on a witch, you knew right well that some witchwork shouldn't be spoken of."

This statement is given with a waver that Marisol has long tried to keep out of her voice. It sneaks through at odd moments and when it does, the Witchmother June that lives in Marisol's head sighs. A witch always makes the choice not to be afraid.

Jack looks up while pinching a piece of cold meat from a thigh bone. "Whatever you did last night is your business, but you should have swung into town on the way home. You said you'd bring back coffee."

Marisol takes a long swig of beer to hide her smile, but Luis frowns in her peripheral vision.

Luis keeps his shirts washed and his hands clean, but the pitted skin of his knuckles are filled with red dust that won't scrub off. Every morning, he eats two scrambled eggs with pepper while watching the sun come up through the kitchen window. He closes his right eye when he's mulling over a problem, and his left when he's remembering the sound of his companions singing to three-thousand longhorns between the sandstone bluffs of New Mexico.

Marisol knows she should say something. She *wants* to say something, but the beer hasn't had enough time to soften the knot inside of her, and her mind keeps returning to the tree branch, snuck into the house beneath her poncho and hidden beneath her bed.

EIGHT

Marisol lays up for a long time, turning the branch in her hands and listening to ranch dogs snore through the open window. Luis and Jack Boyd haven't left the kitchen, and Marisol enjoys the distant rhythm of their conversation, pausing every few moments and restarting after the thud of a bottle against the countertop.

Her room is small and filled with herbs in red clay pots. It smells of dirt and of bird nests in the attic overhead. Jack Boyd keeps the house clean, but he can't bring himself to sweep away the tiny blue eggs sheltered in the rafters.

The branch feels like any other Marisol has held. The tingling in her scalp returns, but the branch does not respond to any of her secret words or sigils. But there is something odd about it, Marisol finally decides, and it's more than just its color.

The branch has no reflection, and because it is so black, no shadows to define its edges. If Marisol could not feel that the branch was three-dimensional, it would seem like nothing more than a crack in the world with no color, no mass, and no purpose.

A burst of wind rattles the house, and dust falls to Marisol's bed. She imagines the trembling home from the outside, all pale blue and white trim. Doors close as Jack Boyd and Luis retire to their rooms, and Lena is left to drift the halls alone, humming an old Shaker hymn in reverse.

Lena had left behind a collection of knit socks and scarves and mittens, and though she is not a vengeful ghost, they all smell intensely of burning hair. Marisol prefers the fraying shawls she inherited from Witchmother June. All that lingers in them is the cedar in June's incense and the faintest trace of rosemary oil.

Marisol pulls a swathe of dark silk more tightly around her shoulders.

"I'll figure you out," Marisol assures the branch and after, when she sleeps, her dreams are notably absent. Instead, there is just black, pressing hard against Marisol's eyelids, unbroken and unceasing until dawn.

CHAPTER
NINE

Marisol wakes and opens her curtains to find the tree has not moved.

This hardly shocks her, but Marisol has grown so used to this wind-battered landscape it would have been a relief to see an unbroken horizon again. Marisol takes careful inventory of the scene: a hare crouched in the cabbage garden, dogs lifting their noses into the wind, Luis riding Fiona out to find the herd. The marigolds are forcing their way back up, gleaming like gold nuggets in the mud.

The branch is still on Marisol's nightstand. She hides it beneath her sheets and goes to find Jack Boyd.

He's at the property's eastern edge, fixing a length of fence knocked over by the storm. Jack Boyd squints as Marisol approaches, and she notes the gray half-circles beneath his eyes.

There is a crop of ragweed growing along the

property line that makes Marisol's eyes water. She is *certain* she'd dug it out of the ground two days ago; ragweed made Jack Boyd sneeze uncontrollably, and Marisol had been tired of having to shield her coffee cup every time they shared the breakfast table.

But, it doesn't seem worth dwelling on a shrub that regrew as soon as Marisol had her back turned, not when there is a massive tree looming in the west that had definitely not been there two days ago.

Jack had been up whispering to Lena late into the night. Lena never speaks back, but the house had whined and rattled in the wind, and Marisol wonders if ghosts have many ways of asking to be remembered.

"You really think that tree has always been there?" she snaps before he can ask her to grab a hammer of her own.

Jack Boyd stares. Distant cattle raise their voices, and it sounds like horns from a faraway battle. It is the first hot day of the year. The veins in Jack Boyd's forearms are thick and blue, pulsing across an old scar, a gift from the teeth of an unruly mule.

"You know, my lenders said I'd be a fool to hire a full-time witch over a part-time Lodgeman out of Starcross, and I'm beginning to wonder if they were talking sense. Maybe you've been cursed. Would you know it, if you were?"

Jack Boyd's face is only tan from the nose down.

He is never cruel, but he is honest, which can sometimes be worse.

Marisol ignores his question. It is another one of Witchmother June's lessons—if you don't like your reality, ignore it and try for something better.

"Jack Boyd, don't tell me you can't remember that tree wasn't there yesterday."

Jack Boyd shakes his head and returns his attention to the fence, scaring away a horned lizard that's taken respite from the sun in their shadows. Jack is so tall, Marisol often wonders how he manages to keep balance. His shadow stretches far down the hill like it's trying to keep an eye on the distant herd.

Marisol has long suspected that Jack Boyd is not his real name, or at least, not his only name. She knows only that Jack's mother was a Modoc woman raised by German missionaries. Jack's mother fled south while pregnant, and there is no amount of whiskey that can get him to continue the story after that.

Marisol does not pry. That would shatter an unspoken agreement between Jack and herself, and besides, Witchmother June had spoken plenty on the bloody clashes between the Modoc and the Federal Army all throughout the west. Things were dangerous enough for a woman in California, let alone one with black hair and the wrong sort of skin.

A bit of anger travels the length of Marisol's neck like a raindrop that's slipped beneath her collar. She ignores it.

Marisol predicts Jack's next sentence before speaks it.

"If you're not going to help with the fence, then whip up another batch of incense to smoke out those yellow jackets. They've taken up in the tree stump near Lena's grave again. I saw their swarm take on her shape the other day. Best get rid of them before they figure out how to do more than that."

"I'll take care of the wasps, Jack," Marisol lies.

If you don't like your reality, ignore it and try for something better.

On her walk back to the ranch, Marisol spots a toad squatting atop a rock. When it shifts, Marisol notices that in place of rear legs, it has a long tail that flaps hideously against the rock.

The sight gives her pause. She's seen plenty of two-headed snakes and six-legged foals in the traveling shows that came through Starcross, but it is different in this context.

This is the wild. It is one thing to stand alongside other humans and take barbaric delight in oddities, but in truth, this toad shouldn't have lived to crawl out of the puddle where it'd been born.

Perhaps, Marisol thinks, ignoring reality may not be the best recourse after all.

CHAPTER
TEN

Marisol finds it too difficult to concentrate on any sort of spellcasting in her room because the wasps Jack mentioned keep launching their bodies toward her window, leaving small black corpses smudged against the glass.

"How many of you *are* there?" Marisol finally gasps, once so many dead wasps have collected on the window that sunlight can no longer get through. They disregard her question, but the sound of buzzing on the other side of the barricade does not stop.

Marisol takes the branch to the kitchen instead, where Lena is pretending to drink coffee out of a dented tin mug. Marisol does not know the color of the dress Lena was buried in, but like all spectral clothes, it is now powder blue. Marisol only wears black.

They sit across from each other, color coded like soldiers, in comfortable silence.

"What is this thing?" Marisol asks Lena, once all her spells have fizzled and revealed nothing.

Lena takes a sip out of her empty mug and sticks out her tongue like something has burned it.

Lena's parents had been sheep herders, but Jack Boyd has never had much to say about them. Marisol suspects they were none too happy when their daughter ran off with a poor, half-native rancher.

There is almost no evidence in the house of Lena's life before she and Jack purchased this dusty plot of land near Starcross. Marisol finds this odd, because the ranch would otherwise be an archeological relic of Lena's existence, even if her death hadn't created a ghost.

Lena died when lightning struck the old birthing barn and set the hay on fire before she could escape. Two heifers had been made ghosts as well, but they'd run off before the newly dead Lena could wrangle them. Marisol imagines they now roam the valley, passing through barbed wire, drifting safely over rattlesnakes and creeks, driven into a frenzy by fresh snowmelt.

When Lena smiles, it makes Marisol feel like she has accidentally stepped through a cobweb. Lena's mouth moves, but her words sound like ceiling rafters splintering in the heat of a fire. Marisol cannot understand, but it does give her an idea.

She returns to the hillside, where she'd burnt

the chicken heart two evenings before. Marisol whistles a note that dries the unused logs strewn across the grass and restarts the fire. Its heat sends waves toward the bright noon sky. Marisol passes the branch through the flames quickly at first, so that they are able to touch its bark but not set it alight.

It doesn't take much experimenting to realize that not only will the branch not burn, but the fire seems to twist and squirm to keep from touching it. When Marisol spears the branch through the fire's center, the flames divide evenly, as if they are trying to tear themselves in half.

A mole lifts its head out of a burrow to investigate. Marisol cannot bring herself to look away from the fire but sees its round eyes in her peripheral vision. The moles have a vast country beneath the ranch, stretching wide and low, like a cathedral flipped upside down.

When she'd first begun her apprenticeship, Marisol asked where the dead go, and Witchmother June had said Mole Country. The war had been over for three months, but Marisol could sometimes still smell the town of Lawrence burning when wind moved through their farm just right. At night, she watched exhausted ghosts of Lodge soldiers meeting Kansas soil after weeks of trekking home from the battlefields.

There is a moment where Marisol cannot move. Even her breath seems to pause. The smoke simmers in her lungs too long, and the paralysis is finally broken by a burning cough.

Witchwork has prepared her for many types of strangeness, but this has made her feel nauseous and shivery, as if one of the wasps had stung her on the side of the neck.

"Well, ain't this interesting," Marisol says to the mole.

It nods in response.

CHAPTER
ELEVEN

There were usually two voices in Marisol's head. Her own, which Marisol chose to ignore more often than not, and Witchmother June's. June's voice made Marisol snap to attention, not because June had been particularly stern or authoritative, but because she had been—well, it was not something Marisol could put a word to.

June had always exuded her own strange charisma. Goats bowed their heads as June strolled by. The crows lapsed into polite silence. June commanded respect simply because she was *June*, which made it exceedingly difficult to argue otherwise.

But, today, Marisol recognizes another voice. This one is quiet, barely noticeable, but that is far more sinister than a voice that vies for attention. This voice reminds Marisol of that sharp inhalation someone you love takes before they deliver an insult that feels like a dagger to the gut.

This voice is biding its time, waiting for the right moment to introduce itself, and that in itself is dangerous. Very little good has ever come from magic that can think on its own.

She tries to push it out of her mind. The tree is the most immediate threat, and that must come first.

Both Luis and Fiona are panting as they ride onto the ridge. There is mud the color of Fiona's coat caked into Luis's pant legs, and for a moment, they appear to Marisol as one massive creature struggling up the hill.

Marisol has been meditating on the branch, and only realizes it is well after noon as she looks up to greet them. It is not surprising. Witchwork tinkers with time in odd ways.

Marisol had once spent six days dancing inside a ring of boulders belonging to a trickster spirit. When she'd finally broken the spell, so few seconds had passed that Witchmother June was still half way through warning Marisol not to enter the circle in the first place.

"Mari, that counter curse was useless," Luis breathes before Marisol can ask what has happened. "Get on. Something's attacked the herd."

All crows share the same name and if you know it, they can be persuaded to deliver a message within reasonable distance. Marisol has taught Luis this name, and the phrases that will make most crows sympathetic and agreeable, but Luis has never used them once.

Marisol tucks the branch into her waistband and pulls herself into the saddle, ignoring the way her stomach churns when Fiona shudders beneath them. Sweat has left an uneven black triangle pointing down from the Luis's shirt collar. He smells of gunpowder and bitter weeds.

"What's happened?" she says into Luis's back as they race toward the silhouette of the herd in the eastern corner of their range.

Luis does not answer right away. Marisol cannot see enough of his face to tell if he doesn't have a response or does and cannot decide how to give it. Many years ago, in another life, she had known a neighbor's son who returned home from the war with this same affliction of silence.

She lets Luis be. By the time they reach the herd, she can infer some of what has happened for herself.

Fiona carefully avoids streaks of fresh blood on the grass. Marisol can see where plants have been trampled flat by hooves. The cows have stopped running, but they are huddled together—a mass of flicking tails and ears in shades of red and brown, the color of river rocks.

"Wolves?" Marisol says, dismounting to soothe the cattle. The herd gently separates as they hear her spell. While most return to grazing, a few heifers with young calves squint toward the field, flexing their nostrils.

Marisol can see the ribcage of a freshly killed

cow in the distance, and she tastes something like copper-wire in the back of her throat.

Luis, again, does not immediately answer. He's drawn his rifle, but its barrel is pointed toward the flattened grass. Sometimes, the spell works a bit on humans as well, but Marisol has never disclosed that to either Luis or Jack Boyd.

"Wolves," he says, "No. Wasn't wolves. It was. Mierda, Mari. It was one of *your* things."

There've always been ghosts, of course, but aside from them intruders on the ranch are usually mundane. Coyotes, black bears—even cougars, who Jack Boyd claims have a drop of the devil's blood beneath their tongues—were easily run off by any magic that made enough noise and light.

But when Luis is deep enough in his whiskey, he speaks of the things that had stalked the cattle trains, picking off cows and cowboys alike.

Lodge magicians had performed unspeakable magic on both their own soldiers and those of their enemies. After the war, what monstrosities survived fled west into less populated lands. Ragged women with the heads of owls and burning hearts that shone through their breasts. Enormous centipedes with human hands that moved silently beneath the earth.

"What'd it look like?" Marisol says. She's been gripping the tree branch without realizing it and shakes the soreness out of her hand.

"Mari. Well, I can't fully say. This is going to sound mad, but—it did look a bit like a wolf, but it also looked a bit like a—candle that's melted all over a tabletop."

The last word is nearly lost among Fiona's agitated snorting.

"Round the cattle up, herd them back toward the birthing pasture. Can I borrow that rifle?"

Luis hesitates. He's never once implied Marisol cannot take care of herself, but it's plain that whatever Luis has seen has rattled him. This makes something inside Marisol waver, but witches— whether or not they have the option—choose not to be afraid.

"The thing took two bullets before it ran off and didn't come back. It might be dying out there, Mari. I know you don't like it when I shoot the wolves that wander in, but trust me, if this thing isn't already dead, kill it. I'll be back with Jack Boyd as soon as the herd is safe."

TWELVE

Luis has taught Marisol a fair amount about tracking on their bleary-eyed morning rides.

She likes these mornings. The sky is always a peculiar shade of blue. They share coffee out of a tin carafe and Luis points out scat from a bull elk or a gopher torn apart by a hawk. Overhead, barn swallows pick gnats out of the sky before they can reach Marisol's forearms.

This creature's path is easy to follow, even without witchwork. It has fled in panic and its tracks overlap where it doubled back or stopped to hunker in place, attempting to paw at the bullets in its torso.

The blood trail varies from brilliant, reflective red to a black so deep Marisol is reminded of the branch in her waistband.

This cannot be a coincidence, although whatever manner of magic that brought the tree to the ranch in the first place is beyond her. It certainly isn't Lodge work either. That sort of magic was structured, careful, and never performed without purpose.

The Lodge, for all its hubris, knew how easily magic could break the world. A Lodgeman saw himself as a clockmaker. One could tinker with the mechanism, make things run in reverse or stop temporarily, but remove the wrong gear or apply too much force, and you risk irreversible damage.

Witches were less inclined to worry about such things—or at least, Witchmother June had her philosophy, that if the gears weren't meant to be fiddled with, they wouldn't exist in the first place.

Marisol kneels and pushes her index finger into the dirt. She has traveled a quarter mile from where she and Luis parted, and the trail has either disappeared or become so faint, Marisol cannot detect it without help.

Marisol has already decided not to be afraid, so the thought of this intruder on *her* ranch makes her angry instead. She searches for a question that grass might understand, and when Marisol reopens her eyes there are sharp blades of rye leaning into the wind.

Before Marisol can follow the grass's instruction, something pounces onto her back.

She drops the rifle. Her face is forced down, and Marisol's frightened gasp fills her mouth with dirt. Something wet moves down her waist. For a moment, she is more alarmed by the sudden sensation of drowning than the feeling of claws tearing into her buckskin jacket.

Move, Witchmother June's voice says in Marisol's head.

She does, but it takes all the strength Marisol has to dig her boots into the ground and push her body forward, coughing earth out of her lungs. She hasn't yet seen whatever tackled her, but it makes a noise as she struggles against it—something between a raven's caw and the human-like scream of a fox.

Marisol reaches for the gun, twisting her torso to inch forward. The creature is caught off guard by her resistance, and its weight briefly lifts as it tries to rearrange its grip. Her fingers meet the rifle's barrel, but it takes one more desperate wiggle before she can fully grab it.

She attempts to swing the gun around and bash it into the creature's head, but the hard pressure on her shoulder forces her back to the ground. Still, the moment of freedom has given Marisol a chance to let out a whistle.

It is too fleeting to call up the full power of the note, but it has the effect she wants. A violent gust of wind hits them both, pelting the creature with flecks of gravel. It is just enough of a distraction for Marisol to squeeze her body out from under it and turn.

She aims the rifle before she can fully see what is attacking her and fires. There is a high-pitched wail alongside the ringing in her ears. She stumbles back, cocks the rifle again, and Marisol is finally able to see what she is aiming at.

Coyote, Marisol thinks, at the same time as *bear* and *bandit*, but in truth, it is neither of the three.

She fires. Her shot hits the creature's shoulder and it stumbles back. It is already limping on one of its rear legs, and this motion nearly causes it to topple over.

Marisol takes quick note of the matted blood on its flank, and the sob it gives as it tries to pull itself up and swipe at her again.

She takes a step out of its reach and speaks the same word she'd used to calm the cows.

Marisol cannot tell if it works. The creature does pause, but that may be because it cannot hobble forward more than a few inches before crying out in pain.

Marisol is also panting. She is dimly aware that the gunfire has disturbed a group of quails pecking in nearby dirt. They take off together, sending warning to the rest of the valley with the heavy beat of their wings.

Heat seems to come up from the ground like the breath of a hidden geyser. Marisol feels hot inside too—a burning in her stomach that she is afraid might ignite the rest of her organs if unchecked. The air smells of overcooked meat.

If Luis shot twice, there's just one round left, but this thought is overshadowed by another.

It is one of Jack Boyd's lessons, not Witch-mother June's. A coyote that drinks from a puddle in a churchyard acquires the ability to speak, but a human must never, ever listen.

"Not one step closer," Marisol says, keeping the rifle steady. She does not know if the creature understands her, or if it is simply in too much pain to attack again. The creature's blood has stained the dirt beneath it so profoundly that any flower growing here for the next decade will bloom red.

It gives another sob, collapsing onto its left flank, before dragging itself forward the length of a step. Marisol does not shoot. She doesn't back away, even though the creature will reach swiping distance with another pained haul.

A witch chooses not to be afraid, and the creature's eyes remind Marisol of a person who has entered a room and forgotten the reason why.

Luis was right. Marisol does not like it when he shoots at wolves striking out from their last remaining strongholds in the farmlands, but she knows why it must be done. In this life, Marisol has pledged allegiance to the cattle. Perhaps, next time, it will be the wolves. But this—this thing is something else, and it does not belong.

"Stay there," Marisol snaps again. This time, the creature's snarl softens.

The bleeding or my voice, Marisol wonders, managing brief eye contact. The creature seems to recoil from this with the same force as it had taken from the bullet, but in their brief connection, Marisol sees fear in its expression.

Hazel eyes. Not quite those of a coyote. Not quite those of a human.

"It'll be o—" Marisol begins, when another shot rings out, and the creature falls dead without a twitch.

Marisol hears huffing and the creak of weight shifting in a saddle. Two long shadows, warped by the moving grass, appear over the creature's corpse. These two shadows break into four as Jack Boyd and Luis dismount and their horses are free to step back, nervous at the sight of blood in the grass.

Jack Boyd's horse is an old white stallion named Gerard, who was given beer to treat anhidrosis several summers ago and has refused to drink water ever since. "Mari, you hurt?" Jack pants.

Marisol's wind must have knocked Jack's hat off as he rode. His gray hair is swept so firmly sideways it looks wet despite the trail dust.

Marisol keeps her eyes down, neither looking at the animal nor at Jack and Luis as they form a ring around the corpse. She has become aware of her heart and breath again, even though that strange internal heat has not dissipated. The sun on Marisol's bare skin makes it feel like she is burning from the inside and outside simultaneously.

The unnatural wind has also brought the smell of ripe chokecherries and hay from the farms around them. It is so hot that tonight there will be summer lightning, flashing over apple orchards on the far horizon.

"I'm fine," she says, unable to keep venom out of her voice. The coyote certainly would have attacked her again if it was able, but the sight of dry white teeth between its slack jaws makes her feel ill. "Thank you, Jack. Is the herd safe?"

"Agitated, but fine. You think it was rabid, or—something else?"

Marisol finally looks up and meets Luis's gaze. She hadn't realized how close they've wandered to the tree. Behind Jack, the tree rises, so black it ignores the dappled light moving across everything else in the valley.

Marisol knows she will soon have her first sunburn of the season. By June her skin will be hardened like bark.

"Something else, but it's crude magic. My guess would be some fool rancher has gotten ahold of a Lodge book and thinks he can save himself some money by doing the witching himself. I'll reinforce the wards around your property. Shouldn't have anything else to worry about," Marisol lies.

CHAPTER THIRTEEN

Marisol loves Luis. Sometimes, she wonders if she is in love with him too. But it often feels like all of their conversations teeter on the edge of an old argument that has never been resolved.

They are sitting on the uneven stairs that connect the ranch house to the earth, sharing whiskey out of a tin mug. Marisol had been right about the summer lightning. It dances silently along the horizon until the evening finally cools, and a white owl passes over their heads, taking the last of the sunset with it.

"If there's something going on at this ranch, you should tell Jack Boyd the truth," Luis says after they have been quiet for a while, listening to cows snoring in the pasture. He scratches a mosquito bite on his forearm too hard and it tears open.

Marisol could stop the bleeding, but the whiskey has made her sullen. She cannot decide what she feels. She thinks of a rattlesnake she'd once seen, tangled in the spoked wheels of a stagecoach, and how its parts had all briefly moved on their own before stilling.

"I'll handle whatever it is. Don't worry about it."

Luis takes Marisol's hand, but she does not squeeze back. The new moon is still a night away and the darkness is absolute, aside from the occasional glimmer of an animal's eyes peering above the grass.

Her thoughts wander to Witchmother June sleeping in stark white sheets, after cancer had broken the paths from June's brain to her legs. By then, her skin looked like rawhide, but at twilight, crickets gathered under her open window to chirp out their best rendition of Love's Old Sweet Song.

Marisol is drunk enough that this memory makes her eyes ache, but she is not certain what brought her to think of it in the first place.

"These mosquitos are driving me crazy. Let's go inside, Mari," Luis says, standing without dropping Marisol's hand. Luis's hodgepodge of accents usually hides his Mexican upbringing, but tonight, his voice wobbles like he's singing one of his mother's old songs.

"I'll be in shortly. Just thinking on some things," Marisol says, disentangling their fingers.

Luis stares at her for a moment longer, but in the dark, Marisol cannot see his expression. And, anyway, her attention drifts back to the tree no longer visible in the distance.

CHAPTER
FOURTEEN

Marisol wakes before dawn hoping she can beat Luis to Fiona's stable and ride to the tree before anyone can say a word about it.

Lena is outside, hovering over the old garden plot, tending to her sugar beets. Last year, Jack Boyd harvested them too late and the beets lost all their sweetness, but Marisol wonders if that's just what happens when a ghost grows food on their own.

Lena glows in this darkness, but seems unbothered by the moths circling her body. She looks up as Marisol passes and Marisol instinctively raises a finger to her lips, though Lena will not speak either way.

"Out on some witching business," Marisol whispers. Lena is still the lady of this ranch, and ghosts express displeasure in odd ways. The last time Lena hadn't approved of a decision, an unseasonal tornado had swept in front of Marisol and Luis's path, knocking them both from their horses.

Lena does not respond to this. She is pointing down at the vegetable patch. Ghosts normally settle on one facial expression—terrified or mournful or cruel—and commit to it no matter what sort of haunting they're engaged in. But Marisol has lived with Lena for long enough to understand the sudden drop in temperature and odd tingling in her fingers, like Marisol has dipped her hands into an ant pile.

"Show me later, Lena. I've got to go before Luis needs his horse," Marisol begins, but she can hardly get the last word out through chattering teeth. "Oh, fine. Let me see."

Marisol notices the smell first, like burnt sugar and rotting eggs. It is difficult to see the garden, even in the ring of Lena's pale blue glow, but as Marisol squints toward the earth, all she can make out are sagging black leaves.

"Rotten? That's never happened," Marisol says, and it is true. Lena's vegetables may be colorless and tasteless and devoid of nutrients, but like ghosts, they still resemble what they're supposed to.

And it's not just the sugar beets. The spinach crop has all but dissolved into a single lump of black mud. Potatoes have pushed themselves out of the dirt and have the green hue of solanine, visible even in the low light.

"This has to do with the tree, doesn't it, Lena?" Marisol asks, glancing back at the ranch. The kitchen light is not on yet. Marisol can still get to Fiona before Luis if she hurries.

Sometimes, Lena is as dense as a storm cloud, pent up with hail and lightning, but now she is no more visible than dissolving morning fog.

Ghosts settle on one expression and for Lena, that has always been concern—concern that Jack Boyd doesn't eat enough vegetables, and Luis drinks too much whiskey, and that no one will patch the holes in the jackets, or fix the leaks in the roof, or remember where the money is hidden, and one day, all that'll be left of the ranch is a pile of wood nearly hidden by grass that neither human nor ghost could hope to rebuild.

"I'll take care of it. Jack Boyd hired me to protect this ranch, and I will," Marisol assures Lena, but Marisol cannot help but feel that she hasn't quite grasped the message Lena was trying to send.

Worse than that, Fiona is not in the stable. Neither is Gerard. The air inside smells like fresh tobacco smoke, and there are two sets of boot prints in the soggy mulch. Marisol sees one of Luis's pockmarked cigarette butts crushed in a puddle.

She tries to think back. Had she heard the kettle this morning, or the heavy sound of Jack or Luis shuffling around the kitchen?

Marisol feels like she's swallowed a chestnut seed, and it is bouncing its way into her stomach. She remembers the way Jack Boyd's throat had bobbed while drinking from a glass bottle, and the way Luis had lit a matchstick after dinner while Marisol watched from the porch swing. Luis had only mentioned the tree once, in passing, but—

No, that wasn't true. He'd asked about it over the coyote's dead body, and then again, while chewing through one of Lena's undercooked, flavorless cakes.

Marisol knows she has stood in place for too long. The barn swallows are up and shaking wood dust from their wings. Their nests smell musky and sharp as they're warmed by the first bit of sunlight coming through gaps in the rafters.

Only Molly is left in her pen. She huffs so furiously at the sight of Marisol that the swallows take flight without waking and nearly collide in mid-air. Marisol speaks the Horseman's Word, but Molly's viciousness transcends even witchwork.

The spell only makes Molly swing her massive head, teeth bared.

The dam that normally keeps Marisol's anger trapped inside her chest strains, just a bit.

"Now, you listen. Neither of us is particularly clever, but we make up for it in stubbornness. I don't want to saddle you up either, but this ranch is in trouble. You must feel it too. Are you going to kick me when I do this?"

Molly stamps her hooves in a way that says— emphatically—yes, I am going to kick you, but Marisol tries anyway.

Luis's spare saddle is ancient, but well-kept, and smells of the olive oil that keeps the leather from cracking. There'd once been prairie flowers tooled in the fenders, but they've been so worn away by Luis's trousers that Marisol can only feel where the pattern used to be.

Molly kicks at her water trough. Her breath smells like cider, and her eyes gleam with an ugly, wild spark that Marisol has always hated and quietly admired.

Marisol feels a cramp in her diaphragm. It is an old, animal feeling—the same she gets when she finds a tree freshly gouged by a bear—and in that moment, Marisol understands that if Molly does allow this ride, it is because she intends to run them both off the edge of the world.

"I'm *done* bargaining with you. I am the witch of this ranch, and you are going to take me where I want to go."

This time, Marisol is able to haul the saddle over Molly's back. Marisol dodges a bite as she tightens the straps, but thankfully, Molly does not attempt to kick her again.

Instead, Molly makes a sound like a dog choking on a soup bone, and she shakes, and she wiggles, and slaps Marisol's arms with her tail, but the saddle gets on.

It gets on.

Sometimes, witchwork is just being angry enough to do something impossible. That wasn't something Witchmother June taught Marisol. It's something she's learned herself.

She can feel Molly's pulse as she strokes her neck for the first time. A human heart most often does its job quietly, unnoticed, but a horse's heart is all fanfare and noise.

"Alright," Marisol breathes. "Now, don't you dare buck me off."

CHAPTER
FIFTEEN

The sun rises as they ride, but for a while, Marisol doesn't truly believe it will.

The sky lightens to blue. There are low clouds and the occasional V of geese, heading north to summer in the Oregon territory, but their silhouettes are such a deep shade of violet they are nearly indistinguishable from the sky.

Eventually, heat prickles against Marisol's scalp and the base of her neck. It is finally bright enough to perceive the colorful tufts of sage and buckbrush on either side of the trail. They follow an old cattle path, stamped into the earth by a thousand heavy hooves over time. Whatever spring or pasture this trail once led to is decades gone, but it climbs into the foothills where the tree is waiting.

Molly is swift and fearless, even when gravel slips beneath her hooves.

They reach the place where the trail has been swept away by floods.

The tree is finally in view, but Marisol's focus is elsewhere. Two badgers, frothing from their mouths and nostrils, wrestling in low grass. A set of molted antlers crawling with ants. A screaming hawk flying impossibly tight circles overhead.

Even the grass here looks black and dehydrated. It curls in upon itself like it wants to carve a way back into the earth.

Marisol is acutely aware of the tree branch she'd hastily shoved into her satchel as she left the ranch. It has not moved, she is certain of that, but that does not mean it hasn't made its presence known. That other voice in Marisol's head bristles whenever she thinks of it.

Marisol finally notices fresh horseshoe prints when a breeze ripples the scrub apart. Two riders, at least.

Her throat burns as she swallows. Marisol cannot tell whether she'd hoped that Luis and Jack had come this way or not, but it would have been simpler if they'd snuck out in the night to tend to a sick heifer and decided to let Marisol sleep.

"The tree is affecting everything—like a fouled well," Marisol tells Molly, who only snorts back, as if to remind Marisol that she is still in the saddle through Molly's good graces alone.

With Molly's pace, Marisol thinks they'll reach the tree in no more than fifteen minutes. The sun has not entirely burned off the morning haze. The tree spears upwards, enormous and dark, but the fog at its base makes it impossible to tell where its trunk meets the ground or if it even does.

Marisol thinks California must be the most fertile land for magic in the world. It is easy to churn rain into a flood, to turn a matchstick into a forest fire. It is land that straddles great faults in the earth; unguarded gateways into strange countries for anyone with enough wherewithal to build the right sort of ladder. Perhaps the tree's roots barrel straight through Mole Country and into the underworld itself.

"Easy, girl," Marisol mutters as they approach, but Molly has already slowed. The air is cooler now that they've gained altitude, and the steam of their breath spirals slowly before combining with fog.

There are shapes moving ahead of them, slow and undefined as Lena on a melancholy day when she can't be bothered to materialize a body. Marisol feels at once too close and too far away. She dismounts slowly, uncertain of when her boots will meet the ground.

"Stay here," she tells Molly. "But if I shout, run. Not back toward the ranch, toward Starcross, understand? Maybe someone there will have the sense to send help."

Marisol tries to imbue these words with as much witchwork as she can muster, to *make* Molly understand, but Molly only gives a slow blink. Marisol sees her own face—the pink flush at the tip of her nose, the gray hair in her eyebrows—reflected in Molly's eyes.

She knows Molly will do whatever the hell she wants.

The sky above Marisol is now well and truly blue, and at odds with the feeling of cool fog in her lungs. The clouds have moved on, but the ground beneath her is hidden. It makes Marisol feel like she is walking in place, despite the occasional sharp rock that stabs through her thinning soles.

The tree is so large that distance seems to have little effect on how she perceives it, but eventually, two horses do appear. Fiona and Gerard, hitched to an old stump, huddled so closely to one another that their eyelashes touch.

Jack Boyd and Luis stand beyond the horses, quietly conferring as Jack pushes dirt with the toe of his boot. Luis is holding something that, at first, Marisol believes to be a rifle, but it is only Lena's old garden hoe, salvaged from the shed and marbled by rust.

"You boys best move away from that tree. Could be Lodge magic. Wouldn't want to set a curse off before we know what we're dealing with."

A part of Marisol wishes she'd already drawn her revolver. She's always been a serviceable shot. Her father had made her aim at tin cans on fence posts until she could hit eight times out of ten, but once she'd learned witchwork a gun seemed like a very small thing indeed.

It's the way Jack Boyd and Luis are staring at her. They don't seem surprised, or guilty, or confused. Marisol has run through a thousand scenarios in her mind where she would scold the boys good and no witchwork would be needed, but Jack and Luis just look *happy* to see her.

Marisol's mind sputters, glancing from them to the tree, as if some hidden connection will make itself known.

"Took you long enough to get here. Come on over and help," Luis calls.

Marisol stays where she is. She looks at the tree and the horses, and a red snail with a cracked shell, dragging itself through cool dirt. That voice that is not quite her own and not quite Witchmother June's, that voice that feels a little bit like the first rain pouring into a wildfire, says: *Listen. Help. I need you.*

Jack Boyd and Luis don't wait for an answer before returning to their task. Marisol takes a step to the side, so she can peer around the horses and see what exactly Jack and Luis are up to.

Between them is a small mound of dirt and an exact copy of the black tree, identical to its neighbor in every way but size. This new tree is no taller than Luis's waist, but by the time Marisol fully processes what she is seeing, it has grown to chest height.

"Boys, get *away* from that," she says, but their business with Marisol has concluded, and both have returned their attention to gardening. The old fire in her stomach flares, like she's swallowed a fresh log and chased it with a quart of fuel.

"I spent the last few days warning you about that tree, and here you are, clueless as two pigs in a dance hall. Head on home, let your witch do her job."

The horses sneeze and grunt, like they've been galloping and forced to a sudden halt. Even Molly, who had ridden into the tree's shadow without slowing, gives a high whine, distorted by the fog into something ghoulish.

Molly hasn't obeyed Marisol's instructions to stay put. Marisol hears her hooves grinding pebbles on the path, but then, Jack Boyd has always said that a proper horse knows the way even when its owner doesn't.

The new tree grows as Marisol flounders. She watches Jack and Luis examine their work with proud faces.

Sometimes, Marisol thinks the loneliness of the west settles so firmly into one's bones that some folks forget any language that isn't the musky smell of creosote or the creaking of a sun-bleached saddle. Jack and Luis can brood, and spit, and whistle sadly over the body of a heifer with a broken leg, but when they smile it is usually done with the shyness of a foreigner in an unfamiliar country.

But not now. They look euphoric. Unguarded.

Marisol again thinks carefully about drawing her revolver. But that won't solve the great problem. The initial curiosity she had felt toward the tree, has now been replaced by rage.

Birthing season has only just started. There are stables that need mucking, and hay that needs stacking, and an unfinished fence that does nothing to keep rabbits out of Lena's garden. Marisol should be smoking wasps out of a tree stump at this very moment, not bothering with this *invader*.

"Why don't you two take a rest for lunch? I brought enough biscuits for all of us," Marisol says. The sun has risen enough to dissolve the fog, but she knows she herself has inadvertently called up the wind that's blowing plumes of dust into their faces.

The grasshoppers, shaken out of sleep, give an angry buzz.

Neither Jack Boyd nor Luis responds other than to cheerfully wave her toward them. Marisol had expected this, but it is the sight of the second tree that makes her swallow the sand in her mouth.

That tree towers a full head over Luis now.

Marisol's coughing spooks the horses, but Jack and Luis do not look up from where they've begun to till another patch of soil.

There is a deep magic in the air that has nothing to do with Marisol, and she cannot find a language with which to speak to it. It is like standing on a dock, attempting to scream at fish at the bottom of the lake.

Molly pushes her muzzle against Marisol's shoulder. Marisol is suddenly afraid she is about to be bitten—but, the terse whuff in Molly's throat is not meant for her.

A swarm of gnats scatters, then regroups, as Marisol waves them away from her face.

Jack Boyd and Luis won't leave here willingly,

that much Marisol can tell. She wishes Witch-mother June's voice, or even the soft tug that June had called the Witch's Compass, would come back to her.

There is only that other whisper, no louder than her heartbeat, and for a moment, Marisol knows that picking up the spade would certainly quell the anger inside of her.

It's just a tree, after all, what harm can it do?

Witchmother June always said there was no separation between a witch and her land. It could sometimes feel like two things connected by a length of twine—but in fact, *you* were the twine, as were the wild ponies, and the creosote, and the thrushes. But there are so many knots and loops in the thread, most people couldn't see it was really just one piece.

Witchwork is sometimes unraveling those knots. Sometimes, making new ones.

Marisol feels something inside of her soften. Her jaw unclenches with a pop. She reaches for the spade and steps into the tree's shadow, closer to Jack and Luis.

The air smells of a morning cigarette, smoked in the cold before the fog has burned off. Marisol feels a strange lightness as if some creature living inside of her has finally gathered its belongings, crept out, and left so much space behind, so much openness, that Marisol can now fill with whatever she likes.

This time, Molly does bite Marisol, hard, on the shoulder.

Marisol cries out. She turns to face the horse, clutching the wound. Molly's teeth have ripped straight through Marisol's shirt, but no blood meets her fingers.

The empty space inside herself that Marisol had been enjoying a moment ago, is again filled by a heat so intense that she is afraid she might catch fire.

"Why did you—*oh*. We need to leave," Marisol says, stepping out of the tree's shade and glancing back at Jack and Luis.

Jack Boyd closes his eyes and turns his face to the sky. For a moment, Marisol sees Jack as he must have been twenty years ago, squinting into the sunlight from the driver's seat of a wagon as he and Lena crested a hill and surveyed their land for the first time.

"The tree won't let them go, but we'll get trapped too if we stay," Marisol tells Molly. "We need to go back. Make a plan."

Molly's eyes are bright with their usual fury. They reflect Marisol's face and the tree behind her, dark and curved across the length of Molly's pupils. The horse is as black as the tree, but its opposite in almost every way. Molly never stops moving. Each breath is accompanied by a war-like, celebratory huff. Even the gnats floating around her ears seem to vibrate.

"We'll come back for them, I promise," Marisol says. But she understands that Molly's anger doesn't come from the tree, or the sight of Jack Boyd and Luis fawning over a third sapling rising out of empty dirt. Molly's anger comes from the same well as Marisol's, and it is endlessly bountiful, fed by some unnamed spring far beneath the surface.

"I promise," Marisol insists. Molly steps back a few paces before finally allowing Marisol to climb onto the saddle.

It is difficult to leave. Marisol's body aches and protests like she's forgotten to collect all of her limbs. She is thankful for Molly's haste, and it is not until they have dropped into the valley, well out of the tree's shadow and in hearing distance of the cattle's low voices, that Marisol is able to sort her thoughts.

Sunlight touches the back of her neck, but there is a cold in Marisol's throat like she's swallowed an ice cube.

This tree is more dangerous than she'd thought.

Marisol needs a coven.

CHAPTER
SIXTEEN

She hadn't intended to return to the ranch. Starcross would have been a better choice. The town was too small to have a Lodgehouse of its own, but magicians stopped there often enough on the trail from Salt Lake to San Francisco.

There were always at least a few dollars to be made at the saloon, where ranchers who couldn't afford a Lodgeman of their own, would pay to remove a blight from their crops or cleanse a fouled well. There were plenty of stray curses on this land abandoned by their casters, like a hunter who's forgotten to collect all their traps.

Most any Lodgeman would want to see the tree out of curiosity, and Marisol has been saving every dollar of her pay since she'd come to Jack Boyd's ranch.

He'd refused to take any compensation for her food or lodging, and Marisol had little to spend her wages on aside from an occasional trinket from the traveling merchants. A glass bead in a particular, dream-like shade of green Witchmother June had loved. A leather journal Marisol has never used.

It's fully noon now, and the sky is too bright to look at. Molly refuses to travel any path except the one that leads back to the ranch, and Marisol can't muster the will to overrule her.

If Marisol had indeed left some piece of herself at the tree, then whatever has replaced it is sticky, thick, and useless. She takes a deep breath, and the cramp beneath her sternum aches.

When she finally reaches into the saddlebag, Marisol tosses the black branch onto the hoof-beaten path behind her. It is most likely a mistake. Marisol knows this, even as her empty hand returns to the reins. If Jack Boyd and Luis could grow another tree from next to nothing, there is no telling how a stray branch might take hold, but she can no longer think. Not with a piece of the tree itself whispering in her ear.

They pass the slain cow from yesterday. It has attracted a swarm of black and silver flies that dance across its ribs and through the tall grass. The cow is not the only dead thing in this valley—like every wilderness in the west, it has accumulated its own collection of bones, and fossils, and ghosts. But the sight of this corpse makes Marisol feel dizzy, and she urges Molly forward in any direction.

Lena is waiting for them, nearly invisible amidst waves of heat rising from the dirt. For a moment, Marisol isn't sure if she's truly seeing

Lena, or just remembering that she had been there earlier this morning in what seemed like a different world.

Molly comes to an abrupt halt in front of the garden and refuses to walk farther. Horses don't usually like ghosts, but Lena's quiet presence is so ubiquitous around the ranch that Molly only stills and listens like she's heard a prairie dog's alarm call.

"Lena," Marisol breathes sliding from the saddle. It feels like she's dropped into mud, but the sensation is caused by Marisol's own legs, struggling to support her weight. Her tongue feels dry and swollen as she calls out.

"Jack. Luis."

A cloud passes overhead, and suddenly, Lena is well defined. Lena always looks worried, but today the furrow in her brow frightens Marisol so much that she nearly fails to dodge the agitated wasps coming to greet her.

Lena's toes brush against the black garden. She must have known something was wrong before Marisol did.

That's what a ghost is, Witchmother June whispers in Marisol's mind. *If all of creation is a mess of twine, then ghosts are the frayed bits at the edges. They're the first to feel a tug.*

The edges, the ends, the roots, Marisol thinks. She turns back to the valley. The day is clear and glows with heat, and the tree—the trees—are visible across the property. There are at least five now, three of which have already grown to the size of the original. Marisol clutches her abdomen, squeezing out the urge to ride back, to take the spade Luis had offered her and tend to this beautiful forest.

"It's what *should* be here," Marisol says, when what she means is, *Lena, I have an idea.*

Lena seems to understand anyway.

Now that the cloud has passed, Marisol can only see the faintest edges of her; the curve at the nape of Lena's neck, the hemline of a singed dress that does not exist. The air smells briefly of burning wood and flesh.

Sometimes, ghosts try to be earnest, but they are only terrifying instead.

Marisol does not trust herself to speak again. Her mouth is full of words about the tree, about the lovely dark woods that will soon stretch from the Oregon territories to the Mexican border, and when she attempts to swallow them back, Marisol feels like she is choking.

There is certainly no world in which she'd be able to explain her problem to a Lodgeman without recruiting another gardener.

She motions for Lena to follow. Marisol cannot trust herself to be within sight of the tree any longer.

SEVENTEEN

Jack Boyd always says some people just attract lightning.

He means this metaphorically, of course. What Jack is really saying is that some people can't drink whiskey without getting in a fistfight or handle a gun without shooting themselves through the boot.

But, the truth is, some people *do* attract lightning. It's one of the best signs a girl has a talent for witchwork. So is a talent for breaking horses, or knitting, or growing food in poor soil, or being the sole survivor of a house fire.

Lena had not survived her fire, but Jack said she could grow pumpkins in a half inch of dust. Lena could knit a scarf in one night, and she'd made lovely drawings of the beetles and field mice in journals that remained in the house, exactly where she'd left them.

Marisol hopes this will be enough, but hope is uncertainty, and uncertainty is frightening. She finds a spot on the other side of the ranch that would work well enough for a ritual circle, but by now, every thought is cut in half by an image of black trees spreading across the farmlands and a great sun burning against Marisol's skull.

These flashes are accompanied by a pang of bitterness.

Why shouldn't the forest grow? The only claim we have to this land is a sheet of paper tucked in Jack Boyd's desk. Marisol thinks, even as she forces her hands to spread a ring of salt in the flattest place she can find.

The rest, she must improvise—a beer bottle in the west, a half-smoked cigarette in the south, a cockerel feather in the east, and an old horseshoe in the north.

Lena floats in rings around Marisol as she works. She is the same color as the thunderhead clouds gathering over the hills.

"This type of spell my Witchmother called it a Rooting," Marisol begins, finding she can speak again now that the tree is out of sight. "It's deep magic. It can't be used to get what you want. It obeys the will of the land. Once I start, put your hand into my chest."

Marisol has only ever touched a ghost in passing. It's not polite to touch a thing that cannot touch you back, and besides, having a ghost pass through you feels like a riding crop hitting all of your skin at once.

She does not know whether or not this method will work, but a good witch can improvise. A good witch can make a spell out of a whistle, or a scream, or the taste of blood in her own mouth.

Marisol does not have a candle, so she lights one of Luis's cigarette butts instead. Despite the clouds on the horizon, the air is so still that the smoke hangs motionless in a shape that resembles an enormous coyote.

She kneels.

A Rooting spell has no words. A Rooting spell is about listening, and the first step is to listen to yourself.

Marisol closes her eyes. She counts her heartbeats and feels the way her breath vibrates against her lower lip. Instead of ignoring the prickle of rocks against her knees, she accepts it.

She is sun drunk and saddle sore—she accepts that too.

Listening is not the same as interpreting, or judging, or ignoring. A witch can only truly listen when she accepts what she hears exactly as it is.

There are all the usual sounds of the ranch.

Molly's saddle creaking in the heat, the chickens gently muttering to one another, and the distant rumble of the herd, but there is something deeper too—something that shouldn't be there, like a single instrument playing a different song than the rest of the orchestra. Marisol can hear it in the space between her heartbeats.

"Lena," she whispers, "Now."

But Lena does not act. Marisol tries to listen for the sound of Lena's shifting dress, but it's absent.

Marisol opens her eyes and catches Lena floating at the circle's edge, turned toward the farmhouse.

There is something dark rising over the building. When Marisol realizes they are treetops her spell nearly breaks. She tries to swallow, but her spit tastes of dirt and smoke.

Marisol snaps her gaze back to the circle's head. What she has seen must be a shadow. A strange, architectural cloud moving across the property.

Marisol breaths. She remembers that she is a witch, and a witch has no choice. She must not to be afraid.

She twists. She looks again. They *are* trees.

Marisol's heart sings with joy and dread at the same time. The trees are not just closer, they are here. Lena has drifted back to the circle, but her face shows no more than her usual worry, and Marisol does not know if Lena is reacting to what they've seen.

"Lena," Marisol whispers, "They need me."

This is when Lena plunges her hand into Marisol's chest.

Marisol feels like she's been bucked off a horse. She feels like she's been exhaling for too long, but when she tries to stop, her lungs continue to push and push and push.

The cigarette burns into Marisol's fingers. The sensation brings her half-back to herself. Marisol opens her eyes to find Lena's face hovering over hers.

A ghost's eyes never look sharp. Marisol cannot be sure if they are seeing the world as it is or how it was, like a drawing that moves just enough to make it seem real.

But Lena's eyes are focused now—not on Marisol, but on the trees looming over the farmhouse roof.

Marisol has rarely heard Lena's voice before. Lena hardly speaks, and when she does, it is garbled or backwards, or in some strange language that sounds as if she's clipped the vowels out of every word.

Lena's voice is now clear and patient. It comes from inside Marisol's chest, a message tapped out by the rhythm of her heart. Marisol can even hear Lena's accent. Soft and round, like the northern plains where she'd been born.

When a plant is sick, Lena says, *you have to pull it up from the roots, or the infection will spread to its neighbors.*

The chickens are hollering. The ground vibrates against Marisol's legs as Molly gallops by, bucking like she's trying to toss the saddle off her back. Dirt breaks a section of Marisol's circle, but the air feels so sharp and dangerous that the spell holds strong.

The trees around them are not as tall as the first had been, nor as full, but there are so many that the space around Marisol is entirely black. There are pieces of a dim, blue sky visible overhead, but aside from that, Lena is the only source of light, no brighter than a lantern on its last drop of oil.

Molly is still close. Marisol hears hooves thudding, but the shadows surrounding them tilt in every direction making it difficult to judge distance. The forest is not silent—far from it—but its creaks and groans feel too close, too claustrophobic, like the sound is coming from Marisol's own bones contorting inside of her.

Marisol's fingers ache. The cigarette burns out against her skin, which means the spell has been cast whether or not she is ready. She wants to speak, to ask Lena what has happened, or what they should do now, but all Marisol manages is a strangled gasp of joy.

The trees know what they are trying to do, and they are *defending* themselves.

Lena seems to pinch the veins around Marisol's heart, and in the sudden dizziness, Marisol is able to clamp down on that voice inside that does not quite belong to her.

No, she thinks. *No*. This is Jack Boyd's land, and I am his witch. I will set a trap for you, in the same way I set traps for the foxes digging into the chicken coop, or a rustler trying to round up our cattle in the night, or an old curse left to fester and spread in the summer sun.

There is hot breath against Marisol's shoulder.

Molly has made it through the labyrinth of trees.

There is a scratch on Molly's nose, and blood

sprays against the back of Marisol's neck as Molly huffs impatiently. Her haunches are twitching.

Marisol can feel the rush of adrenaline as if it were her own, rising and rising, then suddenly strangled like a scream clamped beneath a hand before it can begin.

The crows yell for her instead, but the birds blend so easily into the trees that Marisol cannot tell where the flock has landed.

Marisol focuses on the pain in her arm and chest to recenter herself. She is smiling. She can feel that, but the sensation of Lena's hand against Marisol's heart is as cold as a winter morning.

The spell—the forest—the spell, let it spread, Marisol thinks.

She pictures Jack Boyd drunkenly laughing at the dogs, and Luis massaging his callused hands, and Lena kneading dough that will not rise. She pictures a calf squinting at summer sunflowers.

Marisol thinks of crickets bounding through tall ryegrass, and the constellations overhead simmering in the heat, and Witchmother June's voice, muffled by clean linen sheets, saying "I've got nothing left to teach you."

Marisol reaches out with the magic and anger she's kept latched inside of herself. She reaches out, and the first thing she meets is Lena.

For a moment, Marisol smells tilled soil, bread, and wet tomato leaves. She hears the sound of a house settling into its foundation, and it is not so different from that of this forest dancing in an April storm.

There is a tug in Marisol's abdomen, and she understands that it is Lena, speaking in the only way she knows how. Lena is saying, *look here, look here, to save the garden, you have to pull the sick crop out by the roots.*

I understand, Marisol answers. She imagines her fingers growing long, reaching into the soil, barreling through earthworm tunnels, down into Mole Country, and into the deep well of magic that waits beneath the earth for anyone with enough gumption to start digging.

Marisol's hands feel hot and stiff. The ground feels less like dirt and more like a tangled thread, but before Marisol can find the one that has frayed so much it threatens the integrity of the entire structure—something strikes her in the back of the head.

EIGHTEEN

Marisol can't think. Or rather, she can, but only about the pain radiating from her skull into her spine. It seems to travel in beats, bouncing against each vertebra before dispersing into her abdomen.

She tries to blink dirt out of her eyelashes, but by the time she is able to see the speckled gray earth underneath her, something flips her over.

The sky is mostly hidden by trees, but where it shows through, it is white and so impossibly bright that the pain in Marisol's head briefly turns into shocked numbness.

She knows she cannot stop moving. There is a woosh of air as she flips over, and the thud of something hitting the dirt.

The spell has progressed too far to be broken completely, but the suddenness of the blow has disrupted it. The circle feels hot and dark, like water from a fouled spring. The gnats circling Marisol's head begin dropping to the ground.

Marisol kicks out catching Luis in the stomach. He falls back with a grunt, but his grip on the shovel is firm.

He swings again, just missing Marisol's calf as she pulls herself toward the northern curve of the circle, where the cigarette has burnt down to a nub. The short grass around it has turned a crisp black.

"Luis," Marisol gasps. The feeling of Lena's hand in her chest hasn't faded, and Marisol's heart feels like it's been yanked out by the sudden movement.

Marisol wills her blood to keep moving, to draw what energy it can from her last, choked breath. Luis is smiling down at her, but his expression is so openly genuine that she nearly reaches for his outstretched hand.

Luis's eyes are wet and kind. They look exactly the same when he talks about the cattle trains. Marisol knows what he is going to say, it is—

Help us grow,
help us grow—

"*Help us grow*," Marisol finishes.

The words come so easily, so sweetly, like the first deep breath of spring after a long winter, like the songs witches hum to give courage to the wildflowers waiting shyly beneath the ground.

But—no—*no*, Marisol growls, in an internal voice that belongs to both her and Lena.

Marisol digs her boots into the dirt and pushes herself back to the edge of the circle. Luis has also managed to right himself. She searches the ground for anything that might function as a weapon, but her fingers find only the horseshoe.

It has not been disturbed by their fight but moving it might stop the last chance Marisol has to complete the Rooting.

Witchmother June, Marisol cries silently, but June's soft voice is absent.

There is only the sound of roots stretching beneath her and the wind jostling black leaves. Luis is humming, but the sound has become more guttural like a wolf who has caught a blood scent in the grass.

Marisol knows she can be free of this if she listens to the song. To till the soil, plant the seeds, and follow the forest as it heads east, to Starcross, to St. Louis, to Boston, to New York, reclaiming its ancestral lands, reclaiming the Lodgehouses, the flattened farmlands, and the haunted battlefields where nothing grows.

No, Lena says, and this time, Marisol hardly hears it through the melody.

Luis grunts. He stumbles to the center of Marisol's circle and falls to a knee.

For a moment, Marisol is unsure what has happened. She is struggling to break away from thoughts of trees sweeping across black Kansas flatlands. She manages to prop herself onto her elbows and looks up to find Molly standing over Luis's body.

Molly is caked in mud, and her saddle is askew on her torso. Were it not for the brilliant, wet anger in her eyes, Molly might blend in with the forest entirely.

"The spell, now!" Marisol hears, and this time, she cannot be sure if the words are hers or Lena's.

CHAPTER
NINETEEN

As far as Marisol knows, there is no spell to stop the rapid invasion of a black forest in your farmlands, but she can improvise.

The link with Lena burns in Marisol's chest like she's swallowed a cigarette. In the distance, the herd moves with a weary chorus of brays and grunts. It is faint and the only familiar sound in the creaking new forest. Marisol holds it tightly in her mind, turning it round and round, as one might fiddle with a lucky pebble in their pocket.

Find the roots, Marisol thinks, but it is not only her voice, it is Lena's too.

There is a taste of rotten sugar beets in Marisol's mouth. She holds onto that, and the soft earth beneath her knees, and the smell of an angry horse. Then, Marisol turns inwards, passing through the places where Witchmother June usually wanders, and into the core of herself, where there is always magic inside straining to reach the magic outside.

Lena is there too, stretched thin, like she is trying to build Marisol a bridge.

The roots. Find the roots. They must be down here.

And they are. Deep, knotted lengths of wood indistinguishable from Marisol's veins, trying to burrow into the deepest and most secret chambers of herself.

Help me grow, Marisol thinks, but this voice does not belong to herself, or even Lena, and though it does not speak in English, Marisol understands it perfectly.

She has found the roots, but it's too late. They've already taken hold inside of her.

CHAPTER
TWENTY

The Rooting spell breaks again.

Marisol falls back, glimpsing Luis as she does.

He is pushing himself to his feet. His teeth shine brilliantly in his open mouth, marred only by a thread of blood across his left incisor. His eyes are fixed on Marisol like she has been gone for weeks, and just returned from Starcross with chocolate and a liter of tequila.

"Luis," Marisol stammers, hoping she is speaking aloud. Half of her is still trapped in that inner space. "It's the trees. It's witchwork. That's why you want to dig. Fight it. Think of the ranch. Think of your scrambled eggs and the cold coffee in your canteen. Calves rolling in the mud. Jack Boyd's terrible harmonica playing. Luis, think of *me*."

Luis does pause then, but it is only to pick up the shovel he's dropped in the fall. Marisol drags herself away.

Her fingers graze the horseshoe again. If she is forced to move back once more, any progress she has made with the Rooting spell will be lost in an instant.

The feeling of the land is still bright in Marisol's heart. Her breath sounds like the high whine of a bull elk in spring. She can feel the forests that used to be here and should be again, and the soft patter of wolves moving beneath a shadowed cathedral of trees.

Lena drifts back into view, and this time Marisol feels her anger redirected toward the ghost. Why can't Lena *understand*?

A ghost is not the same thing as the person it looks like. It would be more accurate to say that through dying, a person creates a ghost who goes on to have an existence of its own. This Lena is not the woman who once slept next to Jack Boyd and was awoken by the tender, pink light of a summer morning. This Lena is a creature born of this land and she is shaped by the valley, and its thunderstorms, and the mayflies breeding in her garden puddles.

"Luis," Marisol stammers. She suddenly understands what she must do, but the chorus in her head—the voice that begs her to *help us, help us, help us*—means that Marisol must shout through her thoughts. Even so, she can hardly hear herself through the trees in the wind.

"Luis," Marisol repeats, because it is the one word she can say that does not frighten her. Marisol intends the next sentence as well but does not expect it to come out in such an unsteady slur. "Give me the shovel. I want to help."

Luis already looks so ecstatic that his expression does not change, but he does pause. He wipes sweat from his brow and, because it has mingled with blood, it leaves a streak of diluted pink across his forehead.

Luis pats his vest pocket, searching for a stray cigarette and finds none. Marisol finds the entire pantomime unsettling. Trees that are only pretending to be trees. Humans that are only pretending to be gardeners.

"Course you can have it, Mari," Luis mumbles. It is the same tone he uses late at night when he is half-drunk and wondering if he remembered to close the gate to the birthing pasture.

"Give it here," Marisol says. She reaches out. Her hands feel hot and dry like the skin is about to crack around her knuckles.

Luis looks joyful and trusting even as the trees beat out a rhythm like a war charge.

He hands her the shovel, and Marisol immediately uses it to strike him against the temple, knocking Luis to the ground.

Then, she turns and plunges her hand into Lena's chest.

CHAPTER
TWENTY-ONE

Touching a ghost is different from being touched by a ghost. For one, it hurts.

It really hurts.

Marisol wonders if this is some echo of the Lena that was—the Lena that woke with sore backs and whose left ankle throbbed when it rained. The Lena that tried to save the calves, even after her own skin was blistering. In a moment, Marisol feels the sum of a life's worth of stove burns, saddle soreness, cramps, and heartache.

Marisol tries to say *stop*. She tries to say *I'm sorry*. Neither comes out, and there is no more time.

Marisol is sucked back into the Rooting spell as if it hadn't been disrupted in the first place. Her body suddenly feels like it's been buried in cool, dark earth. Something moves in the tight matter around her, but it is not the moles sniffing or the nearly imperceptible patter of earthworms displacing soil. Marisol cannot recognize it, even with all of Witchmother June's training.

June had died from a cancer in her belly that made her shake and gag, but she had never stopped smiling, even when Marisol wiped blood and spit from the corner of June's mouth.

"You think there isn't anyone as ordinary as you," June had said. "And that makes you angry. But you always choose to be kind, even when that's not how you feel inside, and that's what makes witches out of ordinary folk."

Marisol searches deeper. There must be a mass, a parasite, something Marisol can see, something she can cut out. All curses have a core, a source, something that burrows into the thread of the world and starts whittling at the knots around it.

Marisol travels deeper still. For a moment, she senses Lena's old perfume—a bottle of Caswell-Massey from out east that still sits on Jack Boyd's dresser, smelling of old glass and dry honey.

She's close. There are memories here, but they show the ranch long before Marisol arrived. A herd of bison pawing at snow for bits of grass underneath. A hunter, squinting into the blinding field, waiting for his shot.

Deeper still, the valley is an ocean floor, and what Marisol first thinks are bones turn out to be pink shells nestled in black sand. And beyond that, there is only fire and empty space, so much empty space, but—no—

Marisol knows she has reached two things simultaneously. The tree's roots, and the very center of Lena's self. A wild joy moves through Marisol's body, but she is already overstretched by the Rooting spell.

Marisol wonders if it has anything to do with the distant ache in her leg, like an old sprained ankle that sometimes wobbles in your boots.

Lena, Marisol thinks. *I understand what I have to do, but—*

Lena's ghost has never rushed into a burning barn, or chased coyotes with a pitchfork, or stayed up late tending to Jack Boyd's blisters or Luis's melancholy, but her voice is brave. It only wavers slightly when Lena whispers, *Yes, Mari. Do it now.*

Marisol finds the place where Lena and the trees connect, like a stream finally dissolving into the valley, and then, Marisol begins to tug. It feels like exhaling until her lungs are empty and then pushing out another breath she didn't know she had.

Talk to me, Marisol says, in the same voice she uses to speak to the wind, and the cattle, and the weeds. *You're already in my head. Let me in yours.*

The trees do not answer, but Marisol is vaguely aware of another sensation in the physical world—hot breath against her shoulder—but refuses to let the spell break again. Her body can recover, but she cannot let this land be poisoned.

Talk to me, Marisol commands, trying to summon as much of Witchmother June as she can.

What comes out is not June's voice, but it carries the same bit of strength June had gifted Marisol the first time she'd handed her a sprig of yarrow and taught Marisol how to turn it into medicine.

Witchwork had very little to do with curse breaking or summoning tornados to weave through a bad neighbor's grain field. Witchwork was birthing calves, it was spreading paste on a cowboy's saddle sores, it was settling land disputes through clever words and stubbornness.

You shouldn't be here, Marisol tells the trees, *and we shouldn't be either. You have poisoned the coyotes, as we do. You have corrupted the soil, as we do. But you have hurt my friends, and that I cannot allow. I demand you leave.*

The trees finally reply, in the same dreamlike voice that Marisol had heard in her core.

Help us. Help us.

In truth, Marisol wants to.

She has suddenly understood the deep anger inside herself, and why it has persisted ever since her and June's wagon train had crossed the Kansas river. The west was about taking. It was about taming, owning, and these colonizers would chip and chip away until even the deep well of magic in Mole Country would someday run dry.

But Marisol tugs harder. She no longer feels Lena's presence, only her own body distantly existing in the physical world.

Marisol's skin has hardened into bark. Her mouth tastes of sap. She knows that if she were better able to feel, she would be choking, but as it is, Marisol's tongue only seems stuck to the roof of her mouth.

It would be easy to surrender. Marisol's legs have been replaced with tree roots, and they are reaching through her and into the earth, drawing up water and absolute peace. It is a stillness she has not felt in a long time, not since she was a child foraging in the woods near Lawrence with her mother, back when the air smelled of oak moss and spring foals disappeared in the morning fog.

That was before the war, and Marisol had never even seen a ghost, but it was the first time she'd ever felt her place in what Witchmother June called the Knot. This was when Marisol realized she was a witch.

She should push the trees away. A better spell, something more planned, and Marisol might not be forced to draw them into herself more than she already has. But this is not a planned spell, or even necessarily a good one, and Marisol is improvising.

Marisol pulls, and when she has no more strength, she uses her anger. She thinks of the ranch, the taste of hot coffee in the morning, the smell of hay and chimney smoke, and the rolling snore of cattle in the night. She thinks of barn swallows dancing through heat shimmers. The horses warily eyeing the badger digging up earthworms along the fence line. Lena's bees shining like gold nuggets in the flowerbed.

This isn't my land, Marisol thinks, *but it's not yours either.*

Marisol stops tugging, because she realizes she is no longer holding the thread. Lena has taken it from her, and Lena is *knitting*.

There were times, in this country, when they used to hang witches, but it was only a few years before the townsfolk realized their mistake. The witches were also the ones who mended the dresses, tamed the stray dogs, brewed the beer, and nursed the hangovers. And they were cheaper to hire than a Lodgeman. The executions stopped, but it was easy enough to ignore the inherent witch-work in gardening, cooking, healing, hunting, and knitting.

And Lena is a master knitter.

Marisol feels her own connection to the spell begin to fray. She has brought Lena as far as she can.

There is no air here, nothing to breathe, but Marisol still smells sweetgrass and blue wool dye. She tries to speak—to tell Lena that she must beware, that she must not weave herself into the spell, but even as Marisol tries to express this through the ripple of magic between them, Marisol knows there is no other way.

You'll die, is all Marisol manages, and Lena immediately answers.

I was never alive. I am only the memory of Lena, and that will still be here. I am just as much Lena as her scarves, or the streak in the kitchen floorboards where she used to pace when Jack Boyd was late.

Marisol wants to argue, but her connection to the magic has frayed to the point of instability. The sensations of her physical body are now distracting.

Marisol knows she is coughing. She knows she

has inhaled dirt, that there is a pain in her sinuses and the taste of iron in her mouth, but she does not know if these two things are related.

This knot you are making, Marisol thinks, *you will always be a part of it.*

Lena does not answer, and although Marisol can still feel her sturdy essence in the spell, something has begun to happen. The knot is tightening, and Lena she is shrinking—no, condensing, weaving herself through the threads that belong to the trees, binding them.

There is a great shift near Marisol's body. She tries to open her eyes, her real eyes, but she has lingered by Lena's side for too long.

The bits of Marisol's self that haven't separated from the Rooting spell are being dragged into Lena's knot, and suddenly, the feeling of roots burrowing through her veins is back. This time, they feel too large, and there is pressure against her bones from the inside, like an egg about to crack from hatching a writhing young snake.

Marisol hears a distant bray. Molly, huffing, rattling her reins, and in the far distance, tree branches scraping against clouds.

Now, Lena finally says, and her voice is hardly louder than the grass snapping beneath Molly's stamping hooves.

I can't—

Now, Lena demands again, and this time, Marisol breaks the spell. She feels the roots rush back out of her veins the same way they came. They snatch the air out of her lungs as they go, and for a moment, Marisol feels like she is floating high above a great commotion. She reaches out, but her fingers only meet air that feels very nearly like the folds of a linen dress.

Marisol tries to call out to Lena again, but she suddenly can feel no dress, no air, nothing at all.

The world goes dark.

CHAPTER
TWENTY-TWO

"You meaning to tell me there was a forest here? How long ago?"

Marisol is tired of recounting the story, but she is also tired of stacking firewood, so she wipes her brow, leans against the shed wall, and commands the logs to sort themselves.

It is not a witchly thing to do. Witchwork demands as much sweat and soreness as any other discipline, but Marisol's sunburn is peeling, and she's quite sure she's inhaled more woodlice in one afternoon than is reasonable.

"Remember the day you found Molly standing over me? You thought I'd been thrown—"

Marisol thinks about how she should continue this time. No version is ever quite the same, though Jack Boyd never seems to notice. There is no version, however, that includes the small blue seed she'd found in the place where Lena had stood in Marisol's magic circle.

"Well, it wasn't Lodge magic," Marisol says, deciding it's so hot she may as well skip over the story altogether and let Jack get to speculating, which is his favorite part. "Not witchwork, either. In fact, likely not human at all. My Witchmother used to say that a land can only soak up so much blood before it turns bad."

Jack Boyd grunts.

"Plenty of cattle swept up in the floods last year. Plenty of good dogs run afoul of a rattlesnake. Do my pile of wood like that too, Mari. My shoulder aches."

This is not the type of blood Marisol means, and she has the feeling Jack knows it, but she waves the spell along anyway. No emotion flares in her stomach. Some days are too hot and sticky for sorrow. Sorrow is better stored and saved for long nights of wintertime.

Marisol's thoughts drift back to the seed, although she has only taken it out of her locked drawer once since she'd placed it there. It had been as blue and weightless as a robin's egg but crackled with magic that made her ears ring.

She knows she should destroy it, but for now, Marisol will have to settle on never unlocking that particular drawer again. Never.

Jack Boyd gives a wave with the hand curled around his belt loop.

It's Luis, approaching atop Fiona. Lately, Luis talks to Jack and Marisol less and to the cows more.

Even when Marisol does not accompany him on the drives, she can hear his songs echoing over the hills.

She wonders if—like Jack—there is some part of Luis that remembers the trees, but Marisol has decided she will not mention the shovel Luis swung at her, even if he asks. It is the witch's way to forgive, and Luis has a talent for allowing his guilts to build until they rush from him with the force of a mudslide, dragging along anyone that has been sitting too close.

"Mari," Jack says, after a hiccup that breaks the odd silence between them. "Now that Molly's warmed up to you, better take her for some exercise. We could use some coffee and maybe a bit of honeycomb. Head on out to Starcross, Mari, get some little treats for all of us."

"Sure, Jack," Marisol says, finishing the rest of the stack by hand. She feels a bit guilty for such use of witchwork in the first place, and besides, it's good to feel the scrape of gloves against her calluses. There was plenty of potent magic in the soreness of well-used muscles or blisters earned by a long walk.

"Why don't you go with her, Luis?" Jack adds once the work is done and the silence between them again becomes noticeable.

Luis tenses at the sound of his name but does not fully look up from the spade he's been repairing. He gives a single, dust-choked cough. The cowboy's word of agreement.

"You don't raze the place down while we're

away," Marisol says, but she doesn't think the chuckle she forces out is convincing.

TWENTY-THREE

They race toward Starcross in the late afternoon, the sky overhead a serene shade between blue and lilac. Fiona is lighter than Molly and leaps effortlessly over rocks and broken wagon wheels. Luis has always been the better rider, and the gnats that aren't able to dodge them end up plastered to his face.

Luis reaches the old church first, of course, but Marisol had only hoped to come in a respectable second. It's Molly who grunts and slaps her hooves angrily into the path that winds westward 'round the church to the cemetery.

He leans against a fencepost, waiting. Marisol joins him to watch the sunset, while Fiona and Molly graze on burdock amongst wind-polished headstones.

"There was someone else at the ranch," Luis says, accepting Marisol's half-eaten apple. "I know you said the curse would make the last few days seem like a dream, but it's not as if whiskey's never done the same. There was someone else at the ranch, and now, they're gone. I know it, Mari, tell the truth."

Marisol squints toward the distant golden haze of Starcross. The sky is clear, but the air smells of farmland and salty rain gathering strength on the other side of the hills. Witches have no specific code against lying—sometimes, it is necessary to protect others from harm—but the sentence she decides not to speak leaves a foul taste in her mouth.

"Lena Boyd, Jack's wife."

Luis takes a cigarette out of his shirt pocket but does not light it.

"She died, back when I first started at the ranch," he says. He moves the cigarette out of his mouth, so lost in thought he doesn't realize he's inhaled no smoke. "No way you could've known her."

"I only knew her ghost."

"Didn't know the ranch was haunted."

"Most are."

Luis strikes his match, but it nearly burns out before he finally lights the cigarette's tip.

Marisol wonders if he cannot find the right question to ask. A ranch hand's life involves plenty of dreaming, and dealing with magic can be like that too. He'd be as hard pressed to find words to describe the susurration of drying golden grass at the end of summer.

"You've seen her ghost too, you just don't remember. She helped me break a curse on the land, but it wasn't the best spell—I didn't have time. Ghosts are just memories, stuck in a place by the grief of those that loved them. My spell freed both her and you, in a way."

Luis nods like he understands, and Marisol thinks that maybe he does. Luis may not know about witchwork, but most everyone knows something about grief.

"I've been dreaming of trees. That a part of your curse too?"

Marisol snatches the cigarette out of Luis's hand and sticks the chewed end in her own mouth. Grandmother June had forbidden Marisol from smoking, and, to be fair, it is incredibly unpleasant.

Marisol's nostrils burn and she has to suppress a cough that feels like a kick to her ribs, but even with her tongue pressed furiously against the back of her teeth, she manages a smile.

"Yeah," she says. "But let's go into town and get proper drunk. Then, we won't dream anything at all."

CHAPTER
TWENTY-FOUR

They are still drinking much later on the porch with Jack Boyd. The air smells of Lena's rotted garden, horse sweat, and distant hickory smoke. As the sun finally sinks beneath the hills, a great white owl glides silently past the barn, waiting for mice to begin their journey home from the fields.

Marisol is only half-drunk, but their conversation has been so tender and carefree, that for the first time, she considers retrieving the blue seed from her room and chucking it into the campfire.

"—but, there's a thing, and there's the way you think of a thing, and those two can be quite different. Quite different, indeed. How do you know the world you know is even a lick like the world that is?"

"Jack Boyd," Luis laughs. "You were just talking about Jonah Shiver's cousin, come in to visit from Broken Jaw. How pretty she is and well-spoken too.

A real scholar, you said, studied medicine back east in Boston."

"Oh, give the old man a break. He's had plenty of years for this life to catch up to him," Marisol says, rotating her glass so that the golden firelight seems to fill it back to the brim. "Besides, he's right. Witchwork is all about finding the balance between what is and what you think of it. But you shouldn't drive yourself mad about it, Jack Boyd, that's what you pay me to do and I need the work."

"Just glad you're not from the Lodge. You'd ask for a bonus every time I began to philosophize. You know, Lodgemen used to come into our town, back in Missouri, before Lena and I bought the ranch. They always claim to be above charms, trinkets, but anyone of them would sell you a lucky horseshoe for a nickel. Lena let 'em have it anytime they tried to squeeze cash out of a widow or a young prospector heading west."

Something troubled passes over Jack Boyd's face as if realizing he has spoken out of turn. He scratches at a bruise on his forearm. A moth that has been circling overhead briefly lands on his hair, but he does not notice.

"Oh, Jack. You are most certainly paying me to listen to your philosophizing. It's just worked well enough into my salary that you don't notice. Let's go in, why don't we? I've had enough of these bugs. Luis can ride out alone in the morning, let's you and I stay up late. I want you to tell me more about Lena telling off those Lodgemen."

• • •

Later, Marisol sleeps in the armchair. The bristle of one of Lena's blankets tickles her nose, and whenever it wakes her, Marisol sees the long shadows cast by the porch light. They look so much like trees.

"You alright, Mari? Seems like you were dreaming."

Jack sounds soft and no louder than the patter of late rain, tickling the rooftop.

"I was, Jack. But I've woken up now. We all have."

"You witches say the strangest things."

Marisol laughs into the musty wool.

Maybe tomorrow night she'll burn the seed.

Maybe.

"You certainly ain't wrong, Jack."

Acknowledgments

Endless gratitude to Skot Olsen—my partner in life, first reader, finder of plot holes, and brewer of tea. It is his support and encouragement that made this story possible.

A huge thanks to Leza, Christopher, and the rest of the team at CLASH. I'm grateful this book found a home at a press that takes chances on the weird and uncategorizable.

And finally, to all my friends and family: thank you for always tolerating my book-buying habit and unexplained disappearances into the home office.

About the Author

Karla Yvette is a writer and visual artist, living in the Pacific Northwest. Her work is inspired by folklore, the occult, and focuses on strange women in even stranger places. *The Black Tree Atop the Hill* is her first novella.

ALSO BY CLASH BOOKS

WE PUT THE LIT IN LITERARY

CLASHBOOKS.COM

FOLLOW US

TWITTER

IG

FB

@clashbooks